Home Girl

BY ALEX WHEATLE

Published by Akashic Books
©2019 Alex Wheatle

Hardcover ISBN: 978-1-61775-795-2
Paperback ISBN: 978-1-61775-753-2

Library of Congress Control Number: 2019935273

First printing

Black Sheep
c/o Akashic Books
Brooklyn, New York, USA
Ballydehob, Co. Cork, Ireland
Twitter: @AkashicBooks
Facebook: AkashicBooks
E-mail: info@akashicbooks.com
Website: www.akashicbooks.com

More books for young adult readers from Black Sheep

Around Harvard Square
by C.J. Farley

Game World
by C.J. Farley

Changers Book One: Drew
Changers Book Two: Oryon
Changers Book Three: Kim
Changers Book Four: Forever
by T Cooper & Allison Glock-Cooper

Broken Circle
by J.L. Powers and M.A. Powers

Pills and Starships
by Lydia Millet

The Shark Curtain
by Chris Scofield

I would like to dedicate this book to all children in care, care leavers, and those who may have found shelter, a place to rest their head but not necessarily a home.

CHAPTER ONE

Trading Places

"He's a perv!" I yelled. I fixed my seat belt while switching the car radio to a grime station. I knew she hated that. "Why don't you believe me?"

Louise looked at me like she wanted to give me a koof. But she couldn't. She was my social wanker. She had issues starting the car. Her hands shook. "He says he was only standing outside the bathroom with your towel," she said.

"Every time I step into the bathroom he's pedophiling around," I spat. "*Have I got my shampoo? Have I got my bubble bath? Have I got my soap?* Does he think I'm dumb enough to step into the bathroom without my tings? I'm telling you he's a perv with a big prick P!"

Louise finally started the engine. She sucked in a nervous breath. She always did that when I dropped curses on her bony behind. "He . . . he says he was only trying to help," she stuttered.

"Jack up your ears, Louise! He's not helping me. I know the mission he's on. I can bring my own stuff to the bathroom."

Winding down her window, Louise blazed a fagarette. She pulled on it like she wanted to kill it with one drag. She looked out to the street. A hood-slug wearing a black hoodie walked a pit bull. She pulled away. This was the east ends of Ashburton where even the hounds peeped over their shoulders and paused before stepping around corners. I watched Louise puff her smoke out the window. By the angle of her brows I guessed she wanted to be at home sinking red wine and watching a Bridget Jones movie. She screwed up her face.

"Can I have one?" I asked.

"No!"

"Why not? You know I fire up anyway."

"You're not smoking while you're with me."

"And you're not supposed to be blazing in the ride with me."

Louise pulled on her cancer stick once more. She then blew out the window and stubbed it out. She placed the remaining half in her glove compartment.

At my feet was my banged-up cuddly meerkat toy. Its mouth was lengthened by a tear, one claw was missing on the left paw, and one eye was looser than the other. I picked it up and placed it on my lap. I stroked it twice and smiled at it.

Memories.

I threw Louise an evil eye-pass. Lily Allen's "Smile" crackled from the car radio. No bass. Louise turned down the volume. I turned it back up even louder. Louise knew she was gonna lose this game. She gave me one of those *really* glances and shook her head.

"Where're you taking me?" I asked.

"I don't know yet."

"Don't know? The moon's showing her dimples. Some social worker you are."

"Playing little Miss Madam everywhere I take you doesn't help. I'm fast running out of options."

"Not my fault you always place me with freaks and prick fiddlers."

"The Holmans have been fostering children in Ashburton for over twenty years. They're very dependable. No one has ever made a complaint about them before . . . until this evening."

"All the other kids must've been too scared to spill something," I said. "She was always trying to hug me. What's that about? Always up in my face she was with her welcome-to-*The-X-Factor* smile." An image of my mum bust an entry into my head. I remembered her smile. I tried to erase it but I couldn't. "*Is everything all right, Naomi?*" I took the piss. "Monkey on marbles! I lost count of how many times she asked me that. She made the hairs on my arms wanna leave me. And then *him*! Kim warned me about bad-minded men like him. *Anything you want, Naomi, sweetheart. Just ask.* I knew what he wanted. If he got any closer I would've clanged him with the biggest no-entry sign I could find."

"Are you sure of that, Naomi?" Louise asked. "They were only trying to be friendly. And I've told you before, you shouldn't listen to everything Kim says."

Even then Louise didn't believe me. Her casserole didn't have any dumplings. *What do I have to do to make this woman see the pig in the sky?*

"The other day I was watching *Titanic*," I said. "I always leak tears when I watch that part when Leo sinks into the sea. *She* comes over and hugs me like I agreed to be her

Surrey Gate mum. I told her if she pollutes my personal space again I'm gonna clong her with a casserole pot when she's sleeping. When I finish with her she'll still be seeing tweety birds when she's having her varicose veins done. I'm telling ya, Louise, they've got something of asylum ward twenty-one about 'em."

Louise kept quiet. Maybe the truth finally slapped her sensible spot.

"I'm hungry," I said. I wasn't lying. My stomach snorted. "Where're you taking me? And I don't wanna go to no Alabama Chicken Cottage or Mississippi Hen Hut. Their chicken is off-key."

Louise didn't answer. She kept her eyes on the road. Ten minutes later, she pulled into the car park of a McD's restaurant on the Ashburton ring road. She took out a five-pound note from her purse. I liberated it from her, picked up my meerkat, and was gone before Louise could say the N of Naomi. I looked back when I reached the McD's entrance. Louise shook her head, took out her mobile phone from her handbag, and punched a number. She retrieved her half-smoked cigarette from the glove compartment, sparked it, and looked out the window.

I had just sunk the last morsel of a cheese quarter-pounder when Louise parked her slim butt opposite me. She looked like she had joined in on one of those charity fun-runs but her fitness wasn't up to spec. "Your man not coming around tonight?" I asked.

"Leave it, Naomi."

"He might be cheating on ya, goring someone else."

"Naomi!"

"If that was me I'd churn his balls with one of those food-blitzer things when he's sleeping."

Through a straw I sucked my chocolate milkshake trying to roadblock a giggle. I couldn't quite manage it. A spattering of chocolate spewed out over the table and over Louise's brown leather jacket. A passing black teenage girl carrying a tray of burgers and fries laughed out loud. I put my drink down and wiped my mouth and nose with the back of my hand. Louise's eyebrows switched forty-five degrees and something funny happened to her lips. She was on the edge of the cliff wearing five-inch-high stilettos. I might've gone too far.

"Sorry," I said.

Louise huffed and puffed to the counter. She returned moments later with a handful of napkins and a coffee. I had wiped the table clean. I leaned back into my seat with my meerkat squashed between my arms and stomach.

Louise groped for her phone in her jeans pocket. She closed her eyes and took in two mega breaths. She scoped me hard. "Would you mind staying for a week or two with a black family?" she suggested. "I was thinking of this second-generation British, West Indian family. It's not ideal but it won't be for long. Just until I can place you somewhere more suitable."

"A black family?" *Monkey on ball bearings. What's she on?*

"Yes," Louise nodded. "As I said, only for a short while. They're very good. And you've got black friends you get on very well with."

I shrugged. *This is new. It could be interesting.* "I s'pose.

11

As long as they're not too hugalicious or prick fiddlers."

Louise jabbed her mobile. I watched her every move. She picked up her coffee and walked out of the restaurant. She kept an eye on me through the window. *What's the frucking point? She's gonna give me the lowdown anyway.*

I hot-toed outside to join her. Louise turned her back on me.

"Put it on speaker," I urged.

Louise ignored me.

"It's about me, right? Put it on *speaker.*"

Louise did what she was told.

"Hello? Hello, Colleen, it's Louise. Thank God you're in."

"Hi, Louise. Everything good with you?"

"Not exactly. I'm in a spot."

"Oh, what's up?"

"Can you do me a big favor? I have tried everybody else and I'm fast running out of options. I know it's late in the day but I really need your help."

"It's after eight so—"

"I have an emergency case," Louise interrupted. "I really need an emergency foster carer for the next two weeks or so until I can find somewhere permanent."

"Two weeks is no problem. I'll just clean up our spare bedroom. I haven't used it for a while. Anything about the case I need to know? I'm not having you shove any self-harmers our way without you telling us. That last case really scared the kids. Tony had to give the bedroom walls a new coat of paint."

Louise offered me a worried glance; I made a face at her.

"No, nothing like that," Louise replied. "Well, er, there's something but we'll talk about it when I arrive. That last case, I didn't even know she was a self-harmer. It wasn't on her file and she didn't have any scars on her arms."

"You should've looked at her legs."

"I know that now. I'm so sorry, my mistake."

"Who's loving razor blades?" I wanted to know. "Is it Taneka Taylor who used to be at the unit? Her life was always on a detour."

Louise covered her phone with her hand. "Not now, Naomi."

"So how do you know this emergency case isn't a self-harmer?" Colleen wanted confirmation.

"I have known the case for a while."

"I'm not a *fricking* case," I raised my voice. "I've got a name. Naomi Brisset."

Louise side-eyed me. She was back on the edge of the cliff.

"How old?" asked Colleen.

"Fourteen." Louise eye-drilled me. "Going on twenty-nine," she resumed. "There's something you should know."

"Oh? What's that?"

"She's Caucasian. Normally I wouldn't . . ."

What the fruck is Caucasian? Why's Louise talking all foreign all of a sudden?

I gave Louise one of my best *what the freak are you talking about* glares. Silence for ten seconds.

"Can I call you back in a minute, Colleen?" said Louise. "I won't be long."

Louise spotlit me for five seconds without leaking a

word. Her eyes were desperate. "So, are you really okay staying with a black family? It's either that or the secure unit. I'd rather you stay with a foster family—"

"I'm not going back to the secure unit!" I squeezed my meerkat close to my stomach. "Can't stand the staff there. Hate 'em."

"Do you really hate them, Naomi? You were a bit tearful when you left."

"That's cos I was leaving Kim and Nats. They're my best friends."

"Hmmm." Louise was never sweet on Kim and Nats. "So what do you think about staying with a black family? It wouldn't be for long."

"They got kids?" I asked.

"Yes, they have."

"How old?"

"Sharyna's ten and Pablo's six. They were adopted. They used to be in the care system."

"You were their social worker?"

"Yes. Please give me an answer, Naomi. I haven't got all night."

"Wanna wheel home before your boyfriend gets pissed on waiting for ya and hits on someone else?"

"*Naomi!*"

I thought about it. *A black family. They'll definitely be cooler than the Holmans. They might let me blaze a rocket. The mum might be able to put plaits in my hair like Solange Knowles. They could get my dancing on point. Might learn some top-ranking insults like those black chicks at my last school.*

I smiled. "Yeah. I'm good to play this game."

"Are you sure? I don't want you accusing me of not listening to your opinion before a placement again."

She was right on that one.

"I suppose so," I said. "Unless you wanna give me my own place. I'll be good on my lonesome. Dunno why you're always munching your knickers about it when I bring it up. When I'm fifteen I'll meet a sweet bruv and we can make a life—"

Louise had her *really* face back on.

"How many times do I have to tell you, Naomi?" she said. "You're a minor. The local council are responsible for you until you reach *eighteen*."

"They didn't call me a minor when I looked after my dad!"

Shaking her head, Louise stepped away. She jabbed the redial button on her phone. "Hello, it's Louise again."

It was still on speaker.

"Hi again, Louise."

"I wouldn't ask if I wasn't desperate, Colleen, but I have two emergency foster carers on holiday and another who's about to give birth. It's not a problem that my case is Caucasian, is it? Her name's Naomi. Naomi Brisset."

"Naomi," repeated Colleen. "Nice name."

I curled a grin. *Of course it's a nice name. My mum gave me it.*

"Tell her I was named after Naomi Watts," I said. "She was in *King Kong* and a horror movie."

Louise ignored me. "Will Tony be all right with, er, you know?" she asked.

"Course," Colleen replied. "Won't bother him at all. He'll be cool."

"You sure?" Louise pressed again. "It's just that Tony has always made a point about wanting to foster black children."

"He wants to help all kids," Colleen insisted.

"Okay, Colleen." Louise breathed out relief. "We'll be around in half an hour or so."

"Hold on, hold on," Colleen said. "Any dietary requirements I should know about? Remember last year? You sent us that kid who wouldn't eat rice, potatoes, meat, or anything with seasoning in it."

"Naomi's not fussy about her food. I have her file with me."

"I don't like mince," I called out. "Reminds me of worms. No shepherd's pie either. Oh, and I don't like macaroni cheese. That reminds me of yellow worms."

Louise offered me a *seal your gums* glare.

"Looking forward to meeting her," said Colleen after a pause.

We returned to McD's. Louise sipped on her coffee and sank into her seat. "Seems like Colleen's looking forward to meeting you," she said.

"Why wouldn't she?" I grinned. "I'm lovable."

I hugged my meerkat tight.

CHAPTER TWO

A New Hope

We burned rubber along the Ashburton circular. I stared out the car window looking at road signs. *Monk's Orchard, Spenge-on-Leaf, Crongton, Notre Dame, Cranerley, Smeckenham.* We turned off at the Shrublands exit. I thought about my dad. I wondered what he'd think about me staying with a black family. He wouldn't care. After all, he sank liquor with anyone. Once, I had to drag his alcoholic ass out of Lord Jazzbo's, a cocktail bar that had a samba night on a Thursday, a disco night on a Friday, and a reggae night on a Saturday. They had this speciality drink called Rumwave. Dad loved it. I sampled it once too. It gave me a double-bitch of a hangover the next morning. That was the last liquor I ever had.

We reached Shrublands.

Flowers niced up the roundabouts. Four-by-fours sweetened up the wide roads. Cats slept on fence posts. Hedges were trimmed neatly.

"Black people live here?" I asked.

"Yes, they do," Louise replied. "The Goldings are a nice family. They've done well for themselves."

"They didn't make their Gs from selling dragon hip pills, did they?"

"No! They certainly didn't. And *don't* even go there with that one, Naomi."

"All right," I said. "Just jokes."

"I hope it's just jokes, Naomi."

Louise's eyebrows had hardened. I could tell she was getting proper frustrated at the whole deal.

"It won't be too long you'll be staying here so just bear with me," she said. "I can't have you there for too long anyway. The council machine will have me flying through hoops and asking me to fill in a million forms for that to happen."

"Who's in the council machine when they block the toilets?" I wanted to know.

Louise shook her head. "You don't want to know," she replied.

We pulled up outside this pretty house. The front lawn was well shaved. The white front door had gold numbers nailed into it. Twenty-three. Louise jabbed the doorbell. I can't lie, my insides quaked. I took a few steps back. *Here we go again.*

The door opened. This neat-looking black woman appeared. Mid to late thirty-ish. I liked her peacock-colored earrings.

"Good to see you again," said Colleen. "Please come in. Just boiled the kettle."

At first, I kinda liked the idea of staying with a black family. But now I wasn't feeling too sure.

"Naomi!" called Louise.

I stood on the spot studying Colleen for a long second before shuffling slowly toward the door. She had shoulder-length brown dreadlocks. *Oh, good. Might be able to listen to some original dancehall tunes.* She waved us into the house busting a grin. "What do you want to drink?" she asked. "Hot chocolate? Orange or apple juice? Coke? You hungry?"

She made me feel self-conscious. I took out my mobile although I didn't know what to do with it. "I wanna coffee," I replied. "Four sugars."

"Three sugars," cut in Louise. "Remember we made a deal?"

"But you didn't give up the—"

"Not now," Louise snipped my flow.

I pulled a *screw you* face.

"Come on then, Naomi," said Louise. "Let's get inside so Colleen can close the door. It's getting a bit nippy."

It was cold. I wanted to brag off my *Grime Therapy* T-shirt but I had to wear a hoodie over it.

I entered the hallway. I spotted two kids parked on the third stair. The younger one, a boy, giggled. He must've been Pablo. His name sounded like something you do with balloons. The older girl had her face between her hands. She must've been Sharyna. Pretty. She scoped my every move. I took in my surroundings. It wasn't like my mum's place. The amber-colored paint on the walls looked as if it had been rolled on just days ago. The hallway was grimeless and I could sniff floor polish. I didn't recognize the black man in a framed picture with cheeks the size of melons. They needed another photograph to fit in his stretched trombone.

At the end of the hallway was the kitchen. A black man

sat at the kitchen table. His shoulders were IMAX-screen broad. A tiger tattoo manned-up his forearm. I guessed he was Tony. Colleen invited Louise and me to park our butts. Tony stood up and smiled at me. One gold tooth. "Hi, my name is Tony," he said. He reached out his hand. I looked at it like it was an escaped anaconda. My nerves spat like sausages on a too-high gas ring. I looked at his plate of dinner. I couldn't recognize the food. Then I checked something on my phone.

Colleen reached for a biscuit tin on top of a cupboard. She took off the lid. "Anyone want a nibble?" she asked.

Louise accepted two custard creams.

"No chocolate ones?" I asked.

"Sorry, darling," replied Colleen. "I'll make sure I get some tomorrow."

From a leather case, Louise took out my file. A strained elastic band held the flimsy folder and untold papers together. She slid it over to Tony, who ignored it, took a sip from his fruit drink, and introduced himself again. "Just call me Tone."

I didn't know what to say. *Monkey on a skateboard. This is really happening.* Colleen sat beside Tony. "And I'm Colleen," she smiled. "Colleen Golding. We're glad to have you with us."

The Holmans said the same shit.

I glanced briefly at Colleen and then concentrated on my phone. I tried to focus on a game but it wasn't happening.

"Sharyna! Pablo!" Colleen called out.

Pablo hot-stepped in first. He was still giggling. Then Sharyna entered the kitchen as if the world's paparazzi were waiting for her. All nervous smiles and sideways glances. She had her arms behind her back and her chin was held high. "Hi, Naomi," she greeted in a grown-up voice.

I busted out a smile. I loved her long braids. "You know my name," I said. "You all right? Top ratings for your plaits."

"Thanks," Sharyna replied.

I think she blushed but I couldn't quite tell.

"That's Sharyna for you," laughed Tony.

Louise chuckled and took another custard cream. I scoped the creases around her eyes. Some of the other kids on her files had obviously stressed her out till her balloon was about to pop.

Colleen offered me my coffee. She laughed nervously. "Your coffee all right, darling?"

I sampled it. It could've done with more sweetness.

"It'll pass," I said. "Could've done with a chocolate biscuit to go with it though."

As the grown-ups chatted, sunk more biscuits, and scanned my file, I allowed Pablo and Sharyna to check out my phone. Sharyna and Pablo were then called to wash the dishes. When Pablo had dried the last one, Colleen turned to me. "Are we ready for the tour?"

A tour? The house is pretty but it's not Buckingham Palace.

"S'pose so," I said.

"Follow me then," said Tony, carrying my bags.

Leaving Louise and Colleen in the kitchen, Tony led me up the stairs, followed by Sharyna and Pablo, to my room. I held on to my meerkat. Tony opened the door and I stepped in slowly. I stood for some long seconds under the doorframe. I looked at the double bed. *This is new. I don't usually get a double bed to crash out in.* Tony fidgeted beside me. Sharyna and Pablo remained in the hallway.

Yeah, not too bad. I'll see where my life rolls from here.

I went and placed my meerkat gently between the pillows. I checked out the furniture. "Where's the telly?" I asked.

"The last girl we had staying with us didn't watch too much telly," explained Tony. "She read a lot of misery books."

I stepped toward the window and peered out into the back garden. I could just about make out the shape of a shed. I thought of Dad. If he could get his life up to spec he could live in a house like this. "Do I look like I read a lot? I wanna telly."

"Ask me like that and you won't get it, young lady."

I turned around. I picked up my meerkat and pressed it tight against my chest. "I want a frucking telly! What do you expect me to do when I'm up here? Play noughts and crosses on the walls?"

Sharyna and Pablo crept closer to the door. I lasered my eyes into Tony's forehead but he must've had a deflective shield cos he remained calm. I heard two pairs of feet hoofing up the stairs. "You won't get a TV if you talk to me like that," Tony said again.

Louise rushed into the room. There were custard cream crumbs about her mouth. I nearly busted out a giggle. "Everything all right?" she asked, looking at me and then to Tony.

"Everything's fine," replied Tony. "We're just getting to know each other."

Almost bouncing into Louise, Colleen stumbled in. "Anything wrong?" she asked.

"No," I said. "I just wondered if it's all right me having a telly in my room."

Colleen and Tony swapped glances. Tony shook his head and dropped my bags on the floor. He smiled and said under his breath, "We have one of those."

"Er, yes, the spare TV's in my room," said Colleen.

Tony shook his head again. Louise glanced at him. "I'll get the telly," he offered.

I dropped my attitude. "I want a DVD player too," I said. "I've got nuff DVDs in my bag. I'd love to watch 'em. Sometimes I can't sleep. I get nightmares."

I wasn't lying. I had issues with my sleeping as long as I could remember. Tony smiled a funny smile.

"Attitude, Naomi," said Louise. "Remember we talked about the right tone when we're talking to people? And I think we're missing a word."

Louise keeps playing that same tune. I'm not a frucking idiot. I get it. I clutched my meerkat even tighter and rolled my eyes. "Pretty *please* with bells on wrapped in a pink envelope."

"Yes, you may," replied Tony with a posh voice. I flung him an evil look.

Tony left the room. Colleen smiled nervously. "Do I need to wash any of your clothes tonight?" she asked. "Maybe a school uniform?"

"She's not attending school until next Monday," explained Louise. "She has Thursday and Friday off to help her adjust to her new surroundings and to give her time to bond with her new family."

"So you'll be with me during the day," said Colleen. "We can get to know each other."

"Woo hoo!" I mocked. "This is all a bit too much."

That wasn't called for. She's only trying to be nice. Allow her.

Returning with a portable TV, Tony waited until I cleared the books from the desk. He dropped his posh voice. "Thank you," he said.

"Where's the . . . ?"

Sharyna entered carrying a DVD player. She placed it beside the television and gave me a gorgylicious smile. *How can I carry on spitting attitude after that?*

"Thanks," I said. "What's your name again?"

"Sharyna."

"Maybe when they leave us alone we can watch some spine curlers."

"That would be so—"

Louise cut off Sharyna's excited response. "She's only eleven," she warned.

"I watched horror films when I was six," I said. I wasn't lying. Mum used to love 'em too. We'd sit down in our raggedy sofa munching Haribos. "The new *Evil Dead*'s the gorilla's knuckles."

"Sharyna, would you like to show Naomi the rest of the house?"

"Yeah," Sharyna smiled. "I'll show her my room first."

Half an hour later, I was in my room running my fingers through Sharyna's braids. She didn't mind. We were getting on neatly.

Louise popped her head around the door. "Can I have a minute?" she asked.

"Sure," replied Sharyna.

Louise waited until Sharyna closed the door. "Will you be all right here?"

"As long as *he* doesn't prick fiddle around me."

"I think you're getting a bit paranoid."

"They're all alike," I argued. "Kim warned me about men who foster kids. Loads of 'em tried it on with her. She told me not to trust 'em. You see it all the time in the papers and on the news."

Louise gave me her top-ranking *really* look. "Not all men are like the ones in the news," she said. "And Kim doesn't know everyone. She's not the oracle on everything."

"Oracle? Stop talking foreign. If he tries game on me I'll stab him in his prick. I'm not playing!"

Louise patted me on the shoulder. "I don't think that'll be necessary. You must stop thinking that everything Kim says is true. She sometimes . . . stretches the truth."

"So do social wankers."

Louise shook her head.

"Don't blame me if you get a 9-9-9 later tonight," I added.

"Stop worrying. Mr. Golding's one of the good guys."

"There ain't no good men who foster kids. They've all got . . . what d'you call it . . . an agenda."

Louise placed her hands on her hips. "You think I'd put you with someone inappropriate?"

"You put me with the Holmans. He was the ultimate prick fiddler and I could tell on my first day with them that she was all wrong by her purple leggings and pink plimsolls."

"Hmmm."

"Don't *hmmm* me," I said. "I know that means you think I'm talking shit."

Louise couldn't help busting out a smile.

"When are you coming again?" I wanted to know.

"Let me see. It's Wednesday today. I'll see how you are on Friday morning."

"Don't I get pocket money?" I asked. "These Golding peeps might not give me squiddly jack. Look how he munched his boxers about the telly."

"I'm sure they will."

I held out my hand. "Say they don't? I don't wanna be part of no Austria program."

"Austerity program," Louise corrected me. "They'll give you what they think is appropriate."

"Say they *don't?*" I repeated. "And your appropriate is not on the same level as *my* appropriate."

Louise gave me another *really* look, shook her head, and took out her purse. It had nuff cards in it. *I wonder how much they pay social wankers.* She handed me a ten-pound note. "*Don't* spend it on cigarettes," she said. "Some of this can go toward the chocolate biscuits you want."

I placed the note in a zip compartment of my backpack.

"The Goldings are good people," Louise went on. "They've been fostering for the council for years."

Monkey on skis. Doesn't she realize she's repeating herself? She's going senile already.

"That's what you said about the Holmans," I said.

"You'll be okay here for a week or two until I can find a better arrangement."

"You said that and all."

"Be good." Louise smiled.

She opened the door but paused before leaving. She offered me another smile. I can't lie. I was sorry to see her go. *Why can't* she *foster me? I would squeeze all kinda notes outta her.* I picked up my meerkat and held it on my lap.

CHAPTER THREE

Bathroom Issues

It was late-night o'clock. I sat on my bed with my pink towel draped over my shoulder. Colleen watched me from the doorway.

"He's downstairs," Colleen insisted. "You can check my room if you want."

"He might be in Pablo's room or Sharyna's room," I said. "Have you got an attic? He might've bounced up there."

"Tone!" Colleen called. "Holler something so Naomi believes you're downstairs."

"I'M DOWNSTAIRS, Naomi!"

"See!" said Colleen. Impatience nibbled her cheeks.

Kim told me to get my prick-fiddler radar out on this issue.

"Unless my husband has learned a new trick of sending his voice to different parts of the house, he's downstairs," assured Colleen.

"Will he stay downstairs while I'm having my shower?" I wanted confirmation.

"Of course he will."

"Promise."

"I PROMISE, NAOMI!" Tony yelled. "With bells on wrapped in a pink envelope."

That's the living cheek! Using my own lyrics against me. At least he's got jokes inside of him. Kim would've loved the way I insisted that Tony had to park his toes downstairs while I'm flinging off my BO. I picked up my meerkat and stood up. Without a word, I breezed past Colleen and into the hallway. I paused for a short second to glance down the staircase before stepping into the bathroom. Nerves spat and crackled inside of me as I opened the door. I closed my eyes as I took a step forward. It was okay. Just a standard bathroom. The tub was clean. I could sniff some kinda cleaning liquid. I let a long breath go and closed the door behind me.

I didn't love baths but I needed to think. Sadness munched my heart. It had been the longest day. I placed my meerkat behind the shower hose so I didn't have to look down. I wished it could smile. I closed my eyes and allowed the water to bounce off my head.

Two scrubbings later, someone slapped the door.

"You okay, Naomi?" Colleen asked.

"Is he still downstairs?" I responded.

"Yes, he is. Don't worry. He won't come up until you're ready."

After eleven I was in bed with my meerkat beside me. Tiredness licked me. Colleen watched me from the doorway once again. "If you want anything, don't be shy to ask. And if you're hungry or thirsty during the night just go down to the kitchen and help yourself."

I nodded. "Leave the light on," I insisted. "And leave the door open . . . but not too much."

"You have a lamp beside your bed on the cabinet."

"Not gonna use it. Leave the main light on."

"Okay, good night then."

"Can you do my hair in the morning like Alicia Keys or Solange—she's Beyoncé's liccle sis."

"I'll try."

"And don't forget the chocolate biscuits," I said with a smile.

Louise forever told me to smile more.

"I won't," Colleen replied.

I think I'm gonna be all right. Colleen's on point.

I turned to face the window and hugged my meerkat. *I should really give it a name, but what name? It's not like I've got anyone to name it after. I can't call it Mum. I don't think she'd like to be rechristened an animal.* I closed my eyes but I couldn't sleep.

Later on that night, Colleen checked on me. I pretended I was asleep. Half an hour later, I rolled outta bed and twinky-toed along the hallway to the Goldings' bedroom. I made the same move at the Holmans' on my first night there. I wanted to download what peeps said about me.

The door was half-cracked. The news was on a low volume. Colleen spoke, ". . . can't complain we got a quiet one this time," she said. "She's a bit fiery."

"You can say that again," said Tony. "But I can't relax the rules too much just because she's here for a short time."

"No, you can't," said Colleen. "But as you say, it'll only be for a week or so till Louise sorts something out."

"It can't be for more than that anyway," Tony said. "Remember Louise was telling us that we'd have to fill in all sorts of race-awareness forms for a longer stay."

"It's gonna be different," said Colleen. "Are you sure you can handle it? And then there's your dad."

There was a long pause. Someone on TV was talking about issues in the Middle East. I wondered what the drama with Tony's dad was all about.

"As long as she doesn't harm herself," Tony finally replied. "We'll deal with my dad when we come to it. Might not need to."

"I'm gonna get myself a nightcap," said Colleen. "Do you want anything?"

I heard Tony laugh. "Don't let Louise find out about your late-night drinking," he said. "That'll lead to a social services inquisition."

I wondered what inquisition meant. *I might have issues but I'm not cadazy enough to barb-wire my wrists.* This Tony doesn't rate me.

I soft-toed back to my room but I still couldn't sleep.

CHAPTER FOUR

Morning Rush

I sat up in bed watching the comings and goings of my new foster family as they got ready for their nine-to-five. I laughed when Pablo pulled on different-colored socks in the hallway. I giggled when Tony waited impatiently outside the bathroom for Sharyna to finish showering. I was dressed in my *Stormzy* T-shirt and my pink jogging bottoms—my sleeping garms. I decided to get up and bounce downstairs. I took my meerkat with me. I wasn't paying attention last night but I noticed framed pics hanging from the stair-case walls of black women washing clothes in a river and carrying fruit in baskets on top of their bonces. There was a photograph of black men garmed in raggedy prison uni-forms nine-to-fiving on a rail track. Underneath were the lyrics, *We also built your cabins and planted your corn, only to be treated with scorn.* I paused. "I s'pose in that country they haven't got any shopping trolleys or washing machines," I whispered to myself. *Maybe Angelina Jolie, David Beckham, and those peeps on* Comic Relief *could do something.*

I found Colleen in the kitchen making sandwiches. She wore a baby blue–colored dressing gown and a red, gold, and green headscarf. "Morning, darling," she greeted. "Sleep well?"

"No," I replied.

"Maybe you will on your second night. Always difficult to get comfy in a new bed."

She wasn't wrong. I tried to count all the beds I'd crashed in since they'd taken my ass into care.

I was distracted by the magnet souvenirs stuck on the fridge door. There was a Rastafarian sleeping in a hammock. He had a fat rocket in his gob. There was a sombrero-wearing man with a cheek-tickler mustache, Barack Obama getting all cozy with his wife and a smiling skinny camel from Tunisia. *Where's that?* I wondered what magnets Dad would have on his fridge if he didn't have his drink issues.

"I wanna coffee," I said.

"Just let me finish the sandwiches for everyone's lunch and I'll be with you."

"I can make it myself," I offered. "I'm not a special-needs case."

"The coffee and sugar are in the cupboard."

I filled the kettle and put two teaspoons of coffee and three teaspoons of sugar in an *I Love Washington DC* mug. After pouring in the hot water, I stared at Colleen for a long second. She watched my every move. I then fetched the milk from the fridge, poured a little into my mug, and stirred it. Colleen's spotlight pissed me off. The coffee spilled onto the table. "Sorry," I said. "But you're gonna have to fling me some trust. I can do stuff myself. I looked after my dad for the longest time. The only thing I didn't do for him was wipe his ass."

Colleen reached for a cloth in the sink and cleaned the spillage. "That's all right," she smiled.

I sat down, tasted my coffee, and decided to put another teaspoon of sugar in it. "Why do you wanna look after someone else's kids?" I asked.

Placing the sandwiches, apples, and juice boxes into two containers, Colleen replied, "I . . . I couldn't have a family myself so I—"

"Your thing wasn't working?" I cropped her flow. "I knew a woman like that who adopted this four-year-old kid in my old unit. Her thing didn't work. She didn't wanna talk about it when my mate, Kim, dared me to ask her. Is it because the man wrecks it when he does his thing?"

"Er, not quite," said Colleen. I'm sure she blushed. "Some women cannot have children because of health reasons."

"My mum didn't have that issue with me," I said. "She had me, innit. Obviously. I remember a social worker saying she shouldn't think about having any more though."

"Oh? Is that so?"

"Yeah. Mum got pregnant by the guy living in the spare room. Foreign, he was. He had his skills. He'd help me with my math and fixed the pipe beneath the kitchen sink. Sometimes he'd fling us a few notes to help top up the gas meter. I couldn't pronounce his name so Mum told me to call him Rafi. He used to make me coffee when Mum was out of it. Strong, his coffee was. I had to put nuff sugar in it. He didn't like it when Dad paid a visit—nuff swearing and mauling. That's when the social services placed my ass on the at-risk register."

"I see," nodded Colleen.

"Things were kinda going all right until Mum lost Rafi's baby," I continued. "She tried again but had to have an abortion. Rafi didn't love that. He raged at her in his funny tongue and sacked her cos of it. It sent her off-key. Don't think she ever regained her dumplings after that. She used to spend nuff time in the bathroom to think things over. You read my file so you know what happened next."

Colleen nodded. She had stopped what she was doing and stood still. She paid the fullest attention. *Did I spill too much? Oh what the lardy ho. It's all in my file anyway.*

"Have you got the chocolate biscuits yet?" I changed the subject. "Chocolate digestives, bourbons, or fingers are my fave. Oh, and marshmallows with the liccle dose of strawberry inside."

"Tea cakes," said Colleen.

"Yep, that's right. Love 'em. Have you had any abortions? Do they hurt?"

Colleen looked at me all weird and then swallowed spit. "Er, no. Haven't got the biscuits yet either. Haven't had a chance to get out of the house yet. Maybe you can come with me?"

"Can you get that strawberry yogurt that has that strawberry dip in it? Tastes wicked on chocolate biscuits."

Pablo hot-toed into the kitchen wearing his black school trousers and purple-colored school top. A blue Nike bag that hung from his shoulders kissed his knees. His shoelaces were untied, his belt flapped, and his shirt cuffs were unbuttoned. Too cute. Colleen shook her head and smiled. "What am I going do with you? Come here."

I bust a laugh. "I'll do it," I offered.

Slightly uncertain, Pablo swapped glances with Colleen as I tied his laces, secured his belt, adjusted the strap of his backpack, and buttoned his cuffs. He gave me a top-ranking smile. "Thank you. What's your name again?"

"Naomi."

"Thank you, Nomi."

He ran out again. "Hold on, Pablo," chuckled Colleen. "Aren't you forgetting something?"

Pablo turned around. He game-showed a grin and returned to the kitchen. Colleen handed him his packed lunch. "You'd forget your feet if your ankles weren't attached to them! Have a good day. *Don't* kick the tree in the playground and don't make faces at the dog at the end of the road."

Pablo laughed and hyper-toed along the hallway. "Sharyna! I'm ready. You told me to be ready but you're not ready!"

"Coming!"

I sipped my coffee. I wondered what it would've been like if I had a liccle sis or bruv to look after.

"When I was in the juniors I had to make Dad's packed lunch before I went to school," I said. "I had to wake him up and tell him where I left it. If I swear a lot you have to blame my paps—every morning he'd bruise the air with his Cs and Fs. Then he'd go straight to the bog. He might as well have taken his bed in there. Sometimes I had to piss in the sink. And when I came back from school I had to clean up the bog cos Dad was usually sick in it. And when I asked him for the funds so I could buy Domestos, did he give me it? *No!*"

"Not . . . nice," said Colleen. She had her sympathy face on.

I heard footsteps stomping down the stairs. Tony wore blue overalls over a black T-shirt. His thick gray socks had holes in them. A stumpy pencil was wedged between his left ear and head. "Morning, Naomi," he greeted. "Morning, Colleen. Sandwiches ready?"

I side-eyed Tony. He kissed Colleen on the cheek. I couldn't remember my dad or Rafi ever doing that to Mum in the morning. "Not quite," Colleen replied. "Apple or orange?"

"Both," Tony answered. He sat opposite me. "And how was your night?"

"Not too blessed," I said. "I couldn't sleep."

"That's kinda natural with all the excitement of moving to a new home."

"Excitement?" I repeated. "Are you on something? This isn't my home. Haven't had a proper home since . . . This is just somewhere I'll be resting my bones for a week and maybe a bit. This time next year you'll forget who I am. I haven't got a diddly where I'll be by then. But I'm used to it."

Tony swapped glances with Colleen. "We'll both do what we can to make this place a home for you, Naomi, for as long as you're here."

I thought about Dad again. Then I placed my mug on the table, bit my top lip, and crossed my arms.

"I've gotta get going," said Tony. "You two have a good day."

I side-eyed him as he disappeared. I knew he was trying to be on point but Kim's warnings swirled around in my head.

"Sharyna!" Tony called.

A minute later, I heard the front door closing. Tony's

pickup truck pulled away. I peered into my coffee mug. "Does sex with him hurt?" I asked.

Placing a frying pan on the stove, Colleen blushed again. "Er, erm. When, er . . . when you're in a loving relationship, sex should never hurt."

"My friend Kim says it hurts. *Take that frucking thing outta me*, she said to the last boyfriend she had."

"Language, Naomi."

"Sorry," I said.

"Perhaps . . . perhaps your friend Kim wasn't in a loving relationship?"

Social wanker and sex educational class speak.

"Lost count of the amount of bruvs Kim's had," I said. "I don't think she loved any of 'em. She's got a girlfriend now. Can I have sausages as well as eggs? Oh, and baked beans if you got 'em."

"Of course."

"You gonna do my hair today?"

"Yes, after we go to the supermarket."

"When did you first have sex?"

"Are these appropriate questions to ask an adult?" Colleen placed her hands on her hips and locked her eyes on me. "I know you've had experiences that a fourteen-year-old girl shouldn't have to go through, but you're still fourteen."

"Louise is always telling me to talk about these issues in a grown-up way," I said. I wasn't lying.

She dropped two thick sausages into the frying pan. *Good. I like 'em fat.*

"Louise told you that, did she?"

"Yeah, she did," I replied. I put on Louise's voice:

"There's nothing wrong with talking about sex if you're mature about it."

Colleen half grinned. "Okay," she said.

"Well, spill then."

Colleen took in a breath. "I was far too young," she said. "Fourteen."

"Fourteen," I said. "Are you sure you never had an abortion? Anyway, that's not the youngest I've heard. I know a girl who got spermed at thirteen. Connie Richards. Right little prick-sponge she was. She'd fruck a guy—"

"Language, Naomi."

"And it was her fault for getting spermed," I carried on. "She told me she wanted a baby. She wanted something to look after. Her social worker shoulda given her a bunny rabbit or something. Felt sorry for her in a way though. Her mum was always out and she was forever looking after her baby sis. The bruv she'd done it with was manky-looking—they'd never have him on *Love Island*. He had little volcanoes around his mouth and you could've deep fried dinosaur wings in his greasy hair. Dunno how she slurped tongues with him. I'm gonna get myself a bruv when I'm fifteen and he's not gonna look like that. No way, José. I'm not that desperate."

Colleen turned over the sausages. I thought I spotted a quarter smile spreading from her lips. "Fourteen . . . is very young to know what you want," she said.

"What were you on when you were fourteen?" I asked.

Rinsing her hands before joining me at the table, Colleen sighed. "I was living in a children's home," she revealed.

"No jokes?"

Colleen nodded. "My dad didn't stay around. My mum couldn't cope. You know, that kinda story."

"Left you on the steps of the town hall, did she? Happened to my mate Bridget. She's always going on about it. It really messed her up, like if a boy she fancies doesn't look at her she wants to kill herself. Stupid cow! Bit of a loudmouth *EastEnder* mama she is. I mean, how the fruck can she remember being left on the steps of the Ashburton town hall when she's only seven months old?"

"I wasn't left anywhere."

"Then what happened?" I wanted to know.

"I was six when I went to the children's home," Colleen said. She full-stopped and scoped me hard. I think she was working out if she could trust me with her personals. I smiled like a clown at a kid's fifth birthday party.

It worked.

"Mum got me up early that day," Colleen continued. "She put me in the bath and washed my hair. She blow-dried it and plaited my hair into little China bumps. She dressed me in my church clothes—a yellow dress, white socks, and pink sandals. God, I loved that yellow dress. I looked as innocent as a choir girl."

"Yellow dress, white socks, and pink sandals," I repeated. "I bet the prick fiddlers were watching ya. And there's a lot of 'em in church—it's where they chill. Kim's always warning me about 'em. She told me they're usually people you know, uncles and older cousins and all that. *If he buys you sweets, he really wants treats.* Kim's always saying that."

Colleen gave me one of those *Naomi hasn't got all the*

cucumbers in her salad look. She went on: "To this day, I don't know why, but Mum ordered a taxi. We were only going half a mile to the social worker's offices. We could've walked. She had these one-p and two-p coins in a whiskey bottle. She took them all out, arranged them in little see-through bags, and put them in her handbag. She paid the cab fare with them. I'll never forget the white gloves my mum was wearing that day. She got them in the market and she would wash them like they were the queen's knickers. Mum and her white gloves. Lord have mercy."

"I would've spent the money from the whiskey bottle on makeup and stepped," I cut in. "Kim says mascara makes my eyes smolder."

"Makeup isn't the only thing to make a young girl beautiful," Colleen said. "What's inside is more important."

"But peeps can't see your insides, can they?"

After I washed up my stuff and wiped the kitchen table clean, Colleen drove me to the supermarket. I didn't like the old-school music she played in her ride but I kept my gums on hold. *When I get to know her better I'll educate her in all things grime.*

I did most of the shopping, picking out yogurts, biscuits, crumpets, microwave meals, and fizzy drinks. I didn't wanna be rude but I gave funny looks at the ackee, black-eyed peas, and red kidney beans tins that Colleen collected. Following lunch at a Chinese restaurant where I oinked out with spring rolls and special fried rice, Colleen hot-wheeled me home and started braiding my hair in front of the TV in the lounge. I watched a music channel.

"Looking forward to going back to school on Monday?" Colleen asked.

"No, I'm not," I replied. "And it's not a school. It's a Pupils Referral Unit for kids who've been expelled or have issues—that's how they talk. We don't have problems, we have issues. Sometimes there are more staff there than kids. Doesn't stop the fist-offs though."

"Why don't you like your, er, unit?"

"Most of the other girls don't like me." I wasn't lying.

"Can't believe that's true," Colleen said.

More social wanker speak.

"It is!" I raised my voice. "The only two who chat to me are Kim and Nats. Kim's mum had issues with drugs you get from the chemist. You know, those pills to help you when your balloon's about to pop and those ones that help you sleep. They frucked her up big-time. If it was Monday, she'd think it was Saturday."

"Language, Naomi."

"Sorry . . . and Nats was raped by the son of her dad's girlfriend."

I felt Colleen's fingers stiffen. She full-stopped for the longest time. "That's terrible," she said.

"Yeah. And what's more, Nats's family didn't believe her. They're corner-of-the-curb dickheads."

"Swearing, Naomi."

"Sorry."

"Sometimes people cannot help the way they behave," Colleen said. "Circumstances and background have a lot to do with it."

"I haven't got any issues or circum-whatsits," I said. "I'm normal."

"Of course you are," Colleen said.

"D'you think bruvs will like my braids? I bet Kim's gonna be jealous. It'll kill her if peeps looked at me more than her."

"They shouldn't be interested in you just because of your hairstyle, Naomi."

"The black girls in my unit take it double serious. Always talking about hair, they are. I think Nats wears a wig or some kind of . . . what d'you call it?"

"Extensions?" suggested Colleen.

"They call it a weave but it looks like a wig thing to me," I said. "It came off in a fist-off once—some new girl was cussing off Kim at the unit. Nats went cadazy. It was a shock to me cos before that Nats was as quiet as a ballet dancer's tiptoe."

"Quiet ones bottle it all in," Colleen said.

"They took us swimming last year but none of the black girls went. They were shitting themselves about the chlorine polluting their hair. In fact, the only time you can split Nats and Kim up is when her key worker takes her out to get her hair done."

"I was no different when I was young," Colleen said. "I obsessed about having the biggest Afro—"

"Hold on a sec," I blocked her flow.

I hot-toed into the hallway and looked at myself in the mirror hanging from the wall. I lifted one of my braids and twirled it around my index finger. *Too cool.* I busted out a grin before skipping back to the lounge. "Double thanks for this," I said. "You're a legend. How long will it take to finish it?"

"Another couple of hours or so. I think it looks cute."

"It does," I smiled. "Bruvs will love it. Wish I had longer legs though, and my tits could be bigger. They're not as big as Kim's, which is weird cos she's skinnier than me. Anyway, by the time I kiss fifteen they'll have ripened a bit and I'll be able to get myself a decent bruv—someone who's oil-slick and acne free."

Two and a half hours later, Colleen had almost completed my hair. The sound of a key crunching in the front door was a cue for Colleen to relax her fingers. "That's Tony dropping off Sharyna and Pablo," she said. "He's picking up some stuff for his work but he'll be home soon. I better get the dinner on. Can I finish up later?"

I nodded. "Thanks again."

Sharyna and Pablo bounced into the lounge. "Uniform off," Colleen ordered. "Get out your homework if you have any."

Ignoring their mum, Sharyna and Pablo checked out my hair. "Cool," said Sharyna. "It looks great."

Goodness flowed though me.

"Thanks," I said.

Pablo circled me twice. He looked confused.

"What do you think, Pablo?" Colleen asked.

Pablo didn't answer. He lapped around me and scoped me as if I'd grown another head. The laces on both of his shoes were undone. The tail of his shirt covered his backside and he had blue crayon stains on his cuffs.

"Well?" I said. "What ratings do I get?"

Pablo laughed, placed his hand over his mouth, and laughed again. He took his hand away from his face and asked, "Are white girls allowed to have plaits?"

"Of course they are," smiled Colleen.

Sharyna laughed but I couldn't help wondering what older black girls would think of my braids.

A long session of playing Connect Four with Pablo later, Colleen served up a strange dinner of grilled chicken, rice, yams, cabbage, green bananas, and carrots. It definitely didn't look like the casserole that I had cooked for my dad. Napkins were neatly laid on the table. *This is all new.* I picked mine up and pushed it inside the collar of my Rihanna T-shirt. Pablo grinned but Sharyna kept a square face. Tony and Colleen swapped glances. I had on my plate chicken, cabbage, and carrots, but I couldn't take my eyes off the green bananas. They didn't look green to me.

"You boil bananas?" I asked.

"They're not like yellow bananas," explained Tony. "It's not a fruit. It's a vegetable."

"They look the same to me," I said. "I usually have them sliced in custard. I used to make it for my dad. He loved it. But this looks . . . now don't get offended . . . all wrong."

"Try it," said Colleen.

I studied it again. Steam came out of it. *I'm not gonna put my taste buds through mad agonies.*

"Sorry," I said. "Don't wanna offend but it's not for me."

Pablo giggled. Sharyna glanced at him and she caught the chuckle bug.

"Nomi, you *must* eat your vegetables," Pablo said in a squeaky tone.

All eyes on me. I stood up, collected a serving fork, and skewered one. I dropped it onto my plate and cut off a small piece. I picked it up with my fork and brought it up to eye level. I put it inside my gob and chewed. I thought about it and munched again. I looked to the left and then to the right. "It's kinda hard," I said. "Don't taste nothing like a real banana. More like a funny-tasting potato."

Pablo burst out laughing, spraying his side of the table with carrot and bits of chicken.

"Do you want to try the yam?" suggested Tony after he cleaned up Pablo's side of the table. "That's a bit like a potato too."

"It's a bit gray-looking," I remarked.

"Give it a go," Colleen urged me on.

Forking a flat piece of yam, I dropped it on my plate and cut off a small piece. I put it inside my mouth and tasted it. "It's hard," I said. "Like a hard spud."

Pablo and Sharyna burst out laughing again.

Ten minutes later, I finished my dinner. My plate was clean. Colleen busted out her biggest smile yet.

I helped Tony with the washing up as Colleen played a board game with Sharyna and Pablo in the lounge.

"So, what did you do today?" asked Tony.

Standard foster-parent speak. He's making an effort so I'll allow it. But I'll be on prick-fiddler guard if he wants to buy me anything.

"Nothing much," I replied.

"Did you go out?"

"Yeah."

"Where did you go?"

"Shopping."

"Did you get what you wanted?"

"Yeah."

"What else did you do?" Tony asked.

Isn't it obvious? What do I have to do? Swing my head and lash him with my new braids?

I shrugged.

"We had lunch at that new Chinese buffet place on High Street!" shouted Colleen from the front room.

"Great!" Tony smiled. "What did you choose to eat, Naomi?"

"Chinese."

"Did you try any of their herbal teas?"

"No," I answered. "I don't drink flowers."

"We both had spring rolls and special fried rice," added Colleen from the hallway.

This convo is too boring.

"I'm gonna fly upstairs and watch one of my DVDs," I said. I turned to Colleen. "You promise you're gonna finish my hair in the morning?"

"Of course."

"Louise is gonna be proper shocked," I grinned, then breezed past Colleen and climbed the stairs.

A film and a half later, I skipped downstairs to get myself some juice. I passed the lounge and found Tony sitting down on the floor on a cushion. Behind him Colleen was parked in an armchair massaging his shoulders. Again, I never saw Mum doing that for Rafi or Dad. I guess they were raging at each other too much to have time for that.

"Everything okay?" Tony asked.

"Yeah," I replied. "Sharyna and Pablo are in my room watching something."

Tony and Colleen traded glances. I left them to it.

When I had sunk a long glass of Coke, Sharyna and Pablo sat open-mouthed on either side of me, propped up by pillows. I had the lights out and the curtains drawn. They watched onscreen a crusty-built bruv with one eye, a stained white vest, and raggedy jeans make a grisly mess of a tied-up teenage girl's baby toe with a power drill. The blond chick screamed and screamed again before she zonked out. *Serve her right. She shouldn't have had sex with her boyfriend in the backseat of his secondhand Honda.* Pablo covered his face. Sharyna's fingers dug into her cheeks— her eyes went all brown-yolky fried eggs.

Someone squeezed the door handle.

My head snapped toward the door. Tony's eyes shot cannonballs at me before he marched over to the TV and switched it off. He then glared at Pablo and Sharyna. "Bed!"

A big grin erupted on Pablo's face. "Good night, Nomi." He got up and cutey-toed to his room.

Sharyna took awhile to move. She climbed out of the bed and stared at the floor.

"I'll talk to you in a minute, young lady."

"Yes, Dad," Sharyna replied.

Tony's gaze fired back to me. He looked like he hadn't had his pumpkin juice for the longest time.

"They were bored so they slapped on my door wondering what I was up to," I said. "They wanted to watch what I was watching. They haven't got a DVD player in their rooms. It's not like you haven't got the Gs to give 'em DVD players."

Ejecting the DVD, Tony held it in his left hand as he disconnected the DVD player from the TV. He waved it in the air like he just didn't care. "*This*," he said, "is inappropriate. You obviously can't be trusted. Kids of six and eleven should *not* be watching *this* kind of thing."

DVD in hand, Tony stepped out of my room.

"Where are you going with *my* DVD?" I asked. I jumped out of my bed and chased Tony into the hallway.

"To somewhere you can't find it," he replied.

"But it's *mine*. Hasn't got your frucking name on it!"

"You're *too* young to watch something like this."

"It's still *mine*! Who are you to take away my tings? Did you buy it? No! So give it back! Liberties!"

"This is *my* house and you'll live by *my* rules."

"I didn't ask to come here, prickhead! Bomb your fricking rules! Gimme my DVD back."

"Keep on insulting me, young lady, and you'll never have it back."

"You call this insulting? Keep your toes still cos I haven't even launched my cuss attack yet."

Pablo's bedroom door opened—I could see half of his head and his grinning teeth.

"You can have your DVD returned to you when you apologize for showing it to the younger children."

"So you're not giving it back?" I challenged.

"You could be here for a day or ten years," Tony said.

"You *have* to learn boundaries, Naomi. Learn what is acceptable and what isn't."

I turned my back on Tony and stomped along the hallway. I turned into Tony and Colleen's bedroom. They had DVD box sets on a shelf opposite their bed. I swiped *24*, the *Hobbit* trilogy, and a load of others. I dropped a couple on the floor as I hotfooted out. Tony was still in the hallway. Colleen trotted up the stairs.

"She was showing a horror film to the kids," Tony snitched.

Colleen gave me a *why did I decide to be a foster carer* look while Tony shook his head. "She has to learn boundaries," he repeated. "Even if she's here for just one night."

I brushed by them and entered my bedroom. "You've got something of mine and I've got something of yours. And you're not getting squiddly jack back till I get what's mine."

I slammed the door behind me. The doorframe vibrated and I crashed onto my bed. I found my meerkat and hugged it well tight.

Some minutes later, someone tickled my door.

"It's me, Colleen . . . can we talk?"

"No."

"We do have rules, Naomi."

"So?"

"And they must be kept. We can't allow Sharyna and Pablo to watch horror films. They're not as . . . grown up as you. They have had different experiences from you. Can't you understand that? We don't want them to have nightmares."

I understood. But *he* jacked my property.

"Tell *him* to give back my DVD!" I shouted.

"You'll get it back when we both feel you've learned your lesson," said Colleen.

They aren't giving an inch. By now the Holmans woulda made me a snack, brewed me a sweet coffee, and given me funds to buy a brand-new DVD. All with a toothpaste-commercial smile.

"And he'll get his stuff back when *he* learns his lesson," I spat.

"We'll talk in the morning," said Colleen.

"Not talking to *him*," I replied.

"I really don't want to argue with you, Naomi," Tony said, coming up after Colleen. "But rules are rules."

"Good night," said Colleen.

"Good night," repeated Tony.

"Good night, Nomi," Pablo called from the hallway.

Too cute.

I sat on my bed with my knees tight against my chest. I rocked to and fro, my eyes closed. I must've been doing that for half an hour till I got bored.

"Tony, you're a dickhead," I whispered. "A stupid frucking super-duper dickhead."

I closed my eyes.

I was in charge when I looked after my dad. I could go to bed what time I liked. Watch what I loved. Do what I wanted. Now social workers and strangers are telling me what to do.

CHAPTER FIVE

A New Collection

I didn't roll out of bed till Pablo, Sharyna, and Tony had all left the house. When I heard Tony's truck drive away, I pulled the curtains open. The morning sun forced me to scrunch up my eyes. I looked out into the back garden and heard this annoying bird tweet-a-tweeting nearby. There was a mini-size goal toward the back of the garden beside the shed. An orange ball sat in the corner of the net. A neatly shaved rectangle of grass was surrounded on three sides by flowers and plants. The steps from the back door led to a small pond shaped like the number eight. *Very neat. Louise said Prickhead's a landscape gardener or something. At least he's top-rated at his nine-to-five. I couldn't even remember what was at the back of my old flat—never landed a toe out there.*

I checked out the DVDs that I had jacked from Tony's bedroom that were scattered on the floor. I picked them all up, sat down on my bed, and went through them. *The Shawshank Redemption, The Magnificent Seven, The Sting, Some Like It Hot, Saturday Night Fever, Sarafina!, Babylon, Burning an Illusion. Monkey on ropes, hasn't he got anything from this side of the millennium?*

I decided to look for Colleen. Carrying the DVDs, I

went out into the hallway. I skipped downstairs and heard the sound of a washing machine. The noise came from the basement.

I opened the creaking door and went down a short flight of steps. I could sniff dried mud, grass, oil, and washing powder. The air felt damp. I remembered something from my past. It chilled my blood cells. *You don't have to go in there again, Naomi.* It was Dad's voice. *I can see it's traumatizing you. If you want, I can fill a bowl with warm water for you and you can have your wash in your bedroom. You can always have your wash in there if you like.*

I shook my head and the memory bubble burst.

One side of the basement floor had a world of machine and gardening tools stacked in it. I spotted a broken wheelbarrow in a corner.

Colleen was busy separating the colors from the whites when she noticed me. She was wearing her red, gold, and green headscarf. Pink monster-faced slippers snoogled her feet.

"Oh, you scared me," Colleen chuckled. "Do you want your breakfast now?"

"I'll make it," I replied.

Colleen glanced at the DVDs in my hands. "Did you sleep well?"

"Yeah, better than the night before."

"What would you like for your breakfast?"

"I'd like bacon and scrambled eggs."

"Gimme a couple of secs and I'll put—"

"I can make it myself," I cut her flow.

"I'm sure you can."

"I always cooked breakfast for Dad," I said. "That's if there was any breakfast to fry." I turned to climb upstairs. "I almost forgot." I handed over the DVDs. "Here, you can have 'em back. There's nothing there that'll tickle my like cells. It's all ancient . . . Sorry for last night."

"Thank you, Naomi. The reason why—"

Before Colleen could finish her sentence, I had turned around and made my way up the stairs. I didn't wanna offend but I wasn't up for a lecture at that time of the morning. And I was well peckish.

Scrambled eggs and three strips of bacon later, Colleen joined me at the kitchen table. I glanced at her before adding more brown sauce to my plate. A tall glass of Coke sat beside me.

"Thanks again for returning the DVDs," Colleen said. "And apologizing. I was going to say that the reason why we don't allow Sharyna to have a DVD player in her room is because having a DVD player is another distraction for her. It's hard enough to get her to switch her TV off at night."

"You've got a DVD player in your room," I reasoned. "It's one of them Blu-ray ones an' all. And Pablo hasn't even got a TV."

"Me and Tony don't have to do any homework," said Colleen. "And we aren't learning to read. When we first fostered kids they had everything they wanted in their rooms. Games, TVs, the lot. But you learn with experience."

"They slapped on my door," I said. "I was just trying to show 'em that we're mates. I didn't want 'em to be scared of me . . . sometimes I get that."

Colleen nodded once. "I understand," she said.

"It's good that we're chiming on that one," I said.

"It's just that I don't think they've seen anything like—" Colleen stuttered "—what you showed them yesterday evening. Sharyna had a bad night."

"But Pablo loved it," I defended myself. "His cheeks were having a chuckle party."

"I don't think he did like it, Naomi. Sometimes kids at his age *pretend* to like things."

More social worker speak.

"Horror films never bothered me," I said. "Been watching 'em since I was six. Mum used to go down to the Woodside market and get 'em for a pound fifty each. Later on, when Dad was out of it and I couldn't go to school cos I had to look after him, I'd spend the afternoon watching 'em. Then at the unit, Kim knew this Korean bruv who sold DVDs. He wanted five pounds each but Kim would only give him three. She hustles good like that."

"Not every kid's like you, Naomi. Many will get nightmares."

"I'm *not* a kid!"

Shouldn't have raised my voice. Louise is always going on about it.

I dropped my tone. "Did Sharyna have a proper nightmare?"

"No, but it took her a long time to get to sleep," said Colleen. "I had to read something to her."

"She should've said something. I would've turned it off."

"She's not going to say anything, Naomi. She wants you to think she's cool."

I couldn't argue with that. *Why wouldn't Sharyna wanna be cool like* moi?

I sank the last of my Coke. Colleen watched me lick my lips and place the glass down on the table. "What time is Louise coming to pick you up?" she asked.

"About twelve," I replied. "She's taking me out to lunch. Been asking her for months to take me out to that TGI place in Cranerley but she's not busting out her purse on that one. Don't tell her I said so but Louise is the Duchess of Cheapo. Kim's social worker took her to TGIs and Nats's social worker took her to a Harvester when she kissed fifteen. I ghetto it out with Louise on McD's or Zubaretti's Fish and Chips off Ashburton High Street."

"Do you want me to finish your hair before you go?"

"Course . . . I mean, yes please! Don't wanna go out looking like a reject from *Pirates of the Caribbean*."

"Okay. Get your shower and I'll be ready for you."

I washed up the frying pan, plate, and glass, and dried them too. I stacked everything back in the cupboards as Colleen watched me. "Thank you, Naomi," she said.

The local TV news was just finishing its lunchtime shift. Another gangland murking in Crongton. Some fifteen-year-old bruv nicknamed Joe Grine was found punctured in the Crongton stream near Gulley Wood. *Monkey on a nail bed, Ashburton is toxic but wouldn't like to live in Crongton with all that warring going on.*

I grabbed the TV remote control and surfed the music channels. *Too many commercials.* The doorbell rang. Colleen went to answer it.

I heard Louise from the hallway. I thumbed the volume down and pricked up my ears so I could tune in to their convo. "Sorry I'm a bit late," Louise said. "I had a bit of paperwork to catch up with. Everything all right? Any problems?"

I couldn't help but bust a giggle. I covered my mouth.

"Er, yes," Colleen admitted. "We had a bit of an issue about Naomi's choice of DVDs. She invited Pablo and Sharyna to watch one with her."

My *Mad Killer Driller* DVD wasn't getting much love.

"Oh," Louise replied. "I should've confiscated them from her. Unfortunately, her friends seem to have a liking for them."

"She got a bit upset when Tony took it away," said Colleen. "She went off to our room and took a load of our DVDs, but she gave them back this morning and apologized. So it's all been sorted."

"Good," said Louise.

"Coffee?" offered Colleen.

"That'll be great. Where is she?"

Monkey on bubbles. They're so fricking polite it's a wonder they don't wipe each other's asses.

"In the front room," Colleen said.

I switched off the TV, bounced in front of Louise in the hallway, and hot-toed to the kitchen. I clicked on the kettle. "Coffee, Louise?"

Louise didn't answer. She also forgot to sit down. Instead, she stood very still, hands on hips, and scoped my hair.

"What's your ratings?" I asked, twirling my thumb and forefinger around a braid.

"It's . . . nice, Naomi."

"Colleen did it for me. It diversifies my shoulders neatly."

"Yes . . . it's definitely different," said Louise. She finally parked her butt.

"Biscuits?" offered Colleen.

"Not today," said Louise. She studied my plaits like Tarzan was swinging through them. "I don't want to spoil my lunch."

"TGIs?" I suggested.

I might as well try it, she can only say no.

"Let's not go there again," replied Louise. "Too expensive."

The Duchess of Cheapo strikes again. I'm gonna give her a Duchess of Cheapo hat when it's her birthday.

"Kim's social worker took her there."

"I'm not Kim's social worker."

"No, you're not!" I raised my voice. "She's not a tight-arse. Her purse gets to come up for air now and again."

"Hmmm?" said Louise. "I'm not generous?"

"If you were, we'd be scorching rubber to TGIs."

Dunno what Colleen thinks about our banter. She's standing there with her arms folded. But hey-de-ho, that's how Louise and me chit the chat.

"There's no satisfying you, is there?" Louise went on.

"There would be if you took me to TGIs," I giggled.

I made Louise her coffee. One sugar and not too much milk. She took a sip and glanced at my hair again. I didn't think she wanted it to be my passport pic.

"So where're you taking me then?" I wanted to know. She took a custard cream before giving me an answer.

"Monk's Orchard."

"Monk's Orchard? What you taking me there for? It's full of foreign nannies, cats with glammed-up collars, and little old ladies with little skinny dogs."

"There's a lovely café there," Louise said. "Friar's Tuck."

I pulled a face. "Friar's Tuck? I'm not having my lunch in a church canteen. Those church bruvs are the numero uno of prick fiddlers. The reason why they wear those long baggy black garms is to hide their erect—"

"Swearing, Naomi," Colleen blocked my flow.

"Sorry," I said.

"It's not in the church, Naomi," Louise said. "It's just off High Street. They do nice desserts too."

I thought about it. Louise snatched another look at my braids. "All right," I agreed. "But if any of those little gray-backs give me a dirty look then don't blame me if I boot away their walking sticks and make a salami outta their skinny hounds."

I swear I heard Colleen giggle, but when I looked at her she'd straightened up her face.

"I'm sure they won't say anything," said Louise.

An hour later, we pulled up on a quiet street in Monk's Orchard and headed for Friar's Tuck. A fat brown cat lazying on a windowsill scoped me. It was a small café with only eight tables. It was mostly filled by graybacks sinking teas, nibbling cakes, and filling in crosswords. We took our seats by the window and I picked up a menu. I looked at it for five minutes. "I'll have the chicken and mushroom pie, mushy peas, chips, and an extra-large Coke."

Louise took her jacket off, placed it on the chair beside her, and studied my hair again. "Whose idea was the new hairstyle?" she wanted to know. "Was it yours?"

"Yeah, Colleen finished it this morning."

"So neither she nor Tony suggested it?"

"No, it was my idea. Different, innit? Kim's gonna die with jealousy. She's always wanted to have her hair done like black chicks. Nats is lucky, she's black and she can do her own hair. Once, me and Kim skipped school and went to one of those hair salons in Ashburton. You know, the ones where the hairdressers rent a seat for the day. We wanted to get plaits then but Kim pussied out on going inside. I would've breezed in though."

"It looks good on black girls but . . ."

"But what? Doesn't it look sweet on me? Sharyna loved it to the max. And Pablo. Aren't you gonna order?"

"Er, yes, but you shouldn't lose your identity, Naomi."

"Identity? Didn't know I had one. What's my identity then?"

Louise fidgeted in her seat. "Well, er," she stuttered. "The point is, Naomi, is that if you adopt another race's identity, you might start losing your own. The council has all sorts of rules about not allowing emergency foster parents to influence the cultural identity of the children they look after."

"Not allowing the *what?*" I asked. "Don't know what you're on about with all that cultural thing-a-me-jig. I just wanna look presentable and on point. Aren't you always telling me I must take pride in my appearance?"

"Yes I am, Naomi, but—"

"But what?"

Louise sucked in a long breath. "You might lose something of yourself, the real Naomi Brisset," she said. "For example, would you expect a black boy who doesn't know anything about Scotland to wear a kilt?"

"What's a kilt? It's not a tartan condom, is it? I think you're losing your dumplings in your casserole, Louise. The real Naomi Brisset wants plaits like Solange Knowles and Alicia Keys. Don't you think they look gorgylicious? Kim and Nats do."

"Yes, they're very attractive."

"Then why are you munching your knickers about my braids? If we get a good summer this year I'm gonna try and get myself a decent tan. I'd love to look like Rita Ora."

"Rita Ora hasn't got a tan, Naomi."

"You sure? Looks like she's got one to me. Either that or she sleeps on a kick-ass sunbed in her bedroom."

A waitress came over and took our order. Louise went for a boring salad. *What's the friggin' point of wheeling all the way to Monk's Orchard for a salad?* I made sure I ordered the most expensive dessert—something called a tire-mousse. Her purse needed a shakedown.

"A new foster family I know are returning from their holiday on Saturday," Louise said. "The Hamiltons. I thought you might be a good match with them. They've got a daughter who's nineteen years of age. She's at university. She could be a good influence on you."

"I dunno about that one," I said. "I wanna see how it rolls with Colleen. She's on point. Did you know she was in care too?"

"Yes, I do know. But what about Tony? Are you getting along with him?"

"I'm not gonna lie on that one," I replied. "He can be a bit of a prickhead. He loves to do his man-of-the-house thing. He reminds me a bit of Rafi. Rafi would try and lock down rules on my ass. But I'm not too bothered about Tony and I don't think he's a prick fiddler. He kept his ass downstairs when I had my shower. And I like Sharyna and Pablo. I can look after them. Maybe they'll ask me to babysit if they go on holiday somewhere? Where do these Hamilton peeps live?"

"Spenge-on-Leaf," Louise said. "Lovely house."

"Spenge-on-Leaf," I repeated. "Isn't that where the first-class peeps live? Kim told me she went out with a bruv from there once. She reckoned he was twenty—"

"Don't believe everything Kim tells you," Louise said.

"Are you calling her a liar?"

"Er, not . . . Anyway, the Hamiltons live near the top of a hill. They've got a lovely view."

"A lovely view. If I wanna lovely view I'll look at postcards."

"Hmmm."

"There was this kid in the home from Swee Lanka. Neat black curly hair he had. His house was by the beach, or the way he went on about it, it was more like a hut— he had to go outside to take a dump. Quiet he was. You wouldn't believe the shit he's been through. His lovely view didn't do him much good. In fact, his lovely view murked his liccle cousin. He showed me a pic of her—she had—"

"That's different," Louise chopped my flow again.

"These Hamilton peeps? What do they do?"

"Tim, Mr. Hamilton, is an architect. His work takes him all over the country and beyond. His wife Susan does voluntary work at the youth club on South Smeckenham Road. She's very experienced at working with kids of all ages. She's been an emergency foster carer for nearly a year now."

"What's an architect?" I asked.

"People who design buildings."

"Design buildings? They must be white, right? I've never seen any black people draw buildings—not even on TV."

"Er, yeah, they are white. The Goldings are brilliant for the short term but don't you think it would be more appropriate to be with your own kind for the long term?"

"Depends if they're on point," I said. "Architect and a youth worker? Don't sound cool to me."

"Then, Miss Brisset," Louise chuckled, "what's cool to you?"

I thought about it. The waitress returned with our lunch.

"Thank you," smiled Louise.

Grabbing my Coke, I sank half of my glass before answering. "Why can't you put me with interesting peeps? And I don't give a fruck what color they are. Grime DJs, wrestlers, clowns, actors, singers, dancehall queens . . . or that woman whose balloon popped on *Big Brother* the other day. She needs looking after."

"*You* need looking after, Naomi."

"I can look after myself!" I raised my voice. I attacked my chicken and mushroom pie. "Wasn't I doing that before you lot came into my life giving me all your boring rules and sending me to live in nuff postcodes?"

Shaking her head, Louise picked at her salad.

When Louise had finished her meal, she leaned in closer to me and dropped her voice to a whisper. "You know what time of year this is, don't you?"

"Course. It's April. I haven't lost all my dumplings, Louise. You gonna get me another Coke?"

"No, you've had enough. When you get to my age you'll have no teeth left."

"Then I've got a long, long wait, innit."

"*Naomi!* Try and be serious for once. You know what I'm talking about."

I thought of Mum. The bathroom in our old flat booted an entry into my mind. It was horrible. I didn't wanna chit the chat about her. It made me feel on the down-low.

"It's been nearly four years," I said. "Seems like it all happened just yesterday."

Louise put on her top-rated social worker concerned look. "Don't you want to do anything to remember her by?"

"What can I do?" I raised my tones. "She's *dead*. We burned her. I can't bring flowers to a . . . what d'you call it? It looks like an old jug."

"An urn," Louise helped me out.

"I can't bring flowers to an urn, can I? That's just wrong. I still can't believe that Mum's ashes could fit in there. I mean, with my mum's size, she woulda never made the cut of *Ashburton's Next Top Model*."

Louise covered her mouth to block her chuckles but I wasn't trying to be funny.

"I can't work you out, Louise," I said. "Didn't you used to tell me to try and forget about what happened to my mum and think about my future? Now you're telling me I gotta remember her. Make up your freaking mind! You're aching my brain!"

"I just thought you might want to do—"

"No, I don't. Carpet-bomb that. I don't wanna remember her."

I didn't mean it like that. I think of her every day. But cos I think of her 24-7, I have to relive the way she died. It was all red.

"Okay, I get your point," Louise said. She reached out and squeezed my shoulder. She still had her nine-week-course social worker expression on. "Is Colleen serving you food that you like?"

"Yeah, we went shopping yesterday. Tried some black people food as well. It fills you up. I had this hard banana thing and this hard potato thing."

"Did they give you a choice? Or ask what you wanted?"

"Yeah, Colleen's on point. She bought my cottage pies and my mash. She bought me some beads to put in my hair as well. She didn't have enough time to put them in today."

Louise examined my hair once more. "She did, did she?"

"Can't have it plain," I said. "I have to glam it up with something. Gonna have 'em in before I roll back to school."

"Is that a good idea?"

"Trust me, when Kim sees it she's gonna want a repeat

of that one. But who's gonna do it for her? She don't live with black people, I do! Nats might do it for her though. Nats will do anything for her."

Louise shook her head. She sipped her glass of water and gave me a hard look. "Now, Miss Brisset," she said. "Mr. Holman. Did he really harass you?"

I took my time to reply. *He never got jiggy with me but I didn't love the way he scoped me. Something definitely wrong with him. He needs more counseling than I do.*

I dodged Louise's glare. "Can I have another Coke?"

"Not before you tell me what happened with Mr. Holman. The *truth*, Naomi. And not Kim's version of it."

I met Louise's eyes. She had a *really, really* look going on.

"He was . . . trying to be too nice," I replied. "It was getting on my nerves. I'm goggleboxing, he sits beside me and asks, *Are you all right?* I get up to go to the bog, *Are you all right?* I make myself a bacon sandwich and he comes in the kitchen, *Are you all right?* I bounce upstairs to my room and he asks, *Are you all right?* I'm sure he was watching me sleep and he's there whispering, *Are you all right?* He was doing my brain in. I was thinking about clonging him with that Nutra Bullet thing they've got. I just wanted him to leave me the fruck alone and go to the hospital where he can ask if people are all right all freaking day! And she was just too weird."

"Did he at any time spy on you or make you feel uncomfortable in a different way?"

I side-eyed my empty glass. "Not really," I admitted. "He was a proper Dr. Strange though. Didn't want to stay there. Not with them."

Louise now had her *Blue Bloods* face on. "What was wrong with Mrs. Holman?"

"Just didn't like her."

"There must be a reason, Naomi. You can't dislike people just because you think they're weird."

I crossed my arms. *I need to* Great Escape *this convo.*

"So do I have to write a report?" asked Louise.

I found my napkin on the table and wiped my mouth. "Not really. If that's what rocks your fanny you can go ahead, but I don't really give a long squiddly. As long as I don't have to go back."

"Hmmm. You could have caused Mr. Holman a lot of trouble."

"But I didn't . . . One more Coke before I go?"

"No, I have to do another visit after I take you back."

"Duchess Cheapo!"

"Thinking of your teeth, Naomi."

CHAPTER SIX

The PRU

No mad drama happened over the weekend. I spent most of my time chilling with the kids. Sharyna loved the *The Karate Kid* but it was a bit tame for me. I wasn't loving going back to school on Monday and it came way too fast.

I made sure I was the one to tie Pablo's laces before he left the house. I was garmed in my black jeans, black polo-neck sweater, and my sky-blue Adidas sneakers snoogled my toes. I joined Sharyna and Pablo in Colleen's ride. "Thanks, Nomi," said Pablo. He sat beside me in the back and smiled at me. He had two missing front teeth. *Too cute. If I was eighteen he'd be the designer kid I'd like to adopt. I don't want all that drama trying to get pregnant like Mum had. Bomb that. You wanna get 'em young before they have too many issues.* I grinned back at him.

"Seat belts on," ordered Colleen. She switched on the ignition and the world's most boring radio station played something that the graybacks in Monk's Orchard might've twirled their walking sticks to. I made a mental note to grime-ucate Colleen on the radio station issue.

It only took Colleen ten minutes to arrive at Sharyna and Pablo's school. Sharyna checked her hair in the rearview mirror and kissed her mum on the cheek before climbing out of the car. Pablo had cutey-toed through the school gates before his sister had stepped on the pavement.

"Have you got his bag?" asked Colleen.

"Yeah," Sharyna replied. "I'll drop it off with his teacher."

"Thanks, Sharyna."

"Bye, Mum, bye, Naomi."

"Bye, Sharyna," I called out.

"He does that every day," laughed Colleen as she pulled away. "A couple of weeks ago, he left his right shoe in the car. None of us realized until I picked him up. He thought he lost it at school but it was in the back of the car. That's Pablo."

I chuckled and fiddled with one of my braids. I'm not gonna lie, the nerve ends inside my belly were pillow-fighting each other.

"You okay, Naomi?" Colleen asked. "You've been quiet all morning."

"Thinking about how boring school's gonna be," I lied.

"I'm sure it won't be that bad."

Social worker speak.

"It's gonna be zombies-rule-the-world bad," I said. "Anyway, at least I'll link with Kim and Nats again. Haven't seen 'em for nearly two weeks."

"They your best friends?"

I thought about it. "Haven't got best friends," I said. "They're the only ones who chat to me, I s'pose. I might as well not exist for the rest of 'em. They think I'm weird."

"If you want you can invite them around."

I busted out a giggle. "Ha ha ha! No way! Kim will

hijack your purse before you have a chance to tell her to sit down. And Nats, she doesn't like stepping in strange peeps' houses. She's funny like that. I was staying with my nan for the weekend and Nats once trod all the way from Notre Dame to see me in Ashburton. She was hunting for Kim. She was going cadazy with worry."

"We could all do with friends who worry about us like that," said Colleen.

I nodded. "Anyway, when she came to my nan's gates, I told her that once she finds Kim she should sink a few of her mum's stress pills to calm her down. And she wouldn't come in. She just waited outside in the rain till I got ready. She wanted me to help her hunt for Kim."

"I can understand that," Colleen said. "She was desperate to find her friend."

"I s'pose so. Kim goes all ghost on us now and again. *Sometimes I need to be on my lonesome to think about stuff*, she's always telling Nats. Nah, Nats got some serious abandonment issues."

"What are the teachers like at your unit?"

"Boring. There's only a couple of teachers there in any one day. Loads of staff though. We don't have too many standard lessons. We have talks and stuff. Personal development, they brand it. Usually it all ends up with everybody cursing and fisting off . . . Were you ever expelled?"

Colleen kept her eyes on the road ahead. "Er . . . yes, I was."

"Yeah! What for? Fisting off with some bitch? Nah, you don't seem the type to maul somebody. Jacking from a shop? Can I come in the front?"

"Of course."

Colleen pulled over. I jumped into the front passenger seat and Colleen rejoined the traffic.

"Going missing from school?" I pressed again.

"No."

"Setting fire to the science lab?"

"Definitely not."

"Allowing a teacher to touch ya? Or a bruv in an older year?"

Colleen narrowed her eyes and gave me a hard look.

"Then what was it?" I wanted to know.

Colleen full-stopped for a second and then swallowed a fat worm. "Fighting."

"Fighting? No jokes? You?"

"Yes, me, Naomi."

I scoped Colleen from eyebrow to toe corner. "You're not a hard-curb bitch," I said. "Or you don't look like one. What trauma licked you?"

"Let's not use the word bitch," Colleen said. "My dad certainly wasn't the best in the world, nor was my mum. But they weren't canine."

"Sorry."

She hot-wheeled on for about half a mile in silence. Needles of guilt pricked my brain.

"I was fourteen," she started again. "And even shorter than I am now."

"I wouldn't call you a hobbit," I said.

Colleen smiled. "I'd just started at a new school—Smeckenham Girls," she revealed. "I was seeing this fifteen-year-old guy who was going to the mixed Coloma School down the road. I thought he was the hottest thing ever in a basketball kit. But we all do at that age."

"When you say *seeing*, you mean linking up with him, slurping tongues, and doing stuff, right?"

"Er, yeah."

"Did he bust your rosebud?"

"Did he *what*?"

"Bust your rosebud," I repeated. "Destroy your virgin status?"

"*No*. It was just ... Anyway, the guy was two-timing me with this other girl that I didn't know about. And as luck had it, she went to Smeckenham Girls too. As soon as I found out I broke up with the guy. But his other girlfriend wouldn't leave me alone. She called me a slag, a whore, a slut. Called me every name under the sun."

"What an uber-bitch. Did you clong the brain matter outta her? Did you make her donate a mug of blood to the curb drain?"

"Language, Naomi."

"Sorry ... did you ..." I struggled to find a word that wasn't a curse. "Did you switch on her? Do her in? Bang her up?"

Colleen took her time in answering. "I could just about cope with all the name-calling," she said. "And I tried to ignore her."

"Then how did it all boot off?"

Colleen took in a long breath. "One afternoon I passed her in the school corridor. I was on my way to home economics—what do they call it these days? Food technology or something? Yes, that's it. We were going to make a Victoria sandwich cake that afternoon. My bag was heavier than usual."

"And then?"

"She made a comment."

"What did she say?" I asked.

"We got into an argument, name-calling and stuff. She said, *At least I haven't got a mental mum, you effing slut!* I totally lost it."

"I woulda cold-potted her with something that roasts fat turkeys. Liberties!"

"I grabbed her hair and just tried to rip it from her scalp." Colleen's eyes got bigger and she stopped blinking. "People were jumping on my back but I wouldn't let go. She was screaming . . . I held on for as long as I could. I was dragging her head along the floor. I remember an ambulance coming. Flour and eggs were all over the place. I lost my little bottle of vanilla essence and my caster sugar. Teachers were pulling me away but I put up a fight because I wanted to find my vanilla essence. I was really pissed at not being able to make my cake."

"I woulda been pissed too," I put in.

"I . . . I didn't even know where my mum was living at that point," Colleen went on. She finally blinked. "But in a way . . . in a way I wanted to make the cake for her. Stupid, really."

"It's not stupid," I said. "You had issues."

Colleen tried to raise a smile. "I ran to the toilets. I wouldn't come out for ages. It seemed like there was a million people outside my cubicle."

I squeezed Colleen's shoulder and gave her one of my

special smiles. The kinda smile I used to give to Dad when he rolled home sober. "I used to try and bake my dad stuff. One time I tried to make him little fairy cakes but the frucking—"

"Language, Naomi."

"—gas cut off before they were cooked. No funds on the gas card. Had to wait to finish 'em two days later. I was really pissed with Dad when he donated half the cakes to his pub mates that night. I let him know about it in the morning by spilling my porridge over his jeans. Anyway, that mega bitch you had a brawl with had it coming."

Colleen thought about it. Her face switched back to foster-carer mode. "No, Naomi," she said. "I was wrong. I was making her pay for everything that went wrong with my life. Making her pay for my mother leaving me and so many issues that I had."

I shook my head. "I still woulda clonged her."

Fifteen minutes later, Colleen dropped me off at my PRU unit. She gave me a five-pound note for lunch and said she'd be back at three thirty p.m. to pick me up. I watched her roll away and wave goodbye before I stepped through the parking lot and to the entrance. I thumbed the entry-phone buzzer and made faces at the closed-circuit camera that was scoping me from a high position on the wall. "It's me! Naomi. Whass-a-matter with you? Don't you recognize me? Let me in."

The buzzer sounded. I pushed the door open. The reception area had an L-shaped beige sofa with diversity cushions just to the right of the door. Dated teen magazines were scattered on a coffee table. Behind a counter, parked on a stool, and goggleboxing a computer screen and a closed-circuit TV monitor was Marie. She scrubbed up pretty neatly for a woman of thirty-nine but her rouge was a bit tomato-ketchupy and her nails coulda shanked a bulletproof vest. I loved her leopard-print top though.

"Morning, love," she greeted. "Glad to see you're back with us. Moving again, was you? You must be dizzy, love, with all the moving about you do . . . Kim's missed you."

"All right, Marie," I replied before turning right into a hallway. I didn't wanna get into a long convo with her. Marie could go on a bit about *Love Island*, wherever she was thinking of going on holiday, her latest boyfriends, clubbing, and whatever cocktails she sunk on a Friday night.

"They're in the lounge," Marie called. "Richard's giving a talk."

Richard's always giving a talk.

The lounge walls were covered in posters warning about drugs, more drugs, and the whole alphabet of sex diseases. It leaked into my head so much that it messed up my appetite for bananas.

A television sat in a corner and above it another poster asked everybody to report bullying. Richard stood in the middle of the room. He was wearing a light-blue shirt with rolled-up sleeves and black jeans. *He'd be fit if he wasn't hobbit size. I mean, Hermione never fell for one of her dwarf-sized professors, did she?*

Crashing in armchairs and giant cushions were my classmates: three black boys, two white, a black girl, a mixed-race girl, and two white girls. Wearing orange leggings, a micro jean skirt, a *Kung-Fu* T-shirt, and neatly topped off with orange spiky hair was Kim. A silver stud sexed up her nose and a gold ring glinted in her bottom lip. She was don't-even-have-to-try pretty.

"Naomi! You've gone all ghost on me," she called out. "Where've you been?"

Everyone in the room looked at me. I felt proper awkward.

"I moved, innit," I replied. I played with one of my braids. "Had issues at my last place."

"They don't give me untold days off when they move me," complained Kim. "Why aren't you moving back in with us? Haven't you tried every other foster family in the whole of Ashburton and yonder? Move back with us, sistren."

"I—"

"Can we save our greetings and conversations until break time?" asked Richard politely.

"We'll catch up later," said Kim. "Who braided up your hair?"

"My new foster—"

"Girls!" Richard raised his voice. "Now, where was I?"

Nats pointed at my braids. "Looks good," she said. "I . . . I thought you'd be going to another school."

"Not yet," I said.

Nats looked a bit disappointed. She still had her anorak on. She was wearing sky-blue tracksuit bottoms and pink sneakers. Her hair extensions snaked past her elbows.

"Next thing she'll be injecting her arse with steroids to try and look like us," spat Cassandra, a sixteen-year-old black girl lying curled up on a cushion in front of Nats. She had brown braids and matching brown lipstick. Her eyebrows were tattooed on. She gave me a brutal eye-pass and kissed her teeth. A cold gust of fear blew through me.

"Take an iced smoothie, Cass," Kim dismissed her.

Cassandra kissed her teeth again and hardened her eyebrows. I tried to delete her from my radar.

"Don't worry about Cass," said Kim. "It looks on point. I might get my hair done like that when it grows a bit."

"Who asked you to jump in the argument?" barked Cassandra.

"What are you?" yelled back Kim. "I can't remember you giving birth to me so *don't* tell me squat. I'll join whatever argument I want."

Nats moved and sat right up close to Kim.

"You think I'd want *you* as my mum?" crackled Cassandra. "I'd murk myself if I came out of your crotches."

Same unit, same issues, same beefs.

It booted off.

As she launched herself at Cassandra, Kim was held and pulled back by Richard and another male member of the staff. Arguments brewed and boiled for the next ten minutes with nuff pushing and barging. Every third word was a curse. I stared at the floor and played with one of my braids. *What else can I do?* Nats tried to calm Kim by caressing her shoulders and giving her a hug. Richard stood in the middle of the room with his arms outstretched.

"Now that we're calm again, I'll pick up where I left off."

I was the only one listening to him cos the others were thumbing their mobile phones.

"We have to learn to resolve our disputes in a calm manner," continued Richard. "When we resort to violence we often regret it afterward."

"I *won't* regret it," interrupted Cassandra.

"Far better to have a frank and honest discussion about the issues at hand," Richard said.

The ultimate social wanker speak.

"I'm gonna be real, Richard," Kim chimed in. "This talk is your most boring yet. When are you showing us the film?"

All eyes were on Richard except Cassandra. She was giving me a chronic side-eye. I can't lie, my nerves clawed the inside of my belly.

"Okay," agreed Richard. "But please watch and consider how a little argument spirals out of control. Try to learn from this."

"Just put in the frucking film," a bruv demanded from the back of the room.

"Any more swearing and the DVD will be ejected," warned Richard.

"Just put the fricking DVD in," another bruv raised his voice. "It's the only reason why I touched down here today."

The class settled down to watch the film. It was about two fourteen-year-old bruvs falling out over a smart phone they had found. It ended with one of them carving the other. Throughout the drama, Cassandra side-eyed me. *This is getting zombies-in-the-hood scary now. What have I done to her? Try not to look at her. Stay with Kim and Nats.*

Richard wanted a discussion following the film but neither he nor his staff put up too much resistance as we decided to take our first break of the day twenty minutes early. I followed Kim and Nats to the canteen. We all bought a bag of crisps, a chocolate bar, and a Coke can each and parked at a table. Cassandra and her sistren Yoanna sat down at the opposite end of the room. I could feel the hate from their eyes.

"So is it a long-term ting at your new place?" Nats wanted to know. "You won't be coming back to the unit?"

"No," I replied, "it's just a temp ting. For maybe a week or so."

"You're living with black people," said Kim. "What's that like?"

"The food's different," I said. "They're a bit stricter. You have to eat at the dinner table an' all that. I didn't even have a TV in my room when I first got there. I had to put up a fierce resistance about that."

"Liberties," said Kim. "What about the dad? Not a prick-o-phile, is he? Watch him, Naoms. I'm telling ya, most of them foster dads are pedos—that's why they're in the fostering game. You reported Mr. Holman, right?"

"Er, kind of."

"What d'you mean, kind of? You told me he was tickling on your bathroom door and on your bedroom door when you were getting changed. That's how they start, Naoms."

"He wasn't," I tried to explain before Kim got into her flow.

"They start by being all nice to ya," she relaunched. "Being polite and all that game. Buying you sweets, sneaking you smokes, and giving you hard liquor. Some of 'em even buy you little presents, earrings and perfume. Remember the one who bought me a phone? The ultimate dick-o-phile! They're trying to get you to trust 'em. But underneath all that malarkey they want to put their grimy fingers up your business. That's what they wanna do, Naoms. They don't even bother to keep their fingers clean. They don't even wash 'em after they've been to the bog. They put one up there and when they get excited they put another up there. Make sure you report Holman to your social worker. Freaking prick-o-phile. If he ends up in prison they'll fly-kick the spunk outta him."

"I will," I nodded.

"And don't let your new foster dad anywhere near the shower when you're in it. He might try and peep through the keyhole and all that lark."

"It's all right," I managed to get a word in. "I've given him warning. He knows not to fruck about with me. His toes have to stay downstairs while I'm in the shower."

"Good!" said Kim. "I still dunno why you're even allowing your social worker to take you to foster homes. You wanna squiggle a fat full stop on that one. What's her name again?"

"Louise."

"You wanna sack her, like yesterday," Kim insisted. "Slap her face with her P45 and boot her outta your life."

"She's . . . all right," I said.

"You're better off linking with us. How many times do I have to broadcast that?"

"It—" Nats started. She stuttered. "It . . . it might work

out all good with your new people. You never know, not all foster carers are—"

"Anyway, your hair looks on point," Kim blocked Nats's flow. "Just like them black singers. Makes you look real pretty-duper-licious. Bruvs will be twisting their necks to look at ya."

"Thanks."

Nats stared at Kim. She didn't look too happy. After two weeks of being away from Kim and Nats, I still didn't quite know where my toes fitted around their relationship. I always felt like the spare tire in the trunk—only to be of use when needed.

"Don't worry what anyone says," Kim continued, raising her voice. "Last time I looked, there isn't any law against white chicks having braids." She reached out a hand and felt the texture of one of my braids. "Must've taken ages."

"About five hours in all," I replied.

"It suits ya," said Kim. "Exposes your big crusty forehead a bit but it works."

"Thanks," I said again.

Nats looked at Kim. "I could . . . I could do your hair for you," she offered.

"You can do your own, Nats," Kim responded, "but can you do other peeps?"

"Of course," Nats said. "I'll do it tomorrow, before we get here. I'll get up at snore o'clock if you like."

"Nah," said Kim. "Everyone will be saying I'm copying Naoms."

"I don't mind," said Nats. "Not a problem. I'll even do it in a better style than Naoms is repping."

"It's all right, Nats," Kim said. "Don't want you getting up early just for *moi*. Chill."

I glanced at Cassandra. She side-eyed me and whispered something to Yoanna. My belly chopped and churned like a mad sea.

"I've made up my mind," announced Kim.

"Made up your mind on what?" I asked.

"I feel the need for new garms."

"My pockets aren't chinking with anything, so good luck on that one," Nats laughed.

"Gonna need a plan C," said Kim. "I was thinking about that bruv who tried to chirp me up the other day on Ashburton High Street. He looked like he had some decent change in his wallet. Next time I see him—"

"But he's gonna want something, Kim," Nats cut in. "You shoulda told him you're with me. In fact, why *didn't* you tell him you're with me?"

Kim thought about it. Nats wasn't laughing anymore. *This issue keeps coughing up, and I'm gonna keep my beak sealed on this one or otherwise I'll be the salami in their crusty roll.*

"I'm tired of wearing cheapo shit from Primark and charity shops," Kim finally broke the silence, ignoring Nats's question. "And Naoms, when I get some funds, I'll take you up the scrubbed-up side of town to buy us some decent brands. I could do with some new knee boots."

Nats glared at Kim, then eye-drilled me.

"And you an' all, Nats," Kim quickly corrected herself. "Not gonna delete you out, am I. You're my girl and you *know* that."

"You better *not* delete me out," said Nats. She was pissed.

"Nats always goes cadazy if I leave her out of stuff," said

Kim. She laughed nervously. "Dunno what she's fretting about."

We stood up, flung our litter into the bin, and stepped outside to the playground. I slurped from my Coke can. Kim was about to take her smokes out of her pocket when suddenly I was licked from behind. I dropped to the ground. It was Cassandra. *Who else?* She booted me in the ribs twice before Kim realized what was happening.

"You're not black!" spat Cassandra. Her face was full of issues. "You hear me! You're not black so don't try it!"

"Leave her alone!" screamed Kim. She jumped on Cassandra's back, strangled her with her left arm, and punched her with the other.

Cassandra wasn't small. She flung Kim to the ground and banged her twice before stomping on her stomach. "You frucking freak! Get your bitching hands off me!"

Before Nats could react she was booted from behind by Yoanna. "You frucking bitch!" The two of them swapped licks and fell to the ground.

I just about managed to find my senses. I took a five-yard run-up and booted Cassandra in the back as hard as I could. Cassandra dropped to her knees. She snapped her head in my direction and let out a mad roar. She rushed toward me with Urban Zombie intent. *Sometimes that Wonder Woman spirit leaves your ass and you know it's time to get your hot-stepper on.*

I ran for dear life into the school building. Cassandra hoof-huffed after me but the doorway was blocked by Richard and two other staff members who had seen the mauling from the canteen.

"She bitch-kicked me in the back!" screamed Cassandra. "I'm gonna burst that white bitch! See if I don't. Frucking white piece of shit! Coming to school thinking she's black. YOU AIN'T FRUCKING BLACK! You think they can save you all the time? You're DEAD! D'you frucking hear me! MURKED! I'm gonna carve a second crease in her white ass. *See* if I don't."

My heart biff-boffed like a mad grime bass line. I panted like I had an asthma attack. I didn't stop fleeing till I came to an empty classroom. I sat in a chair with my face between my knees. I tried to control my breathing. I covered my ears to try to drown out Cassandra's cursing.

"I'll frucking get her and her freak friend and Nats the coconut! Frucking bounty, she is! She doesn't even know she's got half nigger in her!"

Marie entered the classroom. "You all right, love?"

I looked up. I felt tears in my eyes. "Fruck off, Marie! Stop pretending you care."

That wasn't called for.

Marie crossed her arms. "Is that what I get from seeing how you are? I dunno what's wrong with all of you. All you want to do is kill each other. Sometimes I think we should give you sticks and stones, take you to the hills, and let you get on with it.'

"Marie!" I screamed.

"There's no need to shout."

"Then get outta my face!"

Shaking her head, Marie walked backward toward the hallway. "I'll give you a bit of time, love, to get over this. You don't look too badly hurt. I'll be back later to check you over. I'm the first-aider here and I didn't take that course for nothing."

I offered Marie one of my best dark-side-of-the-curb glares. Marie shook her head again, turned, and clip-clopped to reception.

I heard Cassandra shrieking and cursing as she was dragged to the safe room. I closed my eyes.

In my inner vision I could see the medics stepping into our bathroom. They were pulling on their surgical gloves. There was no rush. They were all so very calm. Dad was sort of hugging himself in a corner. Tears were dribbling over his lips.

"You all right, Naoms?" Kim asked gently.

Opening my eyes, I heard Dad's voice echoing inside my head: *God will look after her now. I'll look after you from now on, angel.*

Kim kissed me on the forehead and hugged me. "Come, let's go for a smoke," she said. "Don't worry about Cass. She's on lockdown. You wanna see the nuclear fallout on Yoanna. Nats frucked her up something chronic. They've put Nats in the other safe room. They better let her out soon if they know what's good for 'em. Nats got a bitch temper when she's ready, especially if anyone tries to maul me."

With her arm around my shoulders, Kim walked me to a corner of the playground. We spotted two bruvs smoking rockets in another corner. We met Richard on the way.

"You okay, Naomi? Are you hurt?"

I was too much in a daze to answer.

"She's all right," said Kim. "I'll look after her. You lot took your time coming out, didn't ya? What's your game? Wanted us to talk frankly about our issues? Leave us alone. We'll be on the level soon enough."

I stared at the ground.

"Maybe Naomi should see Marie," Richard suggested. "She's our first-aider."

"*Fruck* Marie," snapped Kim. "*I'll* look after her."

"Maybe Marie can check on her later on?" Richard said in a whisper.

Kim thought about it. "All right. But after *I* see to her."

Richard returned to the building. Kim took out her smokes. She fired one up and offered it to me. I accepted. She kissed me again on the cheek and smiled at me. "You're alive," she said. "Not too much damage and still breathing. You should've seen the state I was in after I had a mauling with my last boyfriend—he didn't love it that I liked Tarzan *and* Jane."

I tried to return the smile. I couldn't manage it.

"Cass should be locked up," said Kim. "There aren't any baked beans in her Full English. Not even any mushrooms. Nobody's safe when she's around."

I took another pull. My throat felt like it was lined with beach stones. I spotted two members of staff scoping us from the canteen window. "I want you to cut it off, Kim," I said. "Cut it *all* off!"

"Come again, Naoms?"

"Cut it off! Look how much drama it caused today."

"Don't let cadazy Cass put you off. What did I tell you before? Don't let others tell ya what to do. *Don't* play their games, Naoms." Reaching out to grab a braid, Kim brought it up close to her eyes and sniffed it. "Remind me who done this for ya?"

"My new foster mum, Colleen."

"How long she take? Five hours? Has any other foster mum spent five hours on your hair?"

"No."

"Did your dad ever do your hair?"

"Are you being funny? No, I used to cut and wash *his*."

"Then you can't snip it off, Naoms. Quit that malarkey."

I finally managed a half smile. I pulled on my cancer stick again. Kim placed an arm around my neck and pulled me toward her. She kissed me on the forehead. I felt like I had a big sister looking after me. "*Don't* sabotage your own hair, Naoms. Dunno how long you might keep it but it looks sweet on ya. So fruck 'em all and anybody who sails in that boat."

We finished our smokes and returned to the lounge. During the next lesson we heard Cassandra being escorted out of the building and taken into a van. She cursed Kim's, Nats's, and my name as she went. I wondered what her personal issues were. We all had them. I tried to blank her out but I felt a tight ball of fear in my belly. It was bouncing around and I couldn't control it.

Midafternoon, I went to the ladies. Nats followed me in. After we done our business, we both washed our hands while staring at ourselves in the mirror above the sinks.

"I swear to God I'd murk anyone who hurts Kim," Nats said. Her eyes never left the mirror. "*Anyone.*"

"I get it," I replied. "You'll always have Kim's spine. You messed up Yoanna big-time."

"Kim might chat like she's of the curb but she's not really," Nats went on. "She's . . . she's soft beneath all of that. Vulnerable. She can't really fight. She doesn't come from the ends. Her mum's middle class."

I wasn't quite sure what to say. Instead, I nodded.

"After what happened to me, I was gonna put a full stop to my frucked-up life," Nats said. "Kim saved me from all of that. I owe her everything."

"I . . . I know."

She looked at me like she was warning my ass about something. "That's why I can't tolerate it if someone hurts her. You understand what I'm saying?"

"Nats," I answered, "I'm not sure what road you're going down on this. Kim's always had my back too. She's been a good sistren. Why would I even *think* of hurting her? I'm not Cassandra. You should be raging at *her*."

Nats thought about it and then smiled. "You're right, Naoms . . . sorry, I didn't mean anything. Just a bit emotional after what happened today. I didn't love seeing Kim in pain."

"Me too," I managed.

Nats dried her hands on paper towels and left. I had to remain in the ladies for a couple more minutes just to allow my heartbeat to get back on the level.

Colleen arrived to collect me at three thirty p.m. on the bang. I said a quick goodbye to Kim and Nats before climbing into the back. I waited for the longest time as Colleen had a convo with Richard and two other members of staff. I just wanted Colleen to hot-wheel me home.

Instead of getting into the driver's seat, Colleen joined me in the rear. She closed the door before she spoke. "You all right?" she asked. She placed a palm on my cheek and looked into my eyes.

"Yeah, I'm all right," I said. "She took me by surprise. Didn't see her coming. Next time I'll get the first lick in. She doesn't scare me, you know. She *doesn't*! I'll do her in next time."

Truth being told, Cass terrifies the living pulses outta me. Nats scares me a bit too but maybe I'm being a bit para about her. She was upset cos Cass launched an attack on us and she went into protective mode. That's all.

"You . . . you still want to, er, keep your hairstyle?"

I thought about what Kim said to me earlier. She said I looked pretty-licious in it. And Colleen put in a long shift to do it.

"Yeah, I wanna keep it," I finally replied.

Colleen smiled and rubbed my cheeks. She then climbed into the driver's seat. "Don't you want to join me in the front?"

"No," I said. "That's where Sharyna sits."

I didn't say too much else on the way to pick up Pablo and Sharyna. They had a calming effect on me and I felt like a big sister again. Pablo showed me a drawing that he had completed of his family. Colleen was sketched with big eyes and electric diversity hair; Tony was drawn with a spade in his hands; Sharyna was looking into a mirror; and I was hugging what looked like a small rat. It slapped a smile on me but for some reason it also made me feel sad inside. *This is what a normal fam looks like, Naoms. You've never had normal.* I ruffled Pablo's hair.

Starting the dinner once she arrived home, Colleen told me, "Tony will be taking you to school tomorrow. Is that all right?"

"Tony?"

"Yes. You don't mind?"

"No, I don't mind," I said. "Just that I'll miss you leaking stuff about your school days."

Colleen smiled. "I have an early doctor's appointment I have to keep," she explained. "And I need to shoot off just after I drop off Sharyna and Pablo."

"It's cool by me," I said. "He's taking me in his truck?"

"Yes. You're okay? Nothing hurts?"

"I've got all the carrots and dumplings in my casserole," I said. "Kim gave me a look-over and then Marie checked me out."

"As long as you're sure."

"Double sure."

I took a seat at the kitchen table and watched Colleen grab a bunch of potatoes from the vegetable stand. It reminded me of watching Mum preparing to cook. "What you making?" I asked.

"I seasoned up some chicken thighs this morning," Colleen said. "I'm going to put them in the oven in a minute. Then I'll be roasting potatoes and steaming some parsnip and cabbage."

"Can I peel the potatoes?"

"You don't want to play with Sharyna or Pablo?"

I didn't wanna let on to Sharyna and Pablo that I was terrorized by big Cass. That ball of dread was still bouncing around inside my stomach. I felt safe around Colleen. I felt the water behind my eyes but I wouldn't leak tears in front of her. Never did that in front of Dad or Louise so I wasn't gonna start now.

"Nah, I play with them later," I said. "But I'm used to cooking. Used to cook for Dad. Most of the time he didn't want it or sometimes he would sink it in the morning. Sometimes he'd eat it cold. I had to fight with him to take the plate off him and smack it in the microwave."

At bedtime, Colleen checked to see how I was doing. My TV and light were still switched on. The end credits of a low-rated horror movie rolled down the screen. My curtains were open. I had curled up into a ball and was sucking my thumb—Dad said I had got into this habit after Mum died. My meerkat was beside me. Colleen smiled at me. She switched off the TV, drew the curtains, secured the window, and left.

CHAPTER SEVEN

Tony's Violin Story

Tony wheeled carefully around the Ashburton one-way system. I could sense he wanted to start a convo but didn't know how to. *Dunno why he's feeling that way. I'm talkable.* "Have you got everything you need?" he asked.

"Yeah."

"I hope you're not worrying about that Cassandra girl. She won't be there."

"I'm *not* fretting. I'm not scared of her."

"Have you got your packed lunch?"

"I don't have packed lunches."

"Have you got mine and Colleen's number on your mobile?"

"Yeah—have you lost your onions, Tony? You wrote it down for me just before we left the house."

Tony half grinned. "Of course I did," he said. "I'm going senile already."

"What's senile?" I asked.

"When you forget stuff."

"I forget stuff," I said. "I'm not going senile, am I?"

"Not yet, Naomi. It usually afflicts the old."

"Afix the old?"

Tony shook his head and laughed. Nothing was said for the next few minutes.

"How much money did Colleen give you yesterday?" Tony started again.

"Five pounds," I replied. "But I need extra funds to buy something for this project."

"Oh, what project is that?"

"We're baking something in the kitchen. Need ingredients for a cake. Yeah, we have to put something in to pay for the ingredients."

With his right hand on the steering wheel, Tony used his left to pull out a ten-pound note from his jeans pocket. "Here," he offered.

Monkey on the hoops. This is too easy.

"Thanks," I said.

Three minutes of silence followed. I felt a slap of guilt hustling ten pounds outta him so I thought I'd ask him about himself. It was the polite thing to do. Louise was forever telling me to take an interest in the peeps who care for me. "What made you wanna mess around with grass, trees, and mud for a job?" I asked. "Sounds grimy and proper boring."

Tony half smiled. Something hit his sweet spot. "I was raised opposite Crongton Park," he revealed. "On the south side."

"You lived in Crongton? Are you sure? You don't sound like you grew up sucking bottles in those ends. Was you a Crongbanger? Have you seen anybody get murked?"

Tony shook his head. "No, no, no. I didn't get involved

in any of that. My dad would've killed me if I did. Crongton's not all about gangs."

"My sistren Kim says Crongton's all about the Gs. Everyone's armed up to their necks. They sharpen their hounds' teeth with files."

Tony gave me a *really* look. Louise must've taught him. He changed the subject. "Whenever I had free time—"

"Free time?" I interrupted.

"Time to do what I wanted," Tony explained. "My old man was always ordering me and my brothers and sisters to do our chores."

"What sort of chores?"

"Oh, you might be hoovering all the rooms, cleaning windows, polishing the furniture, clearing up the garden, washing the dishes, mopping the kitchen, taking the clothes to the bagwash. My parents liked to keep a clean house."

"Bagwash? What's that?"

"Oh, sorry, the launderette. My mum called it the bagwash."

"That's not a life sentence, is it," I said. "That's pretty standard. I did all that stuff . . . and more. Sometimes I had to wash out clothes in the bath with soap."

"I guess no kid likes chores."

"I'm *not* a kid and I had no choice," I raised my voice. "If I didn't do it, Dad wouldn't. It always had to be me. If the social were coming, I had to get up at cuckoo o'clock and do it. I wouldn't put the empty cans or the bottles in the bin. They'd check 'em. I had to dump 'em in a bin around the corner or on the next street."

"Must've been tough," said Tony.

I shrugged. "That's how the flow in my house went."

"Did you have time to play? Time to do normal things?"

"What's normal?" I replied.

"Go out to the park, have friends, go swimming, shopping—you know, normal stuff."

I gave Tony one of my hardest corner-of-the-curb glares. "Are you taking the piss?" I spat. "How was I s'posed to do *normal* stuff when I had to look after Dad?"

"I didn't mean . . . Sorry, I should've realized."

Grown-ups! Sometimes they can be so dumb.

I dropped my harsh tones. "That's all right," I said.

Tony cleared his throat. "What I was trying to say was that I never did normal things with my dad."

"Did he love his liquor?" I wanted to know.

"Er, yeah, the odd drink. Dark rum and Coke. The odd beer. Nothing more than that . . . except at weddings."

"Then what are you bitching about? At least you had a dad who was sober. That's a win."

"Er, yeah, I was lucky," admitted Tony. "But he never . . . he never took us out to the park, the fun fair, day trips to the beach, you know, that sort of thing. He never even came to watch me play cricket for my school. I was the captain! He would just go to work, come home, eat his dinner, and put his feet up. He didn't even ask to see any homework. For the rest of the evening he would just sit in front of the TV reading his newspaper. We only heard him when he shouted at us for playing too loud. That was my dad."

I side-eyed Tony like he was the most spoiled kid in

the world. "Boo bleedery hoo!" I mocked. "If I had a violin I'd play you the longest solo. Be careful, somebody might wanna make a film out of your hard-curb life story."

Tony couldn't block his chuckles. *At least he can take a joke.*

"Did he give your mum funds to buy the food and make sure your gas and electric wasn't deleted?" I asked. "Did he buy you your school uniform? Did he go to the post office and pay the council tax? That's what I had to do. If he did, you had an up-to-spec and fit-for-use pops."

Tony thought about it. "I must sound pathetic to you," he said. "He paid for all those things you talk about. Mind you, if I kicked out my shoes he'd let the whole house know about it for days, and the next-door neighbors. My mum would get so mad with him cussing me that she would give me lickings just to make him shut up."

I thought about my own dad. "That's one thing my dad never did to me," I said. "He never licked me once. I used to hit him though when he wouldn't get up."

"Sometimes Colleen does the same to me," Tony laughed.

"If . . . if he hollered at me to stop I knew he was all right," I went on. "I hated watching him lying down so still . . . I used to think he was dead. I don't love scoping dead people . . . except in horror films."

I thought of Mum.

"Must've been tough," Tony said.

I shrugged.

There was silence for the next five minutes.

I hope he's not one of those leaky-eye sorts who bursts into tears at any sad story. That'll be mega awkward.

"Anyway, what free time I had I spent in the park," he finally said. "I developed a love of greenery and trees. My brothers and sisters thought I was weird. I joined this cub group in Ashburton and I would go camping with them in the summer."

"What? In tents? In a field?"

"Yeah, in tents. In a field. That's where people usually go camping, Naomi."

I pulled a face. "No way anybody's gonna get me sleeping in a field. Torpedo that! Where did you shit?"

"During the day we'd look for a public bathroom or a restaurant."

"What about at night?"

"Er, in the woods, I suppose."

"Eeeewwww! Gross!"

Tony busted out giggles again. It took awhile for his humor to get on my radar.

"I need to ask one of the staff to give me a report on what happened yesterday," he said.

"Nah, you don't have to go in," I said. "I'll get it and bring it home."

"You sure?"

"What? You think I'm too dumb to ask for a report?"

"Not at all."

"Then I'll get it."

"Okay, make sure they put it in an envelope."

Five minutes later, Tony dropped me off. "I'm finishing early today so I'll be back by three thirty," he said.

"All right, I'll see you then."

"Have a good day."

"Yeah, and you have a good time with your mud and trees."

Tony chuckled and pulled away.

A mad rush of fear grew in my chest and up through my throat. In my inner vision, I saw Cass and myself in a stone cell without any doors and windows. There was no escape. A low ceiling forced us to crouch. Her fists were bigger than the belly of a fat snowman. *No one to save you now, you white piece of shit! Not acting black now, are ya? I'm gonna pull those braids outta your scalp and choke your white neck with 'em.* She dynamited a fist against my jaw.

"*Fruck* school!" I said to myself.

I quick-toed to the nearest newsagent and juiced up my Oyster card with the ten pounds that Tony gave me. I bought two Twirl chocolate bars and a can of Coke. I parked myself on the grass that fringed the main road, nibbling my choc bars. There I sat deciding how to rock my day. I switched off my phone and watched the traffic flow by as I enjoyed the hit of chilled Coke. *I gotta do something about this addiction, but not today.*

I came to a decision. I stood up and stepped to the bus stop. I caught a bus to the East Ashburton train station and treated myself to a hot chocolate in a nearby coffee bar. I felt all adult and first class alongside the Formula One–buggy mummies and suits. *Maybe I should've asked Nats and Kim to come with me. But they might not have the funds for the fare. And besides, even if Kim does have some money she'll only spend it on cancer sticks, makeup, or some top that tickles her fancy in a charity shop.*

I took a short train trip to Woodside Bridge.

Emerging from the station, I rolled down a side road that led to a grimy housing project. I entered a corner shop and bought another can of Coke. I didn't love the suspicious eyes on the other side of the counter trailing my ass. "I've *not* come here to jack anything!" I barked.

The watchful eyes focused on somebody else.

I checked my surroundings. It hadn't changed much. The same stinking little shops selling bread past its sell-by date and an untold amount of international phone cards, the same mums bitching about topping up their electric meter keys while buying packets of fagarettes and celeb mags, the same dog owners allowing their ugly hounds to brown-slime the pavement.

Not trusting the elevator, I made my way to the third floor of a council slab. I could hear the reversing and whirring of a truck somewhere behind the block. I passed a black cleaner on the balcony. I didn't think he loved his day. He was wearing a yellow Day-Glo top, gloves that coulda kept an Eskimo's digits warm, and black stomper boots. "*Bonjour, mademoiselle,*" he greeted me with a smile.

"All right, *monsieur,*" I replied.

Smacking the letter box of the last door along the balcony, I rubbed my hands together to keep them warm. I heard footsteps approaching. I knew Nan was checking to see who her visitor was through the spyhole. "It's me, Nan!"

Keys rattled in two locks before the door opened. Wearing a Dean Martin T-shirt, brown cardigan, jogging pants, and red slippers was my eighty-three-year-old great-grandmother, Primrose Burton. "Naromi! What wind has blown you here then?"

I shrugged. "Haven't seen ya for a while," I said. "Wanted to see how you were. Thought you could do with the company. Any crime in that?"

"Oh, not at all, Naromi."

"My name's Naomi, Nan."

"Naromi, Naomi, whatever it is. Anyway, it's a joy to see ya. A mighty joy." She gave me a nice but weak hug. "Come on in out of the draft."

I followed Nan's slow steps into her small kitchen at the end of a short hallway. The stench of old tea bags, piss, and furniture polish polluted my nostrils. I sat down on a wonky wooden chair at the small kitchen table and took in my surroundings. The fridge still had the same postcards stuck on it that I remembered when I was knee-high. They were sent from Brimton Bloats, Morthcore Palace, Pickleness Sands, Dunweir Broads, the Isle of Chark, Lewesborough Flats, and Headington Gramley. The cooker had an old-school, dented, whistle-blowing kettle sitting on it. Blu-tacked around an old Tony Curtis calendar were pictures of Princess Diana. There was a small pine shelf with framed black-and-white family pictures and souvenir tea saucers standing on it. I recognized Mum and Grandma. It still made me sad when I realized I'd never see 'em alive again.

An energy-saving fork-shaped lightbulb showered a weak yellow light and a broken cobweb clung on for sweet life to a high corner of the ceiling. In the middle of the kitchen table stood a pile of opened letters and bills.

"I'm just about to have my crumpets," Nan said. "That's how I start my day. Do you want any?"

"Nah."

"*Excuse* me!"

"Er, oh, sorry. No thanks, Nan."

"That's better. Good manners doesn't cost anything. It's nearly half past ten, Naromi, so when I finish my breakfast, I'll be off out."

"It's a bit chilly out there, Nan."

"My heating is set to go off at half past ten so if you wanna spend time with ya old Nan you'll have to come with me to the library."

"The library?"

"Don't knock it," Nan said. "I used to go to the coffee shop and ask for a mug of hot water. Always looked at me funny, they did, asking me if I'd like to try fancy coffees I can't even pronounce. So I thought blow 'em and their look-down ways! I'll find somewhere else. The heating makes me feel snug in the library. I'll read the mags till noon."

I watched Nan drop two crumpets into the toaster. "So how're you getting on?" I asked.

"Oh, by and by. At least I've got my health. That's all what counts. Mildred downstairs, always in hospital she is. If it's not her legs it's her arms, if it's not her arms it's her tummy, if it's not her tummy it's the arthritis playing up, if it's not that there's something wrong in her head. Always something wrong in Mildred's head. That's what loneliness does to ya, I suppose. I dunno why they bother sending her back to her flat. They might as well keep her in, poor dear. She likes her own bed, you see. But, by and by, I get by. Have to thank the Man Upstairs. Gracious He is. Sure you don't wanna cup of tea? Did I ask if you wanted crumpets?"

"No thanks. I've got my Coke."

"Still drinking the Coke? Your mum should've never given it to ya when you was a nipper. I didn't know she was putting that in your bottle. Someone should've said something. You'll be all gums and tongues next time I see ya."

The crumpets somersaulted out of the toaster and Nan buttered them with shaking hands. "Are you supposed to be here, Naromi?"

I shrugged again.

"You'll get me in trouble again. I don't want the nosy people turning up at my door. You know I don't like the nosy people in my flat. A thousand questions they ask. It's like being on *Mastermind* when they're around."

"What's *Mastermind*?" I asked.

Nan shook her head.

While sinking her crumpets, she picked up a small flask on top of the fridge and poured milk in it. She topped it off with three drops of brandy before screwing the cap on and shaking it. "Keeps the cockles warm," she smiled. "When you're old enough you can join your old nan for a drink—that's if the Man Upstairs gives me a few more years."

"Never drank brandy, Nan. Never drank anything. I know what it can do to ya."

I thought of Dad.

Nan gave me side-eye. "It only turns into Beezlebub juice if you drink too much of it."

I wondered who Beezlebub was when he took a piss behind the bike sheds. Or maybe it was a cartoon character.

I wanted to change the subject. "You get lonely living on your own, Nan?"

"Me? Lonely? That's what they all say! Mildred's forever asking me to come with her to the social club. They do all sorts of things, she says. Pottery, needlework, painting, learning, dancing, and how to use the laptop wotsit. But the thing is, Naromi, it's all old people doing it. Why do they always think I wanna see old people all the time? I like to see young'uns too."

"You still forgetting things?"

"I'm afraid so. I keep forgetting to go to the bloody toilet! But I haven't wet myself for a day or so. Embarrassing it is. Now, wrap up, Naromi, time to go out. It's ten thirty."

I watched Nan wash up her plate and soon realized what a struggle it was for her to move her fingers. "Let me do that, Nan."

"*No!* I'm not a . . . what do they call it? I'm not a carrot! If I stop doing things for myself then I'll become a carrot. If I'm not careful, there'll be a pride of donkeys at my front door. You don't want that for your old nan, do ya?"

"No, Nan."

She pulled on a pair of sneakers, tied on a headscarf, and put on a pink overcoat—well, it was pink a long time ago. She placed her flask in the left coat pocket and shuffled out. She bent in the breeze. I followed her out, making sure she had her keys before pulling the door shut.

The library was a fifteen-minute trod. It was obvious that the staff who worked there all knew my nan. Grabbing three celeb mags, she found a chair near a radiator and read. Every five minutes or so, she sampled her flask. I hoped I didn't have to carry her out.

Wandering around the library, I didn't quite know what to do with myself. I decided on a graphic magazine and pulled up a chair next to Nan.

"Mr. Swales doesn't seem to be in today," she said.

"Mr. Swales?" I repeated. "Who's he when he scrubs his fangs in the morning?"

"You'll like him, Naromi. It's always a joy to see him. Big shoulders, nice smile, wavy Greek hair."

"Wavy Greek hair?"

"Blacker than black, by and by," Nan said. "And kind of curly like the hair on a Greek statue. You ever seen Greek statues, Naromi? A beautiful joy they are. They even carve out the naughty bits. You wouldn't know him but Mr. Swales reminds me of Victor Mature. He was in *Samson and Delilah*. Lovely shoulders he had. I'm telling ya, Naromi, fifty years ago I would've gave him the eyes and a bit more if he took my bait."

Monkey in the pigsty. I don't wanna think about Nan having sex. Have to change the subject.

"How long are we staying here, Nan?"

"Till lunchtime. In the meanwhile, can you do a favor for your old nan?"

"What d'you want me to do?"

"Go up to the counter and ask if Mr. Swales is in today."

I smiled and bounced up to reception. An Asian clerk in a pretty pink hijab was stamping a book as I waited patiently for her to look up at me. She had kind eyes.

"Is a man called Mr. Swales in today?"

The clerk gave me a long, funny look, and then her gaze turned to Nan, who was draining her flask again. She switched back to me with an *oh you poor thing* look. Social wankers were expert at it. "Mr. Swales left us well over a year ago," she said in a near whisper. "We tried to tell her once but Primrose got very upset. Can . . . can you tell her he's on holiday or something?"

I turned around to look at Nan; she was flicking through her second magazine. "I'll tell her something." I returned to sit beside her. I couldn't think of what to say.

"Is he on a tea break or having a pee?" she asked.

"No, Nan. He's . . . he's on holiday."

"Oh, I see. Wonder where he's gone. Probably to where his people come from, where they have black wavy hair and nice broad shoulders. I hope he remembers my postcard. But that's a shame he's not here, I really wanted to introduce you to him. One of these days I'm gonna invite Mr. Swales around for tea and crumpets."

I didn't leak another word until I had flicked through my magazine.

"Nan?" I said. I placed the magazine on the empty chair beside me. "The Man Upstairs? Is He still looking out for me? D'you think He's still blaming me?"

Nan pointed a bent finger at me. "Now, I don't wanna hear that kind of talk, Naromi," she said. "I told you once and I'll tell ya again: you weren't to blame."

"But my mum—"

"She wasn't well, Naromi. She had depression. Had it for years she did. I suppose she did her best to hide it from all of us. It was a shock to us all when we found out she was on more tablets than dear old Mildred downstairs."

"I still feel bad about it," I said.

"Have any of those nosy people been in your ears?" Nan asked. "Telling you something different? If they have, I'll be up in their faces. Never trusted 'em, coming to my front door with their fancy pens, fancy forms, and fancy phones."

"No, Nan, it's just sometimes when I can't sleep at night, I wonder if your Man Upstairs, you know, blames me. I could've saved her. She was taking the longest time in there. If only I checked."

"He's your Man Upstairs too," Nan said. "Gracious He is. He doesn't blame you. Don't worry your little cotton red heart, Naromi."

"My nightmares are all red, Nan. I wish they would stop. I wish I could stay with you."

Nan took another glug from her flask and busted out chuckles. Her laughter turned into a chesty cough. "The nosy people will never allow it," she said. "And if I had to swear to the Man Upstairs I would have to agree with 'em on that score. I mean, I forget things every day. It's a wonder that I remember to wake up. Only yesterday I couldn't find the gas card to put in my meter. On my dressing table it was, and I was turning the kitchen upside down. There were pots and pans that I forgotten I had all over my kitchen floor. I couldn't boil water for my tea and it hurts my hands to wash the dishes in cold water. Can you imagine that? Daft as a woolly sock on a hamster I am."

"I could do all that for ya," I said. "Looked after Dad, didn't I?"

"No, Naromi. Someone's meant to be looking after *you*. Not the other way around. That much I do know. You're still a pup."

"I like looking after people, Nan."

"And you did a grand job with your dad. But he was never your responsibility. Oh no. The nosy people should've given him more help. I don't mean to offend ya but they should've handcarted him away to Alcoholics Anonymous or one of them rehab places. Forgive me, Naromi, but he coulda served shots in a pub by cutting himself."

I busted out some mad giggles. Nan always had jokes.

"Dad never liked the social workers," I said. "Always swearing at 'em he was. *Mind your frucking own beeswax!* he used to holler. *This is my flat! Naomi's my daughter, so fruck off out of it!* Funny thing was, it wasn't his flat. It was Mum's but she—"

"It's no small wonder you have a mouth like a Woodside drain," Nan cut in before I got upset. "You need to rein in your swearing, Naromi. Who's gonna marry ya with a mouth like that? Don't expect any nice Mr. Swales to be asking. My Rita had the same problem. She had the mouth of a chimneysweep's Y-fronts."

"They're always telling me off about my swearing," I admitted.

"It's not ladylike, Naromi. I can't imagine Lady Di ever swearing. Oh Lord no. She knew her Ps and Qs and how to drink a cuppa tea with her little finger up in the air. A joy she was. Killed her they did. One day it'll come out, murdering bastards. They didn't want her to have a desert baby with black wavy hair, you see. Oh no. You can't have the next king of England being the brother of a desert baby, can ya? Anyway, now, what was I on about? You haven't got anything to worry about what Him Upstairs is thinking about ya. He'll understand. Gracious He is."

I flashed a grin.

"Naromi, watch my seat while I go to the ladies. Hopefully they've got some extra rolls in today."

"Extra rolls?"

"Toilet rolls. Saves me going to Tesco and buying 'em. Mind you, library bog paper's a bit rougher than Tesco. Tree bark might be smoother."

Returning with her handbag much bulkier than it was before, Nan dropped herself beside me, drained another glug from her flask, smacked her lips, and picked up her third magazine. I chuckled.

"They've got a computer wotsit room here if you fancy it," said Nan. "You go on, I'll be here. Perhaps Mr. Swales might come in on his day off just to say how you do. Nice Greek hair he's got. Did I tell you he looks like Omar Sharif? He's got desert eyes."

I wondered who the hell Omar Sharif was.

I rode the Internet until twelve thirty p.m. Nan tapped me on the shoulder. "Time for lunch," she said. "Oh, and by the way, I love your hair. The nosy people are not too much good at anything, but if they did your hair I'll give 'em a sticky star for that."

"It was my foster mum, Colleen."

"Oh? Who's she then? She African? Colleen doesn't sound like an African name. It's Irish, isn't it? Irish people don't do plaits, do they? Not that good anyway."

The gusting wind had brought rain with it and Nan

did her best to cover us from it with her small, broken umbrella. We made our way to a café and sat at a table. "My treat," she said. She used a handkerchief to wipe the wet from her face.

"You got enough money, Nan?"

"What do you take me for? If I'm going to the library I always make sure to put four quid in my coat pocket for lunch."

"But I'm with you today."

"Oh, I've only got four quid. Never mind, we'll share some scampi and chips."

"It's all right, Nan, I've got my own money."

"Didn't steal it, did ya?" she wanted to know. "I won't have it, Naromi! Your grandmother loved to nick clothes in C and As and Marks and Sparks years ago. Got caught she did. They took her to the police station. Never been so embarrassed in all my bloody life. Verbal warning she got. I can tell ya for free that when I dragged her home she got a lot more than *that*."

"Nan, I didn't nick the money."

"You sure? That's a fair bit of money for an eleven-year-old."

"I'm fourteen, Nan."

"You are? Since when?"

I paused as a waiter approached. "Can I help you?" he asked.

"Scampi and chips, please," Nan ordered. "And I don't want old chips that you've kept in that heating thing for half an hour. I want fresh chips."

"Yes, of course," the waiter nodded. His attention switched to me. "And for Miss . . ."

"I'll have the same," I replied.

Nan watched the waiter return to the kitchen and as soon as he was out of our radar, she leaned in closer and said, "He gave me cold chips last time I was here. Not having that again. Nothing worse than cold chips. I can tell ya for free I'm not gonna stand for it."

"Nan," I said after a while, "what was my mum like when she was my age?"

"Your mum? She was a little dear she was, a little dear. Now let me see . . . My Rita would always bring your mum around for Sunday dinner—I used to do a beef roast. Lived in Moyston Coals they did . . . Can't remember the number of the bus they had to get. Was it a 133 or a 68?"

"Rita lived alone, didn't she?"

"Where's your English, Naromi?" Nan barked. "You make sure you refer to my Rita as Gran."

"Sorry, Nan. Did Gran have a guy?"

"As soon as he heard about my Rita being with child, he legged it like a big-fisted money lender was after him. Your grandpa's name was Bill. Skinny as a cheap sausage he was. A bit of a charmer. Horseshoe smile he had. Flies could get lost in his dimples. He used to work on the Crewbury docks and he sold all sorts of plunder in pubs. He loved to smoke fat cigars, did Bill. Those cigars had a load more meat on them than he had. Don't ask me how he lifted up all those boxes."

"Your scampi and chips," the waiter announced, placing the plates on the table.

Nan looked at the chips suspiciously. "Fresh chips?"

"Taken out of the fryer just this minute."

"Okay, ta very much. Now, be off with you! I'm talking to my great-granddaughter. Isn't she a looker?" Nan pinched my cheeks.

The waiter smiled and went back to his business.

"My mum?" I asked again.

"Oh, sorry, Naromi. There's me going on about my Rita and Bill and you asked about your mum. A little dear she was. Loved going to Riddlesdown Park in the summer holidays with pink ribbons in her hair. We'd play rounders and have a picnic. Peanut butter and jam sandwiches we had. Oh, and lemon tarts. Mustn't forget the lemon tarts. Your mum was good at rounders. She clobbered the ball for miles and miles. The birds had to watch out. She ran her little red cotton heart out going around the bases. Big grin on her face. All the boys fancied her. My Rita had to shoo them away when they knocked on her door—"

"So she wasn't all sad-like then?" I wanted to know.

"No, not at all. That came later when my Rita passed."

"Must've been horrible."

"Yes, it was," Nan replied. "Grieved forever, your mum did. She didn't wanna go back to school."

"What did they do?"

"The doctors and the nosy people put her on tablets," said Nan. "Don't think they helped her too much. It sucked all the get-up-and-go out of her."

"So Mum had it hard."

"Oh yes, by and by. She never got over my Rita's passing. That's probably one of the reasons why she took so many pills. Poor little dear."

* * *

We stayed in the café for another couple of hours. I bought Nan two cups of tea and I topped up with a can of Coke. Nan told me stories about two-timing bingo callers, gold-toothed market traders, one-eyed cat burglars, and female pickpockets. The wind and rain had quit by the time we rolled home. As we stepped out of the elevator and turned right onto Nan's balcony, we spotted Tony, Louise, and another social worker waiting outside Nan's front door. *Monkey on a cracking ice rink.* They didn't look like they were about to tell us they'd won at bingo.

"Oh shoot!" Nan yelled. "The nosy people!"

I'm not sure why but I started to bust a chuckle as we approached them.

"You nosy people haven't been inside my house, have ya?" asked Nan. She fumbled in her coat pocket for her keys. "I'll have you know I clean it in the evening rather than the morning, so don't you go about titting and tutting. I won't stand for it."

"It's all right, Primrose," said Louise. "We're just waiting for Naomi."

"We just wanted to know she was okay," added Tony.

"I suppose you all want a cuppa tea," said Nan. She opened the front door. "I haven't got enough crumpets to go around, though, unless you want to cut them in half. Two of you will have to stand up. I've only got two chairs around my kitchen table. And I won't have any of your questions."

"Nan, I don't think they wanna step inside and have a cuppa tea," I said. "They've come to take me back."

"She's not in trouble, is she?" asked Nan. "She hasn't been nicking, has she? If she has I'll give her what for. I'm not too old to dish it—"

"No, nothing like that," replied Louise. "We're just glad she's safe and sound. Perhaps she should've told us she was paying you a visit."

"Can I see Nan at the weekend then?" I asked.

"Of course," Tony said. "I'll drop you myself and pick you up."

Nan looked at me with kind eyes. "Bless your little red cotton heart," she said. "Give me a ring to tell me what time you're coming around. I'll put the kettle on and make sure I'll get some crumpets in."

"You'll be all right, Nan?"

"I'll be all right by and by. I'm going to watch an old Barbara Stanwyck film for the rest of my afternoon. That's if I can remember how to work the DVD player. Marvelous she was. Dear Mr. Swales should've been an actor with his Greek wavy hair. He would've been marvelous too."

Nan offered me a big grin as she entered her flat, but before she closed the door behind her, she gave a brutal side-eye to Tony and Louise.

"Everything seems to be all right, so I'll be off," said Louise's social worker colleague. I'd never seen her before.

Tony watched her disappear down the stairs before he spoke. "Everything okay, Naomi? You ready to go home now? Maybe next time you can tell us when you want to see your nan."

"Yeah, I'm ready."

"If you don't mind, Tony, *I'll* be driving Naomi back to

your place," said Louise. "I just need to have a quiet word with her. Is that okay with you?"

"No, not a problem," said Tony. "I'll see you back at my place."

Louise gave me a pissed-off *really* look. That meant one of her long lectures. Never thought I'd ever say this but I wanted to wheel home with Tony.

Louise didn't drop a word until I was in the passenger seat. She sat next to me with her arms folded. "Why did you visit your nan on a school day?"

Okay, how would Kim deal with this situation? Don't let 'em chat down to you, Naoms. Release the rebel in ya.

"Cos I felt like it," I said.

"Are you sure it hasn't got anything to do with that incident you had with Cassandra?"

"*No!* I'm not scared of her! You think I missed school just because of her? No freaking way."

"It's okay to be scared, Naomi," Louise said. "Cassandra won't be attending the unit for a while. She has her own issues to work on."

"How many times do I have to tell ya? I'm *not* scared of her! I haven't seen Nan for a while so I wanted to see her. I don't wanna leave it so long that when I turn up I find out she died."

"That's not going to happen."

I raised my voice: "How d'you know? Nobody expected what happened to my mum but it happened anyway. I dunno if you've noticed but Nan's getting old. And she forgets stuff. How come you people aren't checking up on her?"

Awkward moment. Louise stared through the windshield. I fiddled with the car radio.

"Something must be the matter, Naomi," Louise broke the silence. "Tony dropped you at school. He said you seemed well, in good spirits. He even said you two have started to get along. You haven't said anything to anyone about wanting to visit your nan. As far as I remember you haven't seen her for, what, two years?"

I shrugged. "Doesn't mean I don't wanna see her. It's not like *you* take me to see her. I've asked you nuff times."

"That's not true!"

"Yes it is! You just wanna take me to boring lunches and talk about boring issues. By the way, Nan *loves* my hair."

"I have to do my job, Naomi," Louise said. "And find out if anything's bothering you."

"I'll be a lot better if I can see my nan when I want to!"

Louise took a few deep breaths. I sensed she wanted to puff one of her smokes. I stared through the window. "Is everything really okay with you and Tony?" she asked. "He says you two are getting along, but is it true? Has he said anything inappropriate to you? Has he offended you in any way?"

I tuned the car stereo to a dance radio station. I pumped up the volume and started bopping my head to a banging drumbeat.

"Naomi, I *asked* you a question," Louise raised her tones. "Has Tony behaved in an inappropriate way?"

"He's a bit naggy," I finally replied. "A bit like you actually—but he's all right, I s'pose. What've you got against him?"

That corked her flow. She was silent for the next twenty seconds.

"You sure he hasn't said anything?" Louise had a question mark between her eyebrows. "Or did someone say something to you on the way to school? I have to try and understand your reasons for taking off like that."

I turned up the radio volume a couple of doses more.

"All the same, I'm thinking of taking you to the Hamiltons," Louise spoke loudly over the music.

"The who?"

"The Hamiltons," repeated Louise. "Didn't I tell you about them? I'm pretty sure I did."

"Are they black too?"

"No, they're white."

I shrugged.

"They might prove to be a better fit for you . . . not because they're white, but they can offer you more of their time. Colleen has her hands full with Pablo and Sharyna, and Tony does a lot of overtime."

"If you say so."

"You're still on our adoption list, Naomi. My job is to find you a suitable family for the long term."

"If you say so."

Monkey banging cymbals. When is she gonna shut up? Maybe she didn't have a blessed day. I bet her bosses are cussing her cos she didn't fill in a form right or something like that. Or maybe one of her other kids ran away. That's standard for Louise. I just wanna listen to some hard-curb grime rhymes now.

"If you want," she went on, "I'll arrange a weekend for you to stay with the Hamiltons. They're good people."

"Good people? You said that about the Holmans."

"Hmmm."

I liked it when I gave her her pissed-off face.

"Me seeing the Hamiltons won't get in the way of seeing my nan?" I said.

"No, not at all."

"Can I go on a school day?"

"No! Naomi, I know you've had a hard time of it but you must keep to your boundaries."

"Boundaries? I'm not King Kong living behind a tall wooden fence."

Louise snapped her head toward me and scoped me hard. "You're *not* going to see your nan during a school day."

"Why not? I saw her today. Tony said he'll take me."

"Tony's just relieved that you're safe and sound. Promise me you won't do this again. I do have more *important* things to do than look for you, and so does Tony. He has to work."

I shrugged again. "Why are you all getting your pubes in a tangle? I was gonna come back. You think I wanna end up begging and sleeping in some grimy shop doorway with some ugly hound sniffing the corners?"

I didn't chat too much when I reached home. I had a spaghetti Bolognese dinner and then went to my room. I didn't watch TV or put in a DVD. Pablo came in for a while and we played some game on his PlayStation but I wasn't really feeling it. "Nomi, you're rubbish at this!"

He wasn't wrong.

"I'm not feeling too blessed today, Pabs," I said to him. "I'll be better tomorrow."

Pablo went to his bed.

Sharyna bounced in afterward and spilled that some bruv in her class had passed her a note.

"What did it say?" I wanted to know.

"It just said, *I like you.*"

Sharyna couldn't kill the grin spreading from her cheeks. "What do I do?" she asked.

I wasn't sure what to tell her. No guy at any school or unit had ever passed me a note telling me he liked me. *Gotta be grown up here.* "If you like him back, then when he chats to you, just be nice to him and see what happens."

"Thanks, Naomi."

"But *don't* let him touch you from the neck down."

"I won't."

She gave me a little hug. I wasn't quite sure what to do with my arms. *Don't freak out, Naoms. This is normal. You done good with your advice.*

"Good night," she said.

"Good night, Sharyna."

I couldn't sleep. My door was slightly open but Colleen still knocked. "Can I come in?" she asked.

"Yeah," I replied.

She parked on my bed and it looked like she had prepared all evening what she was about to tell me. "Everything all right, Naomi?"

I shrugged.

"You weren't your usual self this evening," Colleen added.

I didn't respond. I stared at my meerkat beside me.

Colleen tried to smile. She placed a hand on my shoulder. "It might help to talk."

I thought of Nan, Mum, Dad, and the rest of my fam. "She's gonna die soon, innit?" I said.

Colleen moved closer to me.

"Nan hasn't got much time left, has she? I haven't got anybody after her. I don't know where my dad is . . . or they're not telling me."

Colleen wrapped her arms around me and I placed my head below her chin. I had to go into fight mode to stop my tears.

There we stayed for the next half hour. I liked that. Sometimes grown-ups always think they gotta say something.

"I wanna go to sleep now," I said.

"Okay," Colleen said. "Call me if you need me."

She got up and switched off the hallway light. I grabbed my meerkat, pressed it tight to my chest, and bawled my little red cotton heart out.

CHAPTER EIGHT

Ancient Disco

"*Tavares? Chic? Sister Sledge?*" I read, sifting through Tony's disco CDs. I was crashing on his bed, flinging away CDs that were just all wrong. Framed photographs of Pablo and Sharyna smiled down from the walls. Books on childcare, stories about sad kids, and thrillers about killers filled the shelf overlooking Colleen's half of the bed. Books about black people—I recognized Martin Luther King from school when we studied Black History Month—rested on the opposite shelf. "This is ancient," I moaned. "Haven't you got anything that was made after I was born?"

"You said you wanted dance music," said Tony. He leaned against the bedroom door.

"You're a black bruv, right?"

Tony looked at his hand. "Obviously," he replied.

"Then how come you haven't got any new stuff? Have you heard of the Grime Doctors? The Gutter Band? The Road Block Three? Or Medieval Sue? You must've heard of her?"

"Er . . . no," Tony shook his head. "I like the old stuff. Haven't you heard of Nile Rodgers?"

"Who's he when he's smoking rockets in the forest?" I wondered.

Tony shrugged.

"This is gonna go all *Titanic*," I said. "Nats and Kim will be at our gates in half an hour. If I play your stuff their toes will get proper bored and they won't stay too long. I couldn't blame 'em."

"Naomi, you gave us just two days to sort out this little do," said Tony. "Colleen's done wonders in the kitchen. Sharyna and Pablo are blowing up balloons, so at least you can pretend to be grateful."

"I'm well grateful, Tony . . . it's just the music. I mean . . . even pharaohs would say your stuff is too old. I should've told Nats and Kim to bring some of their tunes. Maybe Kim will have something on her phone—she's got a smart phone."

"Oh come on, Naomi! My music's not that bad."

"I don't wanna drop a slab on your feelings, but you need to take a day off, cremate your CDs in the back garden, and step into the fresh millennium."

Tony couldn't block his chuckles.

"It's *not* funny!" Reluctantly grabbing a handful of disco CDs, I made my way down the stairs.

The smell of spiced fried chicken steam-bombed my nostrils as I entered the kitchen. Plates of crisps and peanuts were on the table. A pot of rice simmered neatly on the cooker. Colleen sprinkled black pepper over the salad that included slices of avocado, cucumber, baby tomatoes, homemade potato salad, and beetroot. There was a plate full of chocolate digestives on the counter near the bread bin. Holding a balloon, Pablo was looking at them as if they were the top-ranking treat in Willy Wonka's Chocolate Factory. Colleen had her back turned to him. He looked at the chocolate and glanced at her. He gazed at the snacks again. He licked his lips and sucked in a breath. Suddenly, he Olympic-toed to the plate, jacked two biscuits, hot-stepped out, and bounced up the stairs.

"What did I say?" Tony said as he came down the stairs. "*Don't* put out the biscuits until we serve the chicken and rice."

"I wanted to get everything ready," Colleen answered, then looked at me. "Did any of the CDs tickle your fancy?"

I gave Colleen a *really* look. Louise would've been proud of me. I took my phone out from my tracksuit pocket and dinged Kim. "Have you left yet?" I asked.

"Just about to," she replied. "Nats is putting some stiffening gel in my hair."

"Bring some music with ya," I said. "It's a 9-9-9. If you can't, my liccle party's gonna go down like a fart in a hot lift."

"I'm not bringing my CDs, Naoms," said Kim. "They always go missing when I take 'em out. I haven't got anything on my mobile but I've got my MP3 player."

I turned to Tony. "Can you play an MP3 through your laptop?"

"Er, yes," he replied. "Think I can manage that."

"Thank fruck for that!" I breathed again.

"Language!" yelled Colleen.

"You saved my life," I said to Kim. "Get your ass here in flashtime and make sure Nats comes—she'll go all toxic on me if I leave her out. It's my last day here before I fly to the Hamiltons for the weekend."

"Don't worry," Kim said. "Wherever I go, Nats follows . . . Who are the Hamiltons when they're blowing their noses in the morning?"

"I'll find out tomorrow, innit."

"Be careful, Naoms," warned Kim. "Don't trust no one. Especially the man of the house."

Forty-five minutes later, Kim and Nats arrived. I opened the door and was shocked by Kim's face. Her left eye looked like a wet slug with big teeth had been nibbling at it and her left cheek had swollen to the size of one of Pablo's balloons.

"What pissed-off mother bee sat on your face?" I asked.

"Oh, some bruv who I crashed into in JDs," Kim responded, all casual like. "I was just scoping the latest Nikes and brands. He bullshat me about how he's an apprentice for some top-ranking soccer team, told me I had gorgylicious eyes, and then asked me out. I didn't give him the reply what he wanted so he started to get all wifey-beater on me. Trust me, he looks more frigged up than I do. I bit his cheek, his shoulder, and his hand. If he didn't hot-leg it away I would've fanged his balls."

Nats stared at her feet and was silent behind her.

I led them into the house.

Wearing blue leggings, a micro denim skirt, a Marilyn Monroe T-shirt, and a red beret over her multicolored spiky hair, Kim did a proper inspection of the house. "Kinda cool," she said. She kicked a balloon out of her path. "They could do with one of them house stylists though. But I like the pics on the wall. It's all very Black History Month. Even Cass should give you ratings for staying here. Maybe

I'll ask my social worker if I can be fostered out to a black fam."

Nats followed us into the front room. She smiled when she spotted Sharyna and Pablo swapping insults. "Hello," she said. "Has Naoms been bossing you around?"

"Yeah!" laughed Pablo. He watched Kim as if she had arrived from one of them *Star Wars* planets.

"No," said Sharyna, covering her brother's mouth with her hands.

"It's nice to meet you two," greeted Nats.

"And nice to meet you too," said Sharyna.

Okay. So far so good. Even Nats is being sociable. Kim must've had a one-on-one with her.

Colleen served plates of fried chicken, rice, and salad to everyone. Kim sat next to me at the dinner table. Nats decided to sink her meal standing behind Kim. Pablo plonked himself next to Kim and scoped her up and down with Disney-cartoon eyes. Meanwhile, Tony was having issues linking up Kim's MP3 player to his laptop.

"You want some help, Dad?" offered Sharyna.

"Er, yeah," Tony admitted. "That'll be appreciated."

Half an hour later, Tony and Sharyna had managed to bully the laptop to play music. Rihanna's "Man Down" dropped from the computer speaker as Colleen and Nats moved the dining table tight against the wall to create dancing space.

"The floor's yours," said Tony to Sharyna.

Glancing at Nats, Kim, and me, Sharyna covered her mouth with her palms and blushed. "No, Dad. Not today."

"Go on!" Tony shouted her on. "You're a great dancer."

"Yeah, come on, Sharyna," I said. "I saw you popping moves the other day in your room. You're the living dance-hall queen."

Still with her hands covering half of her face, Sharyna shook her head. Kim and Nats turned to me.

"Naoms, why don't you pop a move?" Kim hollered at me. "Go on, sistren! You know you want to."

I didn't want to.

"Yeah," said Nats. "Take a step, sistren!"

"You can dance?" Colleen asked me.

Monkey up a tree with lions below. My heart woke up and started a mad argument with my ribs. All eyes were on me. I didn't reply.

"Yeah, she's *bad*," said Nats.

"Rewind that track!" yelled Kim.

Sharyna pressed a key to restart the song and flicked up the volume. "Show them your moves, sistren!" shouted Nats.

I folded my arms and stared at the floor. The fire in my cheeks was so intense I coulda sizzled buffalo wings on 'em.

Kim grabbed my arms and pulled me up to my feet. "Show 'em what you're made of, sistren!"

"Why didn't you tell us you can dance?" asked Colleen. "Go for it! The floor's yours."

Running into the center of the room with his balloon, Pablo performed his own wild steps. He completed his routine with a Michael Jackson–like spin, a mad rollover, and an attempt at the splits. He climbed to his feet in a daze but the grin he showboated would've won untold sticky stars from Nan. Everyone clapped and roared their approval. Sharyna clicked the restart icon and Kim and Nats started to chant, "*Dance, sister, dance! Dance, sister, dance!*"

I flexed my toes and stretched my arms. *Monkey in a circus. I haven't danced for the longest time.* I gave an anxious side-eye to Kim. She nodded and blew me a kiss.

I tried to relax. My first steps were proper nervous but then I went into my Beyoncé mode. Kim and Nats clapped. The others joined in. I performed a couple of spins and a street-dance move before jumping back to land on my feet.

"Wow!" yelled Tony.

Confidence *Strictly-Come-Danced* through me. I did a Beyoncé thing with my hips, performed a high-kicking move, and twirled like a mad ice-skater. *Monkey Night Fever.*

"She's brilliant," said Colleen.

"I told ya," said Kim. "She loves Beyoncé to the max. Her favorite video's 'Baby Boy.' She's always watching it on YouTube."

Kim wasn't wrong.

The track came to an end. My lungs told me to sit my ass down. Kim wiped the sweat off my forehead and hugged me tight. "You see!" she said. "No one laughed. Sistrens like us *are* good at stuff."

Out of the corner of my eye, Nats flashed envy. *Why's she raging? She was clapping me on.*

"I keep telling her she should do something with her dancing," Kim said. "But will she listen? No, she doesn't! She's got Teflon ears! Nothing sticks."

"She's not lying," added Nats. Her side-eye jealousy went missing. "Naoms's dancing has always been on point."

"I think she should take it up," said Colleen. "That was so good."

Tony nodded.

The music stored on the MP3 player only lasted forty minutes.

"Got anything else?" Kim asked, still sitting beside me.

"There's that old disco stuff I told you about," I said. "Your great-great-grannies might wake up from the dead and boogaloo to it."

"Slap it on!" yelled Kim. "Better than fruck-all."

"Language!" barked Colleen.

"Sorry, Mrs. Golding," Kim said.

Kim apologizing? That's a new one.

Tony pushed the CD into the stereo. He smiled as Sister Sledge's "Lost in Music" discoed out from the speakers. He did a little dad-dance before total humiliation slapped upside his head. Clapping, Colleen got up and performed the Bump dance with Sharyna. Pablo spun around on his back with two balloons. Nats laughed at him. She couldn't resist picking him up and dancing with him. Kim sprang to her feet and performed this weird robotic dance where she imitated karate chops, kicks, and punches. She scoped me the whole time. *Is she trying to impress me?*

Overdosed on excitement, Pablo ran out and squirreled up the stairs. Moments later he returned carrying two Afro wigs. He flung one at Colleen and threw the other at Tony. "Do the Car Wash!" he screamed.

"Oh no!" Colleen shook her head. "I've embarrassed myself enough already."

"Car Wash! Car Wash!" Pablo insisted.

Dusting off his wig, Tony inspected it before pulling it on; his head was a couple of sizes too big for it. "I can't believe I'm doing this again," he said.

Pablo jumped and cheered. Kim and Nats clenched their right fists and waved them in the air like they just didn't care.

Tony looked at Colleen like someone had uploaded pics of them making out for the first time. "Are we really going to get down?"

"If we do," Colleen replied, "you better make sure I get up again."

To more cheers, Colleen pulled on her wig. Sharyna slapped in the CD. Rose Royce's "Car Wash" funked out from the speaker. Colleen lined up in front of Tony before stepping to the left and stepping to the right in time to the beat. Three paces back, two steps to the right, three steps forward. Tony followed Colleen in not-so-perfect sync. Another two strides forward while shaking their chests. Tony's Afro, with a tear near the hairline, slid off the back of his head. Pablo giggled out his ribs. Sharyna cringed in embarrassment, hardly able to watch the *Titanic* in front of her. I couldn't remember the last time I had laughed so hard. I bopped my head while Nats and Kim pumped their fists. "*Go, Daddy, go, Mummy!*"

The song faded and we all gave Colleen and Tony a mad ovation.

"Again!" screamed Pablo. "Again!"

"No," said Colleen. "If I do that once more you'll have to carry me up the stairs or drop me on the sofa."

Grabbing another balloon, Pablo ran up to Sharyna,

smacked her upside her head, and escaped up the stairs.

Twenty minutes later, Pablo got bored with the music and played in his bedroom while sinking his looted chocolate biscuits. Colleen started a convo with Kim, Nats, and me in the lounge while Tony was on washing-up duty with Sharyna.

"I know Naomi's social worker is trying to place her with adoptive parents," said Colleen. "How about you two?"

Kim looked at me. "Good luck with that one," she said. She switched her beams to Colleen. "Once you're a teenager, no one's interested. That's the low-down truth. People want cute little babies with cute little dimples to adopt."

"Yeah," nodded Nats. "For real. I've been on the adoption list since I was twelve. They might as well have put my name down for the first space rocket to Mars. I don't wanna be adopted now. I keep telling my social worker and my key worker that, but they're not hearing me. *We'll find someone for you*, they say. *Don't worry*, they say. *There're parents out there for everyone.* No peeps want to adopt teenagers, so bomb that shit."

Colleen threw her an *I'm not accepting that kinda language* look.

"Sorry, Mrs. Golding."

"I don't care what they say or promise anymore," said Nats. She gazed at Kim. "As long as I've got Kim with me, I'm good. I don't need *them* anymore. If they try and separate us, I'll go to war on them."

Colleen nodded. "I see."

I think at this point, realization slapped Colleen on her forehead that Kim and Nats were an item. She rode it well.

"People used to come around to the home and look

at us like we're something in a zoo," said Kim. "And then they'll spend the rest of the day reading about ya from some big file. Fruck 'em!"

"Language, Kim! Come on, girls, I have two young children."

"Sorry, Mrs. Golding."

"Naoms stands more chance of doing a dance video with Rihanna than being adopted," said Nats. "Why would they promise something when they know they can't deliver?"

Kim looked at me hard. "You don't wanna be adopted, do ya, Naoms? Can't trust any of these adopting peeps anyway. A lot of 'em are prick fiddlers."

I looked at the floor and shrugged.

"You've got these rich people who can't be bothered to have kids," said Kim.

"Some can't have kids for other reasons, Kim," Colleen jumped in. "Whether they're rich or poor."

I glanced at Kim. She had *that* look. She wasn't gonna let this one go. "Their asses are too stoosh to push," she said. "But when the fancy takes 'em, they wanna adopt a nice little baby to show off to their rich sistrens. They send messages on their WhatsApp group: *Look what we picked up from social services! Aren't we good people?* They push the baby around in a mega buggy in some first-class park and their rich sistrens go *oooohh* and *aaaahh*. Then they buy a load of crap for the baby at Christmas that the baby don't need. Trust me on this one. I've seen it. My mum's friends with a few of those first-class women."

"That's the living reality," put in Nats. "They're like designer babies."

"They have birthday parties so they can buy more crap and invite their stoosh sistrens around so they can show how much they *love* their new baby," resumed Kim. "They text their high-end girlfriends who couldn't make the party, *I bought my baby this and I bought my baby that!* Then when they get home they order the nanny to change the baby's nappy, fling a dummy in its mouth, and make its bottle. That's what it's all about. It's all fru—"

"*Kim!*" Colleen raised her voice.

"Sorry, Mrs. Golding, but it's true. They don't give a wet dummy about you when you get big enough and you can speak for yourself."

"She's not lying," put in Nats. "Those stoosh women should be banned from adopting babies, especially foreign kids."

Kim switched her gaze to me. "In this game, our kind have gotta look out for each other. Too many foster carers are too interested in how *they* look rather than thinking about the kids they say they wanna look after."

Nats nodded. "Speech, sistren, speech!"

I wondered: when I was old enough, would I be able to adopt my nan? I have her interest at heart.

I think Colleen was relieved when Nats and Kim got up to leave. We showed them to the door.

"Are you sure you don't want a lift?" Colleen said.

"No thanks, Mrs. Golding," Nats replied. "We're good."

I stepped to the end of the road with them and watched them walk around the corner. Suddenly, Nats hot-toed back to me. I thought she had forgotten something. "Thanks for inviting me too," she said. She gave me a long hug. I couldn't remember her doing that before. "I appreciate it."

"I appreciate that you could make it," I said. "And thanks for bigging me up about my dancing. With all the drama in my life, I forgot about that."

"I love you, Naoms," Nats said, then laughed. "Obviously not as much as Kim, but it's for real."

"Love you too, Nats."

She then hot-stepped back to Kim.

When I reached home, Colleen was still waiting for me outside the front door.

"So, what d'you think of Kim and Nats?" I asked.

Colleen angled her face. "Hmmm."

"What d'you mean, *hmmm*? Tell me what you think of my sistrens."

"They're . . . radical. Anti-everything. They don't trust anyone."

"Radical? What does that mean?"

"I know social services aren't perfect and that goes for everybody working in it, but Kim and Nats are so . . ."

"So what?" I pressed.

"There are good people working in social services that try and do a lot of good. And Kim and Nats should recognize that."

"And *you* should recognize that they talk it how they see it! It's social services and peeps like you who should fix up. Not us!"

I didn't wanna go to war with Colleen, but in social worker speak she had a pop at my sistrens. *I'm not having that.*

I brushed past her and stormtrooped to my room. Half

an hour later, I felt bad. I went downstairs and thanked Colleen and Tony for giving my party.

Tony chuckled. "It's nice to know that I made a complete fool of myself and you enjoyed it."

"It wasn't all for nothing," Colleen added.

They smell of old-school rules but I'm warming to Tony and Colleen. Wonder what these Hamiltons are like when they pick the sleep outta their eyes in the morning.

CHAPTER NINE

The Hamiltons

"Have you got everything, Naomi?"

"Yeah," I replied from my bedroom.

Dressed in jeans, a Zooey Deschanel T-shirt that Kim had given me, a leather jacket tucked under my arm, and my meerkat held in my other, I answered the door. My rucksack was already strapped to my back.

"Ready?" Louise asked.

"Yeah."

"Hold up!" said Colleen. "You're forgetting your sandwiches."

"I'm sure the Hamiltons will give Naomi anything she needs," said Louise. "You really shouldn't have—"

"I *asked* Colleen to make me something," I cut in. "I might not like the . . . Who are they again?"

"The Hamiltons," reminded Louise.

"I might not like their food. So I've got my corned beef–and–cucumber sandwiches."

"Let's skip," said Louise. "Susan's expecting us at ten."

I waited until my butt was snugged in the passenger seat of Louise's car before I had a go at her. "Bit harsh, weren't it?"

"What do you mean?"

"Having a go at Colleen for making me sandwiches."

"I wasn't having a go at her."

"Yes you were."

"It's not like you're off camping, Naomi," Louise said. "You're overreacting a bit. Do you think the Hamiltons will starve you?"

"As I said, I might not love their food."

"Then they'll get what you ask for."

"They might not. They might serve me turd waffles or farts on toast."

Shaking her head, Louise made the twenty-minute journey from the Goldings' home to the Hamiltons' place. It was somewhere high up near Spenge with a neat view. When Louise pulled up I didn't wanna step out of the car.

"Come on, Naomi, time to go."

I stared through the windshield, held on tight to my meerkat, and released the rebel in me.

"Okay, I'm sorry," said Louise after a while. "I was a bit impolite to Colleen."

I grinned at my victory. I climbed out of the car and looked up at the three-story town house. "What floor do they live on?"

"It's all theirs," Louise replied. "They have a lovely big garden too."

Monkey playing hide-and-seek with the queen's hounds. Louise has found me first-class peeps to live with. Nan would be proper impressed. I'm gonna hustle some good pocket money while I'm here. No more Austria territory for me.

We walked up a flight of concrete steps that led to a wide front door. I looked around. There were gaps between the houses. I spotted a supermarket van delivering food to one of the neighbors. I could almost sniff the salmon and Belgian chocolates. There were no long council slabs in sight.

"Here we are," said Louise.

"What's she like?" I asked.

"Susan's lovely. She's great with your age group. Very sporty. She has been volunteering at the youth club on South Smeckenham Road for years and she goes away on residentials with them. She's very well liked and respected."

"What's residentials?"

"It's where the youth workers take young people to a youth hostel for a weekend. They learn things like canoeing and rock climbing. Perhaps you might be interested in that?"

I offered Louise my top-ranking *really* look. I didn't think she'd go to canoeing and rock climbing ever again. *Doesn't she know me? Adults are so dumb sometimes.*

The door opened to reveal a curly-headed, forty-something woman. Her freckles could've satisfied some young dot-to-dotter and her suntan had gone a bit wrong. She was wearing a white T-shirt, black jeans, and flip-flops. *Doesn't she know it's cold?*

Susan greeted me with a game-show smile. "So nice to meet you, Naomi. Everything's ready for you. I'm making brunch if you want it."

"Making what?" I said. My feet didn't move.

"A late breakfast or early lunch," Louise explained.

I wasn't sure if I could connect with somebody who spilled the word *brunch* in a convo. *I don't think this is gonna end like a Walt Disney film.*

"Come on in," said Susan, grinning like a clown who wasn't getting any love from her audience.

I followed her through a tall hallway. Framed film posters hung from the walls. I stopped to take a closer look. *Bugsy Malone*, *Chitty Chitty Bang Bang*, *Willy Wonka and the Chocolate Factory*, and *Snow White and the Seven Dwarves*. The only one I had heard of was *Willy Wonka*, but that wasn't Johnny Depp in the poster. They must've made an ancient Willy Wonka movie that didn't do too well.

"Come on, Naomi," said Louise.

Stepping down a few steps, I found myself in a kitchen big enough to cook for all the Oompa Loompas, the seven dwarves, and Bugsy Malone's crew. There was a mad variety of blenders, mixers, steamers, and grilling machines. The fridge was so wide you could've deep-froze a dinosaur in it. A wooden table stood in the middle and the glass fruit bowl that sat on top of it was full of grapes, apples, oranges, and blueberries. Jamie Oliver would've nodded.

I took a seat at the table and started on my sandwiches.

"If you want I can make you something hot," offered Susan. "Eggs and bacon? I bought some organic mushrooms yesterday so I'll throw those in if you like?"

I shook my head and bit a sandwich in half. The cucumber was nice and cool. I wondered what Pablo, Sharyna, Tony, and Colleen were up to.

"I've got all kinds of juices," said Susan. "Apple, orange, pineapple, cranberry. If you like I can use the fruit blender to make a cocktail of your choice. It's very easy. I just place them in the blender, switch a button, and—"

"You got Coke?" I chopped her flow.

"Er . . . no."

"I'll have orange juice then," I said. "But I *want* Coke for later on."

"Doesn't do the teeth any favors," said Susan. "They say there's four teaspoons of sugar in every can of Coke. Maybe more."

"I don't care," I replied.

"You'll suffer for it when you get older."

"Then I'll worry about it then."

She's a bit naggy. Worse than Tony. I side-eyed Susan. She grinned away the awkwardness and went to pour the orange juice. I sniffed her fear. *Good, I can use that. The rebel in me's gonna have nuff playtime here.*

Louise sat beside me and patted me on the back. "Susan loves cooking, Naomi. I'm sure you're going to have lots of fun baking on Sunday."

"Yes," nodded Susan.

Monkey on a bike. This is gonna be like the Holmans' situation. She's so eager to please I might ask her to wipe my butt.

"Naomi can flick through my big cake book, decide what she likes, and we can buy the ingredients tomorrow morning," said Susan. "Wouldn't you like that, Naomi?"

God. Does she think I'm six? Hold it down, Naoms, you've just met her. Don't launch any cuss missiles at her just yet. Try and be polite. Otherwise, Louise will jump on your tits.

I nodded. "I s'pose so."

I closed my eyes. In my head I could see my dad in our cramped kitchen. He had a white cabbage in one hand and a bread knife in the other. His breath was polluted with Appleton Special Rum—a bandy-legged Jamaican with a ruby tooth came home with Dad and the rum one long night. For Dad it was love at first sample.

An unsteady pot half-filled with water was waiting on the stove.

"Where's the chopping board?" Dad asked.

"It's beside the sink," I replied. "Dad, you don't have to cook. I don't mind."

"*Don't* have to frucking do it?" Dad snapped. "I'm your dad, for God's sake! Can't I cook for my own nine-year-old daughter? What kinda dad d'you think I am? Now where's the frucking board?"

"In the cupboard beside the sink," I pointed.

"I'll show ya and the social people," Dad said. "I'll show 'em all! I can cook for my daughter. Frucking social services! Coming here with their judgements."

"Naomi," Louise called. "Naomi!"

"Oh, sorry, Louise."

"Daydreaming again?" Louise said. "Susan has just asked you if you want a tour of the house."

"Yeah, okay. Just a bit tired."

"Would you like the tour?" Susan asked. "Or do you want a rest?"

"You haven't got a museum upstairs, have ya, and a liccle shop where I can buy souvenirs?" I joked.

Susan busted out a chuckle.

Starting off the tour in the basement, I spotted a set of golf clubs among three mountain bikes, a small canoe, and more helmets than you would find on a big building site. I couldn't give Susan top ratings for first impressions but I thought I'd better try and still be sociable so Louise couldn't nag the lip balm off me.

"Your man plays golf, does he?" I asked.

"No," said Susan, "I do. He plays badminton."

"Do you paddle in that?" I asked, pointing at the canoe.

"Yes, I do," Susan replied proudly. A big grin stretched her lips.

"You're not getting me in there. Bomb that."

After showing me the shed in the garden, which had a long table, a shelf of DIY books, a desktop computer, a small TV, and garden stuff inside it, Susan led me to the first floor. In one room was an office where Susan's man worked when he was at home. Another room had a lot of books inside of it and a desk. "This is where our daughter Emily likes to study," Susan said. "She'll be home later on."

The bedrooms were on the second floor. "Feel at home, won't you, Naomi," said Susan as she showed me to my room. "If you get peckish then just wander down to the kitchen and get yourself something. Perhaps cheese on buttered crackers? I love that in the morning with my juice."

"Thanks, but I prefer something hot like bacon and eggs."

"If you like, we can visit the leisure center this afternoon, perhaps go for a swim?"

"Nah, don't feel like it."

"Or if you fancy, I can load the mountain bikes in the four-by-four and we can drive to the Smeckenham Hills for an afternoon cycle?"

I hadn't ridden a bike for the longest time. I thought about it. "Too cold."

"Is there anything you want to do this morning?" Susan

asked. She looked a bit desperate. *Maybe she needs to have a sit-down and sink her buttered crackers with a juice of her fancy.*

"I wanna sit down in my room, watch a film, and be left on my lonesome," I responded. "Is that too much to ask? You got a TV in there, right? And a DVD player?"

"Er, yes, I have. Louise told me what you like."

I parked myself on the double bed and took in my surroundings. There was a fat wardrobe big enough to give a boatful of refugees shelter. The dressing table was long enough for a b-ball player to stretch out and have a yawn. Small-framed cartoon peeps watched me from the walls: Daffy Duck, Barney Rubble, Inspector Gadget, and Scooby-Doo. I began to think that Susan was curb-butting cadazy and had more issues than I did. *Maybe she needs fostering and looking after.*

"If you want anything just give me a toot," she said. "I'll be downstairs."

"All right," I said.

I dropped my bag on the floor and hugged my meerkat. *I still haven't found a name for you. One day I will.* I stared again at the pictures on the wall. *Messed up.*

When I heard Susan's footsteps fading down the stairs, I opened a zip pocket of my rucksack and took out matches and a pack of cigarettes that I had jacked from the glove compartment of Louise's car. I closed the door and opened the window. Shutting my eyes, I thought of Dad.

He was asleep on my bed. My meerkat was beside him. It was covered in green-yellowy sick. I washed it, rinsed it, and dried it. The next morning, Dad spotted the meerkat in my arms. He was sober. He winked me a grin. He didn't remember that he had vomited all over my fave toy. I didn't speak to him for days.

Striking a match, I watched it burn and wither. I blew the flame out and flung it out the window. I struck another match and fired up my fagarette. Dad's image was still in my head as I took my first inhale. *I hope he's put a big full stop to his drinking. I hope he's okay . . . wherever he is.*

Smoking the cancer stick down to the butt, I took out one of my horror film DVDs, slapped it into the DVD player, and pressed play.

Half an hour later, I puffed on my second cigarette. I watched a scene from my film where a clown-masked bruv chopped off this young chick's toes with a tomahawk. *Why do so many blondes in the films I watch suffer from so much brain cell shortage? You were warned twice about stepping into the woods.*

I stayed in my bedroom for the rest of the day. I only came out once to make myself a tuna-on-toast late lunch. Susan had asked how I was a few times but I was missing Sharyna and Pablo. I'm not gonna lie, I missed Tony and Colleen too. *Who's gonna do my hair?* And I didn't think Susan's school days would be as dramatic as Colleen's so I wouldn't bother asking.

Someone knocked on my door. I paused the movie, climbed off the bed, and opened it.

Standing under the doorframe was a smiling Susan and this pretty young chick. She was pretty enough to be hunted in the woods by an axe murderer. "Can I introduce my daughter to you, Naomi?"

"I s'pose so," I shrugged.

"This is Emily! I'm so proud of her."

Then give her a fricking sticky star!

"Hi, Naomi," Emily smiled. "I see you're just chillaxing."

Chillaxing? What cool peeps use that word nowadays?

I thought of tomahawk man catching up with her in some remote cabin. "Yeah, just watching a film that a friend gave me," I said. "Your pops here as well?"

"Not yet," Susan answered for Emily. "He's in Brussels, meeting businessmen from Qatar. He's going to design a building for them."

"From where?" I asked.

"Qatar," Susan repeated. "In the Middle East."

"The middle east," I repeated. "Don't make sense. How can it be middle if it's in the east?"

Susan busted out a giggle. "I'll leave you two to get to know each other."

Susan posh-toed downstairs as I pressed play on the DVD remote control. The movie wasn't smacking my like spots but it beat trying to make a sistren outta Emily. I hoped she'd disappear but she parked on my bed wondering what to say.

"Fancy going out for a drive and getting something to eat?" she said after a while.

The ending of the film was rubbish. The dumb chick with missing toes got rescued. It was proper disappointing. I pressed the stop button and ejected the DVD. "Yeah," I said. "Bomb this film. Don't know why my sistren says I have to watch it."

Bouncing downstairs, Emily and I stepped into the kitchen where Susan was seasoning a fat fish. Baby potatoes were waiting on a counter beside a bowlful of greens next to a plate of green herbs. Susan wore an apron with a giant cauliflower printed on it—at least it wasn't a cartoon character.

Louise had always told me that she wanted me to sample a dose of normalness. *This isn't normal.*

I thought of Mum.

"I'm taking Naomi out to get something to eat," said Emily.

"But I'm just about to put the fish into the oven," said Susan. I had to give her ratings for hiding her disappointment.

"She's been cooped up for most of the day inside her room," said Emily. "She needs some fresh air."

"I do happen to be here," I put in. "I *can* talk for myself. But yeah, you're not wrong, I do need to flush out my lungs."

"Okay, then," said Susan. "We'll have the fish tomorrow. Find something decent to eat, not fast-food rubbish. Perhaps that Wholesome Food restaurant on Spenge Court Avenue?"

"Okay, Mum."

I followed Emily to her car, a navy-blue Peugeot 306. *Daddy and Mummy must've given her the funds for it. I'm not gonna be a hater about that though. If I was a parent I'd do the same if I had the grands in my pocket.* Once inside I sniffed the fagarette and coffee stench. Untold scarves, socks, and sneakers covered the backseat. *Okay, this is a bit more normal.*

Emily pushed the key into the ignition and Muse's "Time Is Running Out" spanked out from the stereo. A tiny plastic Buddha and a baby koala bear hung from a chain from the rearview mirror. *She's an interesting chick. Not as stoosh and first class as she looks.*

"My mum means well," said Emily. "But eating her food bores me to death after a while. What do you fancy, Naomi? Pizza Express? A Kentucky? McDonald's? Nando's? I've always preferred the fries from Wimpy."

Before answering, I scoped Emily hard. She had a neatly trimmed soup-dish haircut. A silver ring niced up the baby finger of her left hand. She wore a world of silver studs and clip-ons in her right ear. Jimi Hendrix burned a guitar on the black T-shirt she was wearing and her black jeans, splitting at the knees, were fading to gray. Adidas basketball shoes gripped her feet. She wasn't wearing any makeup but I thought her prettiness could stir something in most bruvs' trackie bottoms. I didn't think she was a virgin and I guessed she didn't know how to flick on a gas ring and brew an egg.

"Chinese," I finally answered. "Or that Thai stuff. Always wanted to sample that. My mate Kim was boasting about her last ex taking her to eat a Thai dinner one time."

"We'll have to find a place and eat there," Emily laughed. "If I come home with Chinese or Thai food, Mum will have a fit . . . I know a place."

We drove to the Southside shopping center in Ashburton, and Emily led me to a Thai restaurant on the first floor next door to the cinema. Picking up a menu, I speed-read through it.

"What are you having?" asked Emily after a while.

I tried to remember what Kim had sunk on her visit to a Thai restaurant. "A large Coke, that chicken curry thing, vegetable rice, and those sweet dumpling ball things . . . oh and a couple of those spring roll things."

"No problem."

"Make sure it's a large Coke," I said. "Your mum hasn't got any."

"At least we have something in common," said Emily. "Our addiction to caffeine. I'm gonna have a coffee."

"Caffeine? I don't do drugs! It's not my game."

The food and drinks were ordered. I sank my meal with a knife and fork but I was proper mesmerized by Emily's use of chopsticks. "Where'd you learn to do that?" I asked.

"Backpacking in Thailand," Emily replied. "I took a gap year—"

"What's a gap year?"

"I finished school and got a place at uni but before I started I wanted to travel a bit," she explained. "Mum wanted to treat me to a holiday. She had her heart set on Australia—"

"Australia! Wow! Isn't that the place where they make *I'm a Celebrity . . . Get Me Outta Here*? Don't watch it anymore though. It's for kids. Australia's ram-jammed with jungles, isn't it? If I'll ever get out there I'll carry nuff bug killer with me. Mozzies scare the skin cells outta me."

"Er, parts of it are jungle, but yep, that's Australia," Emily said. "But Mum coming with me would be ten times worse than a mozzie bite."

I can't lie, I was connecting to Emily. Maybe because she thought her mum was stone-cadonking cadazy too.

"God!" she continued. "She wanted to visit Sydney, Brisbane, Melbourne, Tasmania, and then take a plane and go to Perth. Six to eight weeks she wanted to go for. That would've done my head in. We would've ended up killing each other."

"Wish someone would take me to Australia," I said. "Never had a holiday, not a real one. My social worker Louise took me and my sistren Kim to Butlin's for a weekend last year. Louise's boyfriend didn't like it cos Kim and me tried to catch 'em having sex. We'd crash into their room at three in the morning. They were just spooning though. I s'pose they're too ancient to have a crotch rhapsody and all that."

Emily giggled hard at that one.

"Don't wanna sound ungrateful but I didn't love it," I went on. "The beach was too rocky, the sea was too grimy, and Louise wouldn't let us out of the camp late at night."

"I guess it was an experience," Emily said. "All travel experiences are good in some way."

I shook my head. "Trust me on this one, it wasn't a good experience. Apart from Kim getting into a maul with another chick who at first she fancied, it was boring. The people there were lame too. My other sistren, Nats, was well upset cos she couldn't go. Mad she was. When we got back Nats launched a cuss attack at Louise. She let down her tires, grooved her bonnet with a nail file, and liberated one of her wing mirrors. She would've pissed on her driving seat if we didn't pull her away. Tried to tell Nats afterward that the holiday was boring, but she was simmering for the longest time."

"Mum's still planning to take me and Dad to Australia later this year," said Emily. "If you want we can swap places."

"Your mum that bad?"

Sweet God, please say yes. If she does, then if Louise wants me to be fostered by her I could say Susan's own daughter thinks she's nuts.

"Don't get me wrong," said Emily. "She means well. But she's a bit too much sometimes. When I finished school I wanted to go out and celebrate with my mates and Mum got upset because I didn't want her there. She always wants to *be* there. Gets on my freakin' nerves."

"I hear you on that one," I said. "My dad was the same. The only difference was he tried to be there but his drinking sabotaged him."

"Last year I went to a weekend music festival," Emily said. "She wanted to come with me and my mates to that. You wouldn't believe the amount of arguments we had about me backpacking in Thailand. *It's not safe for an eighteen-year-old girl to travel alone! You might get kidnapped.* God! She was going on every day. I don't even think about bringing boyfriends home."

"You've got a boyfriend?"

"Sort of."

"Sort of? Does that mean you'll let him paw you but you won't let him stick his thing in you?"

Emily blushed and looked at her meal for a long second. "Er, not quite," she replied. "There is a guy, half-Ghanaian, half-Scottish. He's thirty-four—don't tell Mum that. I met him at the Mango Falls bar just off Ashburton Hill. His name's Gabriel. I just wished he'd get his shit together. He's a poet and a singer with amazing talent but he's so freaking lazy. He doesn't get out of his bed till the afternoon. He still hasn't done his demo yet . . . He's got an incredible bod though."

"Thirty-four? Bit old for you, isn't he? He'll get gray hairs soon. You don't want kids with gray hairs."

"I'm twenty in a couple of months," said Emily. "Most guys my age are so immature and don't have a clue."

"I'm gonna get a boyfriend when I kiss fifteen," I said. "My sistren Kim had boyfriends when she was twelve but she was always warring and cussing with them. Maybe that's why she ended up with a chick."

"Oh," Emily said.

"When I get a bruv I wanna look after him and cook his fave meal for him. Then snoogle up on the sofa and watch my fave horror films with him. We'll have four kids. Two boys and two girls. I'll adopt all of 'em. I'd like the oldest to be a girl so she can look after the others if something ever happens to me."

"Having a boyfriend is not the be-all and end-all," said Emily, sipping her black coffee. "There's another guy who I see, a bit younger than Gabriel. Steve. He lives over in Elmers End. He's got more money but he's a bit of a political head."

"What d'you mean?"

Emily let out a big sigh. "He's got a half-decent brain and spending time with him would be bliss if he stopped rabbiting on about the world and its problems. He means well but he goes on about marches and demos 24-7. He wants me to march with him and wave banners in the air like I just don't care. Mum would love him and that's why I've never brought him around. I see him when *I* want to see him. When I can get him to shut up, he makes out pretty good."

"So you're two-timing?"

Emily thought about it. She took another sip of her coffee before answering. "I suppose I am. But boodally-hoo! Why shouldn't I have fun before I become an obedient wife like Mum?"

"Obedient? I wouldn't complain. She's got a neat yard, nice kitchen gadgets, untold fruit blenders, her canoe, golf clubs, her bike, and the membership of a suntan place. She's well blessed."

Emily chuckled. "At social events and dinner parties she plays the loving wife, hugging my dad and kissing him on the cheek, but when they're at home, they're always in different rooms doing their own thing."

"They don't have sex? Mind you, they're way too ancient to have sex. Eeeewwww! My brain just downloaded a graphic. You wanna throw away the bed on that one."

Emily bent up in a mad giggle. "They do . . . sometimes . . . I think."

"At least they're not fighting," I said. "My mum used to fight with her . . ." I trailed off and stared at my food. I couldn't help thinking of Mum's ex-boyfriend Rafi, who hollered, raged, and swore in his own language at her cos she got rid of his baby.

Emily picked up the conversation. "No, they never fight," she said. "It might liven up the place a bit if they did."

"Have they fostered before?" I wanted to know.

"No, you're the first. Mum's latest project in her plan to save all the kids in the world."

"What d'you mean?" I asked. "She doesn't go over to those hungry countries to adopt every skinny kid she sees, does she? You know, like what pop stars do. My sistrens, Kim and Nats, don't love that game."

Emily let loose another chuckle. "No, not quite. Mum's never really had a proper nine-to-five job. She didn't really need one. Dad earns loads."

"If my hairier half earned the grands I'd stay at home too," I put in.

Emily screwed up her face. "In the last few years she's volunteered at a youth club. I think she's getting tired of it now. She tries very hard, putting her heart into everything they do, but the kids just don't like her."

"Maybe she tries too hard," I said.

"The other week some eleven-year-old kid called her a frucking snobby bitch," Emily said. "She came home and had me and Dad up most of the night talking about it. I mean, it was just a pissed-off eleven-year-old kid and she wanted to have a public inquiry into what he said. *Do you think my approach wasn't appropriate* and all that. God! It drove me and Dad crazy. Now she wants to foster kids."

"At least she wants to help people," I said.

Emily raised her voice. "She needs to get a proper job and stop jumping from one thing to another!"

"Ain't fostering kids a proper job? I might wanna flex that way one day."

Emily nodded. "Yeah, it is a proper job. But you gotta want to do it for the right reasons."

I thought of Kim's rant the day before about poshos

wanting to adopt so they can get ratings from their rich friends.

Emily shrugged. "She'll probably want to take us bike-riding tomorrow." Her voice was on the level again. "And if I refuse to go she'll dump a load of guilt sick all over me."

I swigged down my Coke.

Following a breakfast of boiled eggs, brown toast, and a couple of nibbles of the biggest grapefruit I had ever seen, Susan tied the mountain bikes inside the back of her Range Rover. She then went down to the basement and collected three red helmets. She gave one to Emily and one to me. I hadn't seen anyone so happy since Kim jacked a brown suede jacket from a first-class store a year ago. Scoping the blue sky, Susan said, "We should make use of this day, Emily. The sky's much clearer than yesterday. Perhaps we should drive down to the Hobbledash forest and ride our bikes there? We'll get a lovely view. Maybe have our lunch by the lake. Just like we used to. What do you say?"

"No, Mum!" Emily replied. "It takes forever to get there. The Smeckenham Hills is good."

"But Naomi will love the scenery down there and the cool, fresh air will do her a world of good."

"*Mum!*"

Sitting in the front passenger seat, I played with the strap of my helmet as Emily stretched out in the back and napped. I closed my eyes too. On the journey, I couldn't help but think of Tony and Colleen dancing in their front room with their Afro wigs on. I tried to hold onto that little movie in my head but Dad gate-crashed my thoughts.

It was six a.m. After scrubbing my fangs, I went to the kitchen and washed up the pots, plates, and cutlery from the spaghetti Bolognese dinner I had cooked the night before. I cleaned the top of the cooker before mopping the kitchen floor. I then stepped into Dad's bedroom. The quilt had been booted off the bed.

Lying on his stomach with his legs apart and his forearms beneath his grimy pillow, Dad was only dressed in his boxers. I didn't love the hairs on the back of his shoulders. The ashtray, sitting on top of the bedside cabinet, was overflowing with roll-up butts. I took it out, emptied it in the kitchen bin, and rinsed it under a hot tap. I returned to Dad's room and searched the wardrobe, the chest of drawers, the bedside cabinets, and everywhere else for any liquor. I found a quarter-full bottle of Napoleon brandy in a drawer beneath the mattress. There was a stack of unused paper cups there too. I took the bottle to the kitchen sink and emptied it. The alcohol fumes chim-chimneyed up my nose. Returning to the bedroom, I placed the empty bottle on the bedside cabinet Dad was facing. I wanted him to *know* that I'd been hunting for his hidden booze.

Satisfied that there was no more drink in the house, I showered and changed for school. I styled my hair into ponytails and tied the pink and white ribbons myself. I grilled myself a bacon sandwich for breakfast and hunted that down with a glass of water. Only when I had washed up the frying pan and the dishes did I enter Dad's room again.

I slapped him out of his dreams. I brought with me his two tablets and a glass of water.

"Dad. *Dad!* It's half seven."

He rolled to the other side of the bed. He grunted and groaned and scratched his head. He slowly opened his eyes. His chin was all wire-brushy. I didn't like the jungle on his chest neither. He focused and accepted his pills and the water. He sunk it in one gulp and belched a big belch.

"Don't forget to take the other tablets before you eat something for lunch," I reminded him. "There's some cheese and cucumber that I bought yesterday that you can make a sandwich with."

"I—" Dad belched again. "I won't forget."

"It's the day of the Year Six show," I reminded him. "It's gonna be like *The X-Factor*. I'm dancing in it so don't forget. Be at the school by three o'clock. *Don't* even think about being late."

"Of course I'll be there, Naomi," assured Dad. He sat up and picked the sleep outta his eyes. "Why don't you watch TV and I'll fetch you your breakfast."

"I've already had some," I said. "I ironed a shirt and trousers for you last night. They are in your wardrobe. I've also shined your black shoes. Wear 'em but try not to slash on 'em during the day. I'm not having you rolling up to my school stinking of piss! Don't forget to trim your chin and nice up your hair before you go out. Oh, and put some funds on the electric key. There's only fifty-eight pence on it. We're good for gas at the moment."

"You didn't have to iron my clothes or polish my shoes," Dad said. "I'll be there . . . Now come here, give your dad a hug before you run off to school."

He reached out his arms, tilted his head to the side, and curled his lips into that stupid grin he had. I wasn't five years old anymore. I looked at his hands as if they were dripping with acid and backed away two steps. At that moment I could feel his pain but I wanted him to feel mine. "Three o'clock, Dad. *Don't* be late."

I closed the door behind me.

Backstage, Pat Rogers, the cutest girl in my class, fitted on her oversized blond wig. It looked good on top of her toffee-colored face. She took deep breaths as she prepared to sing Lady Gaga's "Poker Face" to a crowd of parents sitting on Wendy House chairs in the school hall. (I liked Pat, bless her tonsils—I wonder what ever happened to her?)

Cross-armed teachers lined the sides as our nervous headmistress, Miss Amanda Compton, fidgeted in her seat in the front row. She adjusted her glasses for the nineteenth time.

Five dancers dressed in black leggings and school T-shirts, including me, were ready to support Pat's singing. It was 3:53 p.m. Stage right, I pulled back a curtain and scoped the audience once again. There were twenty rows to check. No sight of Dad. Not even near the exits. My head dropped as I lined up with my fellow dancers. The track began to blast out from the PA system. I closed my eyes, booted my disappointment to the back of my brain, and tried to remember the choreography taught to me by my PE teacher, Ms. Gabriella Banks (my fave teacher of all time).

The performance began and Pat Rogers forgot the third line of the song. She had a serious brain freeze. Cheered on by the crowd, however, she managed to finish her tune and received a mad ovation. Dancing behind her, I didn't miss a step. Simon Cowell and his crew would've had no choice but to give us top ratings. If Nan was there I would've got untold sticky stars. The curtain came down and we group-hugged. Ms. Banks suddenly burst into tears saying how moved she was by our dancing and Pat's singing. It set me off.

Afterward, I wandered aimlessly backstage. I pulled off my dancing shoes and threw them aside. I found a wonky stool, sat on it, and cursed Dad with every swear word that I knew. Backstage, all eyes were on the next act getting ready: a lion-masked Godfrey Abrahams about to sing a song from *The Lion King*. As Godfrey mangled "The Lion Sleeps Tonight," I couldn't stop the tears spilling down my cheeks.

Surrounded by tall trees and hearing the crunch of the pine cones as I rode over them, I proper enjoyed the rush of wind that swept over me as I bombed downhill. I tried to keep up with Susan who had zoomed a hundred yards ahead. I wondered if she had sank a few dragon hip pills along with her spinach-and-berry brekkie.

Emily was miles behind, cycling like a stoosh chick who hates sweating. The last uphill climb was a steep one and I had to jump off. My calf muscles screamed and my chest was heaving. I pushed my bike to this viewing plat-form that offered a neat view over Smeckenham and the Ashburton Downs. I could make out a windmill kissing the horizon.

I placed my bike on the ground and joined Susan. I took off my helmet and squinted. The sun was proper bright.

"Nothing like a good bike ride," Susan said. "You fill your lungs with air and it gets the heart going. Brings color to your cheeks."

"And it does your legs in," I put in.

"That's because you're not yet used to it, Naomi," said Susan. "Trust me, on your fourth or fifth visit you'll be whizzing up that hill like an Olympian."

"If I come again I'd like to ride a motorbike. Or one of them things with giant wheels. A quad bike or something. That'll be easier."

Susan gave me side-eye.

Five minutes later, from the bushes at the bottom of the hill, Emily emerged. Her helmet tied on the handlebar, headphones the size of dustbin lids covered her ears, she took her time pushing her bike up to join us.

"If you're willing to put the effort in," Susan said, "you *will* ride up that hill and reach the summit."

I guessed that Susan was trying to teach me some kinda life skill or something but it went flapping over my head. She poshy-prattled on but I was thinking of lying on a beach sipping a colder-than-cold Coke.

Once Emily had reached the viewing platform, Susan handed out energy drinks, high-protein bars, and bananas.

"No Coke?" I asked. I glared at the energy drink as if was a meerkat's piss sample. I didn't even bother unwrapping the protein bar. It had better use as a ping-pong bat. "No chocolate?" I spat. "What are you? Some kinda evil choco-hating Jamie Oliver disciple?"

Emily burst out in a giggle but she covered her mouth with her hand.

"Didn't I tell you to get me some Penguin choc bars?" I said to Susan. "You know, the original ones, not those mint things. They're my fave. Even a bourbon would've been good."

"I can't give you Coke or chocolate following good exercise," said Susan. "Far too much sugar. You'll lose all the benefit of what you have just cycled for."

Okay, not gonna hold it down anymore. She's obviously full-metal stonking black-birds-swirling-in-a-tornado nuts.

"Oh, Mum! Give Naomi some Coke if she wants it," said Emily.

Okay, that's saved her for now.

"I haven't brought any with me," replied Susan.

I gave a glare that Susan couldn't avoid. Then I sat down on the ground resting against a semicircle stone wall. As I unpeeled my banana, Susan dropped herself beside me. She looked at me like a chemistry teacher did to me once when I used a lit matchstick to ignite the Bunsen burner. She was also cadazy. "Take that hill as an example of life," she said.

Oh no! Lecture o'clock! When Dad was half-pissed he'd sometimes try to get all clever on me telling me about the meaning of life. I glanced at Emily to save me but she was listening to her headphones and had closed her eyes.

"The hill starts off with many twists and turns," Susan went on. "There are many bumps at the start, sharp bends and places where you could fall off. There are many signs and you have to make sure you follow the right one."

I nodded in the hope that she'd superglue her gums and scribble a fat full stop to this crap. Emily faked sleep. Susan didn't shut up. *When I get back to Louise, I swear I'm gonna give her the longest cuss attack ever. What was she thinking, putting me with this madwoman? She's obviously escaped from asylum ward twenty-one.*

"But if you navigate all that," Susan carried on, "you'll eventually rise to the top and you'll laugh at your difficult start in life . . . Do you understand what I'm trying to say, Naomi?"

"No," I quickly replied. I looked away, hoping Susan would put a heavy cork in it.

"What I'm trying to say is that despite your very . . . complicated start in life, you can be anything you want to be. A doctor, a lawyer, an accountant, a businesswoman . . . maybe even a politician. God! We need more female MPs in this country. The men always make a mess of it."

"Anything I want?" I repeated.

"Er, yes. You can be *anything* you want, Naomi."

"I wanna be a street dancer," I said.

"A street dancer? It's not really a stable career, is it?"

"*That's* what I wanna be," I insisted. "I wanna go on tour as a dancer for someone like Nicky Minaj or Rihanna. I wanna see places like New York, Hollywood, Hong Kong, Paris, and that city where they had the Olympics. Where they've got the Jesus statue."

"Rio," said Susan.

"Yeah, Rio, I wanna fly there and learn to dance the samba . . . and New Zealand where the sports people do that haka thing . . . and that place where you have those fat statues with Chinese eyes."

"You mean Buddha statues," Emily chimed in. Her eyes were still closed.

"You can still visit those places if you study hard and get a good place at university—"

"Oh, Mum," interrupted Emily. "Give her a break! She's only fourteen. And if she wants to be a dancer, so what?"

"I'm only trying to teach Naomi the value of hard work," argued Susan. "Too many kids these days believe that they don't have to put the effort in to get rewarded. All that celebrity TV is to blame."

"Mum! Take a time out. All we can think about now is resting our legs."

"Yeah, my bones feel like they're made of mash potato," I said.

Susan stood up and, with her arms swinging, hoofed-poofed down the hill. She looked out across the valley beneath her. *She's definitely got a bit of the ravens flapping around her skull going on.* I hoped she'd carry on walking till she reached the windmill.

"She's going to have a sulk now," said Emily. "Don't worry, she'll be back to herself in a minute. Sometimes I wonder who's the parent."

During the drive home, Susan stopped off at a corner shop where she bought me a bottle of Diet Coke and a Mars bar. By the time she had returned to the Range Rover, Emily was snoring on the backseat. Jazz played on the car radio. I let it go but if I went for another drive with her, I'd have to deal with the radio station issue.

"Perhaps you should think about a classical form of dancing?" Susan suggested. "Maybe you could train for the ballet? That's a great career."

I shrugged and crocodiled my choc block.

"Those dancers who tour with pop singers are very young," Susan said. "I don't think any of them are over thirty. There's much living after you reach thirty. That's why I'm suggesting having a plan B."

I focused on the road ahead. I didn't wanna get in a long convo with her. Just wanted to get home and watch a horror movie or something. Vampires fanging posho necks would've worked.

"I know school has been difficult for you," Susan went on. "From reading about your home life I can understand why you were so angry. It explains the fights with teachers and other students. The frustration must've built up. You were the one who was supposed to be cared for and yet you were lumped with looking after your dad."

Monkey being interrogated by the feds. How does she know so much about me? She's not my official foster carer. I'm just here for the weekend.

"But if you stay with us you'll get all the support you need. Emily's very bright, my husband knows everything worth knowing about math, and I know a thing or two about English and other stuff."

"You've only known me for two secs and you've read my frucking file?" I raised my tones. "You know all about my dramas at school? And what happened with my mum and dad?"

"Er . . . yes, Naomi. Louise read from your file to me. It makes sense, don't you think? So I could get to know—"

"*I* don't even know you and you know shit about me! *Liberties!*"

Emily stirred in the backseat, sat up, and leaned forward. "What's going on?"

"I'm trying to explain to Naomi that any potential foster carer needs to be briefed about the young person they're taking in."

Susan scoped me with dread. Her bottom lip wobbled so much I thought it was gonna drop off. She had to brake sharply to avoid the van in front of her. We all rocked forward. The seat belts saved Susan and my ass, but Emily fell off her seat. *Kuboof.*

"And I don't wanna be no freaking doctor!" I yelled. "Don't wanna be a lawyer or go to uni. You can toss Guy Fawkes on top of all that. You can't tell me what to do. You're not my mum! I'm gonna be a dancer and if you don't like it you can frig yourself with your bike pump!"

"I was only suggesting, just giving you something to think about—"

"*Stop the frucking car!*" I screamed. "I wanna get out! Telling me to do this and do that! *You're not my dad either!*"

Susan stamped on the brake pedal. Everyone jolted forward again. Emily smacked her head on the headrest in front of her and dropped to the floor again. "For freak's sake, Mum!"

"Sorry," said Susan. She puffed out a long sigh and rested her head on the steering wheel. She then sucked in a deep breath and closed her eyes.

I took the opportunity to escape.

"Naomi!" Susan called. "I'm very sorry! I didn't mean to upset you."

I threw her a brick-hard glare. Then I marched away and threw the Mars bar wrapper over my shoulder. I forgot my Coke bottle but it would've looked kinda tragic if I storm-heeled back for it. Pedestrians foot-braked in their tracks to see what the drama was all about.

"*Naomi!*" Susan called out again.

Jumping out of the ride, Emily hot-stepped to catch up with me. I tried to ignore her but I kinda liked it that she cared enough to quick-toe after me. She rolled with me for a short stretch before she could think of something to say. "I know you're pissed off with Mum but it's a long trek from here."

I paid her no mind and carried on walking. I stretched my strides. Emily had to jog for a bit to keep up with me.

"I don't know about you," Emily said, "but my legs are killing me with all that riding up hills. My body's reminding me of the shots I took last night. If you're gonna walk all the way back I'm gonna have to go with you—duty of care and all that. Do you wanna do that to me? I'll need a wheelchair and a sick-bag by the end of the day. It's not a look I've been going for."

"Tell your mum to stop lecturing me and tell her to stay outta my eyesight."

"I will. I swear, if she says another word to you I'll hit her with her bike and roll her down one of those hills."

I quarter-smiled.

"She doesn't mean any harm," Emily added. "She just

gets carried away sometimes. All that goodwill in her wants to come out of her stomach like an alien."

I tried hard to kill my grin. *Alien* was one of my fave films. I didn't love the sequels too much.

"I'll help you bake a cake this afternoon," offered Emily. She was smiling and doing happy things with her eyes. I wasn't six years old but at least she was trying to bend my lips into a smile.

"All right, I'll come back with ya but I'm gonna hold you to licking your mum with a bike if she starts on me again."

"Promise. Bike versus Mum's head is definitely on—even if she nags you a tiny bit."

I couldn't murder the chuckle that ran away from my mouth.

Avoiding Susan's gaze, I returned to the Range Rover and took a backseat next to the bikes. I crossed my arms and stared out the back window. I was good but I wanted Susan to know I was still raging. Emily joined me. Susan fired up the engine and pulled away.

"I'm very sorry, Naomi," Susan apologized once more. "I—"

"*Mum!* Just drive."

We reached home. I jet-heeled to my room and slammed the door behind me. I could hear Emily telling Susan to just leave me on my lonesome for a bit. I sat on the bed and stared at the blank TV. Suddenly, the TV was showing me the inside of my old flat. *Monkey in Wonderland. I'm beginning to see things. Is this shit happening in my head or the TV screen?* I watched myself on the TV—or at least I thought I did.

I tip-tap-toed to the bathroom and pushed down on the door handle. I stepped inside. The bathroom fan was louder than normal. The soap dish dripped red. Sliding fingerprints marked the white-tiled walls. The scum level inside the tub was stained with blood and grime. I couldn't sniff the lavender oil that Mum usually spilled into her bathwater. Her head hung over the side. Her sleek hair looked nice but there was a small puddle on the floor. It was weird seeing her naked. Her mouth was open but her eyes were closed. The water was very still, like a little pond on a silent, cold day.

I staggered to my bedroom, slammed my eyes shut, grabbed a pillow, and pushed it into my face.

Later that day, it was Emily who helped me bake a Victoria sponge sandwich cake. She gave me ratings for following instructions and mixing everything up to spec. Susan popped in and out of the kitchen to check on us and slowly my rage toward her went down a dose or two. But I had made up my mind about something.

When the cake had cooled, I cut a slice for Susan and offered it to her on a plate with a napkin.

"Naomi did most of the work," said Emily. "She was telling *me* what to do."

She wasn't lying.

"What a nice cake," Susan said, checking the texture. "Maybe one day you can be a chef? Perhaps when you finish school you might consider doing a cooking course or something?"

"*Mum!*" Emily raised her voice.

I bit my top lip.

"Just try the cake and stop going on," urged Emily.

Biting a big chunk, Susan raised her eyebrows and nodded. "This is delicious!"

Emily smiled and clapped. I scoped Susan's face for any sign of fakery.

"Perhaps we can bake cookies or shortbread tomorrow," Susan suggested.

I didn't respond to that one. Instead, I returned to the kitchen table and cut myself a big portion of prime Victoria sponge. I poured myself a glass of Coke, sank half of it, and sat next to Emily. I sucked in a big breath. "I'm not gonna be here tomorrow," I announced.

Susan and Emily swapped glances.

"But—" Susan started.

"I wanna go back to the Goldings," I choked her flow. "When you finish your cake, can you call Louise, please?"

"Of . . . of course," Susan managed. "I'm very sorry I upset you this morning. I've learned my lesson, Naomi. If we're lucky enough to have you again, I'll be more . . . considerate."

"There won't be a next time," I said. *I'm not raising my tones and I'm not swearing. Louise would give me a top ranking for this.* "Can you call Louise when you finish your cake? I'll appreciate it."

"Er, yes, of course."

"That's a shame," said Emily. "We've loved having you here."

"Yeah, I know," I said. "I appreciate it. But . . . but I can't see me fitting . . . I can't see . . ."

Susan's head fell.

"I hear you," nodded Emily. "You can bake a wicked cake though! Do you want me to wrap the rest of it in foil so you can take it with you?"

"Yes, please," I replied. "Thanks for being my trainee."

Emily laughed but Susan stood there as if I'd made jokes about starving babies.

Sitting on my bed beside Emily with my bags packed, I checked the time on my phone. Ten past six.

"You all right?" Emily asked. "You've been quiet all afternoon."

"I'm all right," I said. "Been thinking."

"About what?"

"About my real mum. You know, she was really pretty. My nan once showed me pics of her when she was sixteen years old. It's been years since . . . you know, but I still miss her loads."

"Course you miss her. You wouldn't be human if you didn't."

"I just—" I couldn't stop the tears. "I just wanna be somewhere . . . somewhere where I can imagine her smiling. Instead of always thinking of her in that . . ."

Emily gave me a long hug. "You don't have to say it." She wiped my tears.

I felt a slap of embarrassment. After all, I had only known her for one day.

"You'll find somewhere," she said. "What about the Goldings? Their place could be that somewhere."

"Louise says she wants to find a better fit. I think she

means she wants a white foster family to look after me." I sniffed that Emily kinda felt awkward about this issue so I didn't run with it.

"You must be tired of all this moving around," Emily said after a while.

"You're not wrong on that one! Last night I was trying to count the amount of bedrooms I've snored in for the past year."

"How many?"

"My calculator crashed on that one," I said. "I've had sleeping bags, single beds, double beds, bunk beds. Doesn't matter how comfy they are or how many pillows they give me or if I keep the light on . . . I still have nightmares about Mum."

Emily squeezed me again. It felt nice.

"Maybe," she said. "Maybe you need some sort of closure, or talk about her with someone. Have you tried that?"

"Louise tries to get me to talk about her. She wanted me to mark the day of her death the other day."

"It has to hurt for a while before we get over stuff," said Emily. "Everyone who has ever loved someone goes through that shitty time. I cried for weeks when my gran died. It shows how much we loved them. If you want you can always call me up. One day you'll be good."

"You're not just saying that, right? You'll definitely keep dinging me every now and again?"

"Course I will. Maybe next time I'll take you to that American diner that's next door to the Thai place."

I grinned. "I'm gonna reserve a napkin on that one."

"That'll be cool for a chillaxed girl," Emily replied.

I wished she wouldn't use that word. So last millennium.

We sat there in silence for the next ten minutes. My thoughts swayed to the Goldings and my school sistrens. Kim would want an update on my latest drama.

"I haven't got too many friends, to be honest," I said. "So make sure you keep me on your TV dish. I know that Kim has my spine but Nats goes funny on me sometimes."

Emily smiled and kissed me on the forehead. "I'm sure Nats has your back too."

Half an hour later, the doorbell rang. I grabbed my meerkat and bounced down the stairs. I slowed down when I realized I looked too eager. Emily followed me with my bags.

Her arms folded, Susan managed a smile and greeted Louise with a peck on the cheek. "I'm sorry it didn't work out," she said to Louise. "Maybe . . . maybe I need to read more. I *want* to understand and learn from this."

"Thanks for having Naomi," Louise responded. "Don't blame yourself. Sometimes . . . sometimes it just doesn't work out. I'm sure there's a young person out there who really needs someone like you."

"Can I get in the car?" I cut their flow.

"Of course."

I gave Susan a hug but I could feel her stiffness and disappointment. "Remember that hill," she said.

"I will," I replied. *No I won't!*

Emily dropped my bags into the trunk of the car. Susan remained by the front door, her arms still crossed.

"We'll catch up soon," Louise said to her.

"Yes, let's do lunch. I'll try and talk you out of your coffee habit!"

"I suppose you can try."

I was already in the passenger seat. It felt awkward but I wanted to get back to the Goldings' place in flashtime.

"Don't be a stranger," said Emily, closing the passenger-side door and giving me a bagful of cake slices wrapped in kitchen foil. "You've got my number. When you're ready, give me a call and we'll go out."

"Deffo," I smiled. "Maybe you can take me to Australia or something."

Starting the engine, Louise waved at Susan before pulling away. Emily gave me a thumbs-up and a big smile. I'm not gonna lie, I was sorry to leave her.

CHAPTER TEN

The Shark in Louise's Knickers

Parking on a side street just two turnings from the Goldings' house, Louise killed the engine and turned off the car stereo. For twenty seconds she sat in silence staring through the windshield. She then scoped me hard like she was counting the hairs of my eyebrows. I tried to ignore her by stroking my meerkat—I thought of calling it Emily. "I'm waiting, Naomi!" Louise exploded. "This is going to be interesting, I should imagine."

"What?"

"I'm waiting to hear what terrible crime Susan's just committed."

"She was scratching my nerves."

"Scratching your nerves? By giving you suggestions about careers and education? Let's try her at the Old Bailey! In fact, let's not bother with the trial. Let's hang, draw, and quarter her!"

"What shark got stuck up *your* knickers? She was ordering me around, being bossy."

"You couldn't even say a proper goodbye. You ran to my car like a whippet."

I wondered what a whippet was. I guessed it was a Us-ain Bolt–like shark. "I didn't give her a proper goodbye? I hugged her, didn't I? I don't pretend to like people. That's what adults do. That's what *you* do."

Louise raised her voice: "She took care of you, tried to advise you. Encouraged you. And you can't even be both-ered to stay another day? She didn't show it but she feels terrible."

"Boo diddery hoo! I can't believe the hard-curb life she's had. Let's give her a social worker. Let's send her for counseling. Give her a frucking lolli—"

"Your sarcasm's not working, Naomi."

"So what d'you want me to do?" I asked. "Stay with someone who I don't like? It wouldn't be so bad if Emily would be around but she's at uni."

Louise gripped the steering wheel hard. Maybe she imagined it being my head. She bit her bottom lip before reaching out for a cigarette in the glove compartment. "And *don't* think I didn't realize that you stole my cigarettes when I dropped you at Susan's. They call that theft, Naomi."

She got me on that one. I didn't reply. Instead, I held my meerkat against my chest.

Winding down the driver's-side window, Louise ignited her fagarette and pulled on it like it gave her life.

"Can I have one?" I asked.

Louise gave me my biggest-ever *really* glare.

"She was doing my head in," I said. "Couldn't take to her. Another day of her, somebody would've had to call the feds out on a grimy murder. Trust me, I woulda made full use of that canoe paddle in her basement. And you wouldn't want that drama to happen cos you're always bitching about your paperwork and social wanker inquiries."

I think she agreed with me on that one. She puffed her smoke out the window. "She did everything she could to be nice to you. She made her house your own, gave you your own space to watch your DVDs, took you bike-riding."

"My legs are still screaming on that one."

"I just," Louise stuttered, "I just can't understand. What did she do that was so wrong? Tell me, because for the life of me, I can't work it out."

Monkey in the witness box. It must be one of them fat great white's finning around her crotches. I wonder if her boyfriend has stressed her out lately. "She . . . she was lecturing me," I replied. "She wouldn't stop going on."

"She was trying to advise you on careers after teaching you a life skill. And for that you swore at her, got out of her car, and ran off down the street."

"I didn't run."

"Same difference."

"I just didn't want to stay with her. Are you gonna put me on lockdown and fling away the keys for that? No! And I didn't *ask* to stay with her. It was *your* idea. *Your* mission."

"Susan's a kind woman," said Louise. "She's a dear friend of mine and has worked with children for many years now. I just hope this experience doesn't stop her—"

"From what?" I snapped her flow. "From fostering again? Oh my days! It's a tragedy! Let's get the fiddler to play outside her gates! If she wants another kid so bad why doesn't she just bang thighs with her man again and give birth to one? Another Emily would be a yes-yes for the world."

"Naomi, sometimes you go too—"

"No kid I know would wanna stay with her," I corked her dribble. "Every minute she was up in my face. *Is the pillow all right? Is the juice too warm? Is your room too hot? You sure you don't want me to switch off your bedroom light? Do you know where the downstairs toilet is if someone's in the upstairs one? Is the bog paper soft enough—*"

"I think you're exaggerating, Naomi."

"No. I'm not. And she kept chit-chattering on about the outdoor life. If she loves it so much, why don't she put her helmet on, pack her compass, and stomp to the North Pole!"

"She was only thinking about your comfort."

"I'm fourteen! I don't need someone asking me if my pillow's fat enough and if I need the light on or off."

"It's called showing concern for others, Naomi. That's all."

"Anyway, I thought you said that if I didn't like somewhere you put me, all I had to do was holler out loud and you'd move me. So why are you munching your G-strings about it?"

Louise rubbed her forehead. I had her there. She sat very still staring through the windshield for the longest time. I thought about slapping her to get her out of her trauma zone.

"I'm really at a loss as to what to do with you," she said finally. "I've lost count of the amount of fostering placements you've had . . . How will I or any of us ever be able to find an adoption family for you or even a foster family that'll give you a bit of stability?"

"The Goldings were on point," I said. "Tony chews his boxers a bit but Colleen's okay . . . and I love Sharyna and Pablo. Soon, if I keep up my ratings, Colleen will trust me enough to babysit for 'em."

Louise placed a hand on my shoulder and her rage faded. She looked at me with kind eyes again. "They're not ideal for the long term, Naomi," she said. "I've told you already about the problems of long-term interracial fostering and the council policy on—"

"No you haven't."

Louise ignored me. "And besides, how long will it take for you to find something wrong with them, I wonder? If this continues I'll have to return you to the care unit or a home out of the area. Do you want that, Naomi?"

I didn't answer. I stroked my meerkat again.

"And if you do return to the unit, I'll be a bit concerned about the influence Kim and Nats have on you. I'm trying to keep you away from all that."

I gave Louise a long eye-pass. She didn't back down and eyeballed me with interest.

"The Goldings will do for now," I said after a while. "But I still can't see why you can't give me my own place. I can look after myself. I don't need anyone looking out for me. I looked after my dad, didn't I?"

Louise shook her head.

"Just give me the funds you gave him," I went on. "I won't waste it on liquor. I'll pay the rent. I'll turn off the lights at night. I know how to use a thermostat so I won't blow up the bills. I know how to look out for bargains in the supermarket. Kim's already shown me where the charity shops are where I can get secondhand garms. You can call me Miss Naomi Cheapo."

Louise smiled for a short second but it quickly died.

"I could even foster young kids, maybe just one at first," I suggested. "If you have to, you can come and visit me once a week. I'll even give ya your coffee and custard creams. I'll even have a roll-up waiting for ya. When I put the kids to bed we could watch a horror movie together. It'll be sweet."

For the first time since I'd known her, there was a tear in Louise's eye. She lowered her head and blinked twice before wiping it away. She then cleared her throat. Her cancer stick had grown a long ash end. "You know we can't allow you to do that," she said. "Be sensible, Naomi."

"Why not?" I wanted to know. "I'll give 'em better care than loads of zero-rated mums out there. You should know the score on that one. You work with some—"

"We've been through this before. You're too young."

"But I was old enough to look after my dad?" I argued. "Old enough to give him his pills? And I did all the shopping. It was *me* who always put funds on the electric key and gas card. Me who scrubbed up the whole place when social wankers visited. Me who made sure he went to the doctor's. I did all that stuff."

"I know what you've been through, Naomi. It wasn't right that you had to take that on. You should've received more help. We all admit that. But you're still a child and need looking after."

"I'm *not* a frucking kid!"

Louise shook her head again. Her harsh tones returned: "This is getting us nowhere."

What's the matter with social wankers? Their moods swing more than Tarzan.

"Why can't you listen to me and ask what I want!"

Louise gazed through the windshield again. She then threw her butt end out of the window. "Let me get you back to the Goldings," she said. "I'm taking a day off on Monday so make sure you go to school that morning."

"Tony takes me."

"Hmmm," responded Louise. She restarted the car. "No more day trips to your great-grandmother's flat."

"There wouldn't have to be day trips if a *certain* someone took me to see her."

I tuned into the radio station that I wanted as Louise pulled away. She didn't look at me once the whole journey. I guessed she was really pissed at me or was thinking about something. *I didn't go too far, did I?*

Louise pulled up outside the Goldings' home. "I . . . I won't be seeing you to the door," she said. "You'll be all right, won't you?"

I nodded and stepped out to the trunk where I collected my bags.

"Naomi," Louise called.

"What is it now? I haven't jacked any of your fagarettes."

"It's not that."

"Then what is it?"

Louise was about to say something then hesitated. She stared at the ground. "Sorry," she said.

"Sorry for what?"

"Sorry . . . sorry for placing you with somebody that obviously didn't work for you. I just . . . I just thought Susan might've been a good influence on you. My mistake. If it's okay by you, we don't have to tell the Goldings about this."

I wanted to grin off my cheeks but she did say sorry. Grown-ups don't usually do that, in my world. "If they ask me no questions, I can't tell any lies," I said.

"I guess I had a personal stake in things working out with you and Susan," Louise added.

"Don't know what you mean about a personal stake but don't fist yourself up about it, Louise," I said. "Grown-ups mess up too. Even social workers. Makes ya normal."

I wasn't sure if Louise was about to laugh or cry. She punched into first gear and was off. *Monkey hot-pawing away from hunters.* That was emotional.

CHAPTER ELEVEN

Shortbread and Shortcomings

"I'll make it," I insisted as Tony filled the kettle with water. "Thank you," he said, then parked himself at the kitchen table. There was a packet of bourbon cream biscuits on the counter and he reached for them. He took out two and offered me the packet. I picked out three.

Tony scoped me nervously. "So . . . so what happened at the Hamiltons' place? Didn't . . . did you disagree about something?"

"Louise told me not to spill," I replied. "But it's no biggie. I dunno why she's stamping a big confidential on it. Basically, Susan tried hard but she just couldn't tickle my like cells. Sometimes it rocks that way. Not that she did anything off-point to me, cos if she did I wouldn't have stayed another second. I would've taken a bus home."

I said home.

Tony stared at the steaming kettle. I guessed he wanted to know more of what went down but didn't know how to ask.

"There are some peeps you just can't get on with," I said.

"That's true enough," replied Tony. "There are some people I don't get on with."

"Louise," I guessed.

Tony looked at me for a long second before he nodded. "We've had our disagreements over council policy at times."

"What don't you like about her and the council policy?" I wanted to know.

"As I said, just the odd disagreement. That's all. Nothing too serious."

"At first I thought she was a first-class bitch," I said. "But when you get to know her she's on point. She does care."

"So she should," Tony put in.

The kettle had boiled. I made Tony his mug of coffee. I even stirred it for him.

"Thank you," he whispered. He took a sip and I crunched another bourbon.

"I think she's having issues with her boyfriend," I gossiped. "Louise has been brewing lately. Getting all emotional. She almost leaked tears the other day."

I could see Tony felt awkward. He changed the subject: "Did you like the bike-riding?"

"I did at first but Susan wanted to ride up mountains that got clouds swirling around 'em. Me and Emily were having asthma attacks."

Hearing Colleen come down the stairs, I collected another mug from the cupboard. "I've just made Tony a coffee," I said to her as she came in. "D'you want one?"

"Okay, then, darling. Remember I have mine—"

"Black," I cut in. "Yes, I know. I *can* remember stuff."

"Pablo settled down?" asked Tony.

"Yes, he has," replied Colleen. "He's a little excited that Naomi's back. He now wants to go bike-riding in the mountains."

"I'm gonna make shortbread with him tomorrow," I said.

"Make sure you leave the kitchen how you found it," warned Tony. "And follow the directions carefully."

"We will. I know how to clean up after myself and I've baked stuff for my dad before. I *know* what I'm doing."

I gave Colleen her mug of coffee. She took a sip. "Thanks, Naomi."

"That's all right."

Tony and Colleen swapped something with their eyes. They both nodded. I wondered what mission they had planned.

"Yesterday we were checking out places where they have urban dance classes," Colleen said.

"Oh?" I said. I poured myself a glass of Coke. *Monkey sitting down in class with a pencil and paying attention.*

"We found a place near North Crongton—a community center," Colleen said. "There's a dance club that is based there. It's called Urban Steps."

"Near North Crongton? Kim calls Crongton Shank Town—a place of untold murkings. Is this community center safe?"

"We think so," said Colleen. "There's been no trouble inside that we've heard of. Urban Steps have done performances in schools and for the Crongton council. Some of their members have appeared in a couple of pop and grime videos."

"Appeared in videos? Who were they for? The Wolf Riders? Moleskin? The Beaver Crew?"

"I can't remember their names," Colleen replied. "They last performed at the Crongton Park Country Show. They got a massive ovation—there's a clip on their website. It's a bit of a drive but we wondered if you'd like to try out with them?"

"Yeah. Course! My toes are ripe for this. You know that."

"They have classes on Tuesday evenings and Saturday mornings," said Colleen. "I was thinking we could introduce you to the tutor on Tuesday. She's a lovely woman—a French-Tunisian lady. Beautiful accent she's got. Ms. Ibtissem Almi—hope I pronounced it right."

"But I don't speak French-Tunis-whatever-it-is," I said. "How am I gonna understand her tones?"

"She speaks good English," laughed Tony. "Would you like to join on Tuesday?"

I could use this to nice up my wardrobe. Don't let the opportunity fly by, Naoms.

"I haven't got any dance garms," I pointed out. "Had to bomb my last sneakers I danced in. Gonna need those slip-on shoes, leggings, tracksuit bottoms, and all that . . . and I wanna headband . . . please. And I don't want any cheapo brands—they don't last."

"I was planning to shop for your dance things next time I go shopping," said Colleen. "Louise said it's okay if we buy you stuff—within reason. We just have to give her the receipts. Pablo and Sharyna need some new clothes as well. We'll drive down to Southside."

"Yeah, I'm definitely on that."

"Great!" said Colleen. "We'll go after school or on a weekend. We'll have a meal there too."

"I'm on that too. Can we go to Mega Burger? They've got this new double-bacon-burger thing with cheese."

Colleen screwed up her face. "Hmmm, I suppose so."

The next day after school, I sort of made shortbread with Pablo. I took out all the ingredients myself: unsalted butter, plain flour, and sugar. Pablo had massive fun with the blender. The kitchen had brand-new decorations but I cleaned it up. Colleen kept on breaking an entry into the kitchen. I had to tell her to go missing. "I've got this," I said. "You don't have to be the food police on this one."

As Pablo and I used the biscuit cutters, Colleen and Sharyna went out to get something for Sharyna's science homework. By the time they came back, the oven was a disaster zone. I opened all the windows to let the smoke out and proper scrubbed the inside of the cooker. Pablo giggled his little ribs out as he slopped the burned shortbread into the bin. He laughed harder when Colleen stood by the kitchen door with her hands on her hips. Sharyna entered and placed a hand over her mouth.

"It went a bit wrong," I said.

Colleen's hard-curb stare wouldn't leave me alone.

"Pabs, I've got something for you," Sharyna said.

Colleen didn't move until Sharyna and Pablo had climbed the stairs.

I went to the sink and rinsed my hands.

"Naomi," Colleen said, "sit down."

I dried my hands and took a seat. Colleen scoped me hard. I stared at the floor.

"I—" I stuttered, "I had the gas up too high. I put it on mark eight but it was meant to be on mark three. Pabs wanted to play a game while the biscuits baked for twenty minutes."

Colleen's laser gaze coulda sliced a bank vault.

"I didn't understand why it burned till I looked at the instructions again."

"Listen to me, Naomi," Colleen lowered her voice. "When I was asking you about the instructions and if you want to ask me anything you're unsure about, I'm not thinking you're not capable. Not at all. It's just that if you're taking on adult responsibilities, you should be clear on what you're doing. Do you understand that, Naomi?"

My cheeks sizzled like the oven. I had no defense on this one.

"I know you've had to be an adult for much of your life," Colleen went on, "but there are times when you have to put your hand up when you're not sure. You're still fourteen."

"I get it, Colleen!"

"In fact, I'm at fault too," she admitted. "I should've stayed here to supervise you. God knows what Louise would have made of all this."

Half a grin escaped from my lips. "She'll probably clong you with a million risk-assessment forms. There won't be a full stop on that one. Don't fret, my gums are sealed."

"Promise me that if you're not sure about something, anything, then ask?" Colleen said. "It's not a sign of weakness. It's how we learn."

"So you're not banning me from the kitchen forever?"

Colleen laughed. "Oh, no!" Her face went soft again. "You can fry my breakfast when it's my birthday. Last year Tony made a mess of it. Come on, I'll help you clean up and then I'm taking you all to Southside."

CHAPTER TWELVE

A French Master Class

My dance outfit, white headband, and slip-on dance shoes were inside my new Adidas shoulder bag. On my way to the dance studio, I pressed my meerkat against my chest and gazed through the passenger-side window—the North Crongton streets were grimy. We passed a lot of fried chicken huts, bookies, liquor shops, and cheapo stores.

"Are you okay, Naomi?" asked Colleen.

I have to admit, I wasn't on Colleen's radar. I was thinking what the other girls at the dance class might be like. Would they laugh at me? Behind my back would they be making loser signs and dropping me to the bottom of their rankings? *Say I fall over? Say I make a prick outta myself? I wish Kim and Nats were with me. They'd have my spine. But I might not be as good as they say I am. I swear that if anyone busts out a giggle at me, I'm gonna clong 'em so hard their granny's toenails will feel the vibrations. Then I'll quick-heel outta there and make my own way back even if I have to hike it.*

"Naomi," Colleen repeated as she reverse-parked into a space, "are you okay?"

"Yeah . . . kind of."

"Kind of?"

"What sort of peeps are gonna be in the class?" I wanted to know.

Colleen switched off the engine. "Kids who want to learn about dancing, I suppose."

"I mean . . . are there gonna be peeps . . . like me?"

"What do you mean, *like me*?"

"You know what I mean, Colleen. Kids from a unit. Kids who've been expelled. Kids who have . . . issues."

"Honest answer is, I don't know, Naomi. It doesn't matter what your background is. What's important is that you want to learn to dance, right?"

"But—" I could feel the furies flying the loopy-loop in my stomach. "But I haven't been with normal kids for the longest time. Not since I started going to the PRU. I've been at that place for, what, nearly two years now . . . off and on. The kids at this dance place might think I'm backward. They might look at me funny. They'll whisper things behind my back."

"They don't even need to know about your background," said Colleen. "You're not going there to swap family histories."

"But they might ask me about my life," I said. "Sooner or later they're gonna drop that barbell on me. I don't need that drama. What am I gonna tell 'em? I can't stand it when normal kids talk about their mum this and their dad that and their brother this and their sister that. And all that *my dad's picking me up in his BMW. My mum's gonna buy me a name-brand dress for the school prom. My parents are taking me to Cun-Can-Cun or whatever it's called for their summer holiday.* It presses my rage buttons."

Colleen gave me a *really* look. She must've been taking lessons from Louise. "And you're going to allow that to stop you from doing something you really want to do?" she challenged me. "Come on, Naomi! You can do this!"

I stroked the head of my meerkat. "Kim says I shouldn't trust normal girls, girls who still live with their parents. *They'll always think they're better than you*, she said."

Colleen wrapped her hands around mine. "You shouldn't listen to everything that Kim says. She's only a few months older than you and she doesn't know everything."

"Funny you saying that," I replied. "Louise says the same thing."

"Maybe we're right."

"Maybe you're wrong!" I raised my tones.

Awkward pause.

"I think I know a little bit about what you're going through," Colleen said after a while.

"You do?"

"I remember going on my first school journey," she went on. "My mum was all excited that I got selected but I was dreading the trip. I wasn't in the *in-crowd* and I thought I'd be *Colleen-no-mates*. I didn't want to go but Mum was saying it was a great opportunity, so I went."

"What happened?" I asked. "They cussed you out? Dropped your knickers in the toilet? Pissed on your pillow? Put their raspberry pads in your trainers? That's what Kim did to some girl she had a beef with."

Colleen shook her head. "Raspberry—" she stuttered. For a short second she looked proper shocked. "No, it never got as bad as that. The in-crowd girls still refused to talk to me but I made good friends with another girl—

Tracey Cunningham. We're still close to this day. She's married and has two kids now. And you know what I say about those other girls who spread gossip about me and threatened me?"

"What? Saw off their baby toes with a broken rum bottle?"

Colleen ignored my bottle remedy. "*Screw 'em,*" she said. "If they don't like you for yourself then you don't need them as your mate."

I loved Colleen's little movie but the furies were still booting my ribs. "Say I'm rubbish at the dancing or what this tutor asks me to do?"

"You won't be," reassured Colleen. "You have a great talent. *Use* it."

"But you're gonna say that cos you know me."

"I say it because it's *true.*"

I gave Colleen a half smile before I climbed out of the car. I left my meerkat on the seat on purpose—didn't wanna be given grief about bringing a cuddly toy with me.

"Do you want me to go in with you?" offered Colleen.

"Nah, I'll be good. I don't wanna step in there with you and let them all think, *Look at her! She has to walk in with her foster mum. She must have untold issues!*"

Colleen started the car, tooted her horn, and hot-wheeled away.

For half a second, I thought about skipping dance and visiting Nan. *Where would I get the bus from?* I thought better of it. Louise would puff another box of fagarettes a day.

I took in a mega breath and pushed through the door. I found myself in a short hallway that led to a dance studio.

Notice boards advertising extra English and math classes, yoga sessions, car boot sales, homework clubs, IT classes, Sunday church services, and a lost white cat with black patches covered the walls. *One day I'd like to keep a cat, but if it doesn't wanna sink the food that I cook, it'll have to go out there and hunt for its own dinner.*

A tall, honey-skinned woman dressed in black leggings and a black vest sitting behind a round table was helping a mixed-race teenage chick fill in a form. I watched them silently until I was noticed.

"Hello there," the lady greeted me with a strong accent. "*Bonjour.*"

"Hi," I replied in a whisper.

"Have you come to join the dance class?"

I nodded.

"Can I ask you to fill in the enrollment form? I am the tutor. My name is Mademoiselle Almi. *Comment t'appelles-tu?* What is your name?"

"Naomi . . . Naomi Brisset."

"Naomi Brisset? Oh yes! *Bon.* Your parents came to see me the other day."

Monkey impressed. I want to take her accent home and put it in my hot chocolate before I go to bed.

"They're *not* my parents," I pointed out.

"*Excuse moi*, Naomi. How do you say? Er, foster parents . . . Are you coming to watch today to see how we do things or would you like to take part?"

"I dunno."

"Have you something to dance in?"

"Yeah."

"That is good. *Bon*. After you fill in the form, get changed in the dressing room upstairs and come down to the studio. Stretches and warm-ups start in fifteen minutes. If you want to watch today, just to see what we do, that is good. If you want to join in at any time, that is good too."

The staircase was to my left but I hesitated. I scoped the form and screwed up my face as I read the question: *Next of kin.*

How am I gonna answer that? Dead mum. No phone number there. Dad, the heavyweight rum king of Ashburton and all the bars surrounding it. No digits there either. Good luck on trying to find his drunken ass. Maybe I should write down Louise's, Colleen's, or Tony's name? No, bomb that. I'll leave it blank.

I regretted leaving my meerkat behind. I wished Kim and Nats were with me. Normal peeps didn't bother Kim. Then again, Kim loved to start mauls with everyday chicks. Our weekend trip to Butlin's gate-crashed my mind.

"*Ne t'inquiète pas*," smiled Ms. Almi.

"Come again?"

"That's French for, *Don't worry, Naomi*," Ms. Almi translated. "You love dancing, *oui*? So we all do. You will have good fun."

Sitting in my new dance outfit on a bench in the changing room, I watched the other dancers arrive, get changed, and skip down the stairs. Their ages ranged from around eleven to sixteen. They looked so comfortable and I felt so awkward. Only when the room was empty did I stand up and perform a few stretches. There was a mirror above the sink and I peered into it. I adjusted my headband and said to myself, *I can do this. Colleen thinks I'm good, Kim and Nats think I can bless any dance floor, and my PE teacher at primary school, Ms. Banks, always gave me top ratings—God bless her bunions. She would clench her fist, stare at me hard, and say, "Knock 'em dead, Naomi."*

I heard the pounding on the floor below. Warm-ups had begun, I guessed. I stared at my clothes on the pegs and thought about changing back into them. Kim wouldn't mouse out of this one, I thought. She wouldn't sit up here all on her lonesome. She would bounce down to that dance studio and not give two flying diddlys what they thought about her . . . and Nats would follow her.

I tip-tap-toed down the stairs. I stopped at the double doors that opened to the studio. A dance track with a heavy bassline bruised the floor. I nodded to the beat. Taking in two deep breaths, I entered the studio like I was starring in *America's Next Top Model.* I felt the heat of a million pairs of eyes scoping me from eyebrow corner to little toe.

Sitting cross-legged on the floor with cane in hand, Ms. Almi was drilling the girls in the first five steps of a routine. A boombox in the corner played a Nicki Minaj track. *"Un, deux, trois, quatre, cinq!"* Ms. Almi instructed. *"Un, deux, trois, quatre, cinq!"*

Seeing myself in the long wall-length mirror, I sat down at the empty end of the studio. I fixed my headband again and tapped my feet as I watched the girls go through their moves. I was impressed to the max and wondered if I could match them.

Twenty minutes later, the furies in my belly took a time-out and I decided to join the line of dancers. Ms.

Almi was about to introduce me to the other members of the class but thought better of it. I didn't think she wanted to bring added attention to me. Within minutes I picked up the routine and high-kicked away my stress cells. Ms. Almi smiled at me and killed the music. "*Très bien! Fantastique!* Now relax for a moment."

My legs did this spaghetti-in-a-boiling-pot thing as Ms. Almi approached me. Her pointed toes, lifted chin, and straight back fascinated me. I wondered what it was like to grow up in France and if they had PRUs and children's homes there.

"Very good that you have finally joined us, Naomi, but maybe next week you join us for stretching and warm-ups, *oui?*"

I nodded, relieved that I didn't mess up in my first session. I even let loose a half grin.

"*Bon!*"

When I get back to the PRU, I'm gonna ask them if I can learn French.

CHAPTER THIRTEEN

The Corner Shop Scam

Rolling out of the classroom fifteen minutes before the lesson finished, Kim led Nats and me to the playground where we parked on a bench.

Taking out her smokes from the pocket of her stolen purple suede jacket, Kim offered me one. I accepted. "Thanks."

Not smoking herself, Nats flicked her lighter to fire up our fagarettes.

"So what d'you reckon about Richard's lesson this afternoon?" asked Kim.

I shrugged.

"He's just being nosy," said Nats. "He's just like the rest of the staff. They all want to know every liccle ting about you."

"You're not wrong, Nats," said Kim. "I didn't write one friggin' word. Fruck that for a slabful of grimers."

"Nor did I," said Nats. "How could he expect us to write down something on a piece of paper that no one knows about ya, and then he collects the papers and everybody has to guess who wrote down what? Only three people did it."

"I did it," I said. I sucked hard on my cancer stick and

checked Kim's and Nats's reactions. They weren't too happy-clappy about it. "Richard did say it didn't have to be too personal," I explained. "It could've been a fave singer or something."

"Why did you do it?" Kim wanted to know. "Didn't I tell ya they're just putting their mitts in your business? You know that they're gonna keep all that. They'll probably get Marie to type it all up and they'll slap it in your file and paste it on their spreadsheets. And then they'll get everyone to read it when they have their staff meetings. You can't trust 'em, Naoms. When are you gonna start crooking your ear and giving me attention on that one? I'm not hyping."

"What did you write?" asked Nats. "What is it that none of us know about ya?"

My cheeks microwaved. I stared at the ground.

"Oh come on, Naoms!" urged Kim. "You can't tell us that you wrote something and not spill about it. Come on! Let the rhino shit on the shagpile."

I let them brew for a few more seconds. "I thought it was a good idea," I said. "I think Richard's on point when he said that if we knew a little info about each other, we'd understand each other more and there wouldn't be so many fights."

"You're only saying that cos he tickles your fancy," said Kim. "And they'll always be peeps mauling each other. Richard thinks—"

"I don't fancy him!" I protested. "He's too short."

"His dick is probably short an' all," laughed Kim.

"Fancy Richard?" Nats shook her head in disgust. "Kim's on point, you can't trust any guys, Naoms, even if they're teachers. Anyway, we're waiting. What did you write down?"

They both glared at me hard but I made them wait a few more seconds. "My dad used to jack goods from corner shops," I admitted.

"Is that all?" said Kim. Her eyeballs did a full circle. "After all your hype? That's not exactly the confession of a teenage serial killer, Naoms. The way you puffed it up with your big pause, I thought you or your dad gored a man in his balls or something."

Nats bent herself up in mad giggles.

"It was the way he used to do it," I said.

"How did he used to steal then?" Nats asked.

"He'd use me," I answered. "He'd ask me to step inside a shop and pretend I was in the trauma zone. He used to rub my face and pinch my nose till they turned red and then he'd roll me in."

"What then?" asked Kim.

"I'd start crying. You know, proper-little-cute-girl-in-a-Disney-movie-lost-her-puppy bawling. I'd fall to my knees and the shopkeeper would come around and ask if I was all right. Sometimes they'd just look at me for the longest time and I'd really have to charge up the dramatics."

"Our girl wants an Oscar," chuckled Kim.

"Anyway, when they came up to me I'd ask for a drink of water," I continued. "They'd go and get the water and Dad would bounce in and jack stuff. He'd go for his liquor, bread, cereal, milk, and my Coke—I wouldn't do it if he refused to get my fizz. Oh, and he'd rob a few tubes of extra-strong mints—he never loved the social peeps sniffing alcohol on his breath."

"So when the shopkeeper came back with your drink of water, what would you tell 'em?" Kim wanted to know.

"I'd give 'em my *Paps is sick in bed and the doctor was shaking his head* story, let loose some more tears, and they'd give me a packet of chocolate biscuits or something. I'd thank 'em but by that time Dad was hotfooting home getting ready to make my brekkie."

"That's kinda clever for a guy," said Nats.

"He should've jacked the notes outta the till," said Kim. "That's what I would've done. What's the point in getting yourself on lockdown for robbing a few bits of food and liquor? Bomb that. Might as well go for the jackpot."

"Dad used to feel guilty though," I said. "Sometimes, after he picked up the child benefit funds from the post office, he'd take it and leave money on the shop counter when the assistant wasn't looking. Usually a few twenty-pence pieces. It didn't cover the cost of all the things he jacked though. It made him feel on the level. *I'm not a criminal,* he'd keep telling me. *But you have to eat, don't ya?*"

Kim shook her head. "That's just a dumb-ass mission," she said. "What did he wanna give the change back for? They'll only suspect him of jacking the stuff if he got caught putting the silver on the counter."

"Wassername?" Nats thought out aloud. "Anita Stelling. She got a sentence for stealing some perfume during the Ashburton riots."

"Anita's not been blessed with too much brain juice," said Kim. "It was only a cheapo brand. If you're gonna jack stuff, you might as well go for the first-class shit."

"I'd only munch porridge oats for Chanel N°5," laughed

Nats. "Or if any bruv tried it on me again. I'd definitely do time for that."

After what Nats went through with her foster brother, I'd do time with her if another guy troubled her.

"It's a good little scam that your dad had though, Naoms," said Kim. "When I have a kid, I might play the same game. I'll dress her up all cute so the shop people will go *ahhhh*. Put her in little pink tights, little white boots, and a nice little white jacket. I might slap a liccle pink beret on her bonce."

"How're you ever gonna have a kid?" asked Nats. "You said you'll never bump thighs with a man again. And we're gonna be twined for the longest time, right?" She scoped Kim hard.

For a second I sensed hesitation in Kim's eyes. "Er . . . yeah," she said. "We're gonna be linked forever, Nats, you know that."

Again I was in the awkward zone.

Nats's eyebrows softened. "And—" she stuttered, "and didn't you say a long time ago that you don't wanna go through the living agonies of having a baby?"

"You're not wrong," replied Kim. "Bomb having a baby and all that screaming malarkey. I'm gonna adopt one day. And then I'll work the scam."

"*You* adopt?" giggled Nats. "I suppose it could be big fun being parents together."

I couldn't imagine Kim and Nats adopting. *That'll be a war game.*

"Dunno why you two have got the laughing bends," said Kim. "I'm serious. If there's a liccle chick out there, say around ten or eleven, who has all sorts of issues and woe going on—don't want 'em too young with all that wiping away shit and drying tears. But who better to understand a ten-year-old girl with issues more than me? In fact, the social should be paying me a caravan load of funds for my know-how."

"They won't give it to you, Kim," said Nats. "They only give money once you're over eighteen and if you're living with a bruv—a so-called *stable relationship*. It doesn't matter if that guy is a pedo or something. They keep giving 'em the funds and they do what guys do. They should let lesbian couples raise more kids. It's safer that way."

"My dad had drinking issues but I always felt safe with him," I said.

"Some bruvs are on point," said Kim. "Just a few . . . maybe?"

"I wouldn't trust any of 'em!" Nats raised her tones. "Didn't the pricks give my dad and his girlfriend funds to help look after me? And he had to make sure he had a girlfriend who stayed at home to get it cos he worked in the evenings. And his girlfriend's son was a *prick*! He was *all* nice when the social interviewed him. That's what *they do*. He was the one who made me a coffee and gave me a Viennese whirl at the first meeting. Guys pretend shit but really they're blatantly evil. I swear that if I ever see him again, that trigger's getting—"

"Let's not go into that one again," said Kim. "Don't wanna put Naomi on the down-low, do we, and make her scared of any bruv in trousers? I thought you had got over the hill on that one, Nats? We've talked about it nuff times.

Don't let what that drainhead did to ya sabotage your life."

Nats crossed her arms and looked out to the main road. Then she stood up and stepped away. I wanted to follow her and give her a hug but I thought better of it. *Monkey in a test lab. I thought I had a boxful of issues.*

Twenty minutes later, Colleen arrived to pick me up. She asked me how school flowed for the day but I thought about Nats. *How could she ever trust bruvs again after the shit she's been through? She's blessed that she has Kim loving her and backing her spine though. She lucked out on that one.*

"Louise still wants to get me adopted, right?" I said to Colleen.

"Yes," she nodded. "That's the general plan."

"If she does find someone," I said, "I don't want 'em to have a son in the house who's older than me."

Colleen side-eyed me. "Why . . . why not?"

I nibbled my bottom lip.

She stopped at a traffic light. "Why not?" she repeated. "What's brought this on?"

"Cos if he's younger than me, I can boot him off if he wants sex. But if he's older and bigger than me, I'll look for something to gore him with. I'm not playing. The blue-bloods will call it murder one."

Colleen swallowed something. She managed to keep her eyes on the road. "Have you been listening to Kim and Nats again?"

"What if I have? What Nats had to go through was real."

Colleen concentrated on her driving for a minute. "I'm

. . . I'm sure Louise will take everything into consideration," she said. "Not all young men are like . . . like the guy who attacked Nats, Naomi. You girls have to learn to trust again."

"Some are like that," I said. "Too frucking many."

"Swearing, Naomi."

"Sorry."

We drove in silence for two minutes.

"Wherever you're placed," said Colleen—she tried to smile but it didn't reach her eyes—"the final say is all yours. So don't worry."

"You're not just saying that?"

"No, I'm not," replied Colleen. "It's up to you."

"I'll hold you to that," I said. "There's no way I'm gonna live with a foster bruv who's older than me. I don't want my parts to be fiddled with."

"Louise wouldn't let that happen to you. As I said, wherever is suggested you go is up to you . . . only you."

CHAPTER FOURTEEN

Mutton and Milton

Colleen had taken us to the Ashburton Southside shopping mall. Tony wanted to buy shelves and other stuff in a DIY store. Sharyna and I swapped glances. I decided I didn't wanna spend my precious Saturday afternoon scoping bits of wood.

"Can Sharyna and I check out a couple of clothes stores?" I asked.

"Yes," Colleen replied, "but meet us back here."

"Can I come too?" Pablo asked.

Colleen narrowed her eyes and thought about it. Tony shook his head.

"Let him come," I urged. "We'll keep a close link on him. Promise."

Colleen uummed and ahhed. Everyone looked at each other.

"All right," said Tony. He kneeled down to his son and wagged a finger at him. "Have you learned your lesson, Pablo?"

Pablo grinned and nodded.

"*Don't* wander off," warned Tony.

Pablo wanted to blitz into the game store but he had to wait as Sharyna and I checked out jeans, tops, jackets, and a world of other clothes. I can't remember how many shops we rolled into but one second Pablo was there, the next he wasn't. It felt like all the shit in the world had dropped on my head. It was too soon after the oven issue. *What's Colleen and Tony gonna think of me now? You're not a grown-up, Naomi, you can't even supervise a six-year-old. This is gonna drop my ratings like a penny in a fish tank.* I'm not sure how a brain sweats but mine did—it leaked outta my ears.

Sharyna and I doubled back on ourselves, returning to every shop we had visited including the game store. No Pablo. *Monkey not focused. I should've held his hand. Why didn't I hold his hand? They'll stamp this one down in my file and put it on that spreadsheet that Kim talked about. Louise and her social wankers will never let me foster or adopt in the future.*

"I'm gonna have to spill to Colleen," I said to Sharyna. "I'm gonna have to drop it on 'em."

"*No,*" Sharyna said. "Let's go back to the game store again. He might be in there now."

I shook my head.

We took an escalator down to the DIY store. I spotted Tony holding shelves and a big plastic bag. Colleen carried two pots of paint. We slow-toed toward 'em. My heart fly-kicked my rib cage. Shame karate-chopped my guts.

Colleen noticed us first. "Where's Pablo?" she asked. Her eyes darted everywhere.

Sharyna stared at the floor.

"I . . . I thought he was with us," I said. "Sorry."

"I'll find him," Tony said. "I think I know where he might've gone."

He hot-stepped away as I tried to kill my tears.

I looked up to Colleen. I expected her to launch the cuss attack from hell. "Sorry," I repeated.

"Don't be too hard on yourself," Colleen said. "He's done it to us too . . . lots of times."

I didn't feel any better.

Ten minutes later, Pablo was found kicking a tennis ball against the brightly painted stone gnomes in the Home-base garden department.

Colleen tried her best to keep her voice on the level. "How many times have I told you *not* to run off? I thought you stopped doing that. You had us worried out of our minds."

"I wanted to see the little men," giggled Pablo. "The same little men that Granddad's got in his garden."

"And how many times have I told you not to bring that old tennis ball with you while we're out shopping?" said Tony. "You need to throw that thing away."

"But it's boring just looking at stuff," Pablo said. "Can't we go to the game store? Sharyna and Naomi didn't take me."

"We're going home now," said Colleen. "Maybe your dad can take you to the park later on."

"Can't we buy some of those little men?" Pablo pleaded. "One of them can be the goalie for my football net. It'll be better than Dad."

Tony couldn't block his chuckles and nor could I.

"Don't even go there, Mum," said Sharyna. "They creep me out and so do the ones that Granddad's got. It's like wherever you go in Granddad's garden, them things are staring at you."

"We didn't come here to buy any little men," said Tony. "We've got the shelves and the other stuff, *finally*, so let's head home."

Pablo made a face.

Tony looked at me but I sensed he didn't wanna boot my ass to prison island. "I thought he'd stay with you," he said. "He hasn't wandered off for a while. What young kid wants to hang around a DIY store with their parents when they've got older sisters to follow?"

He said sisters.

"He'll learn to keep us in sight," Tony added on.

"He *better* learn," Colleen put in.

"And I like the way when things don't go to plan, you're always wanting to do good for Sharyna and Pabs," Tony said. "You always see to it that they're having a good time. Thanks for that, Naomi. Most wouldn't bother to try again."

Are they proper thanking me? Monkey performing magic tricks on Britain's Got Talent. *Can't remember any foster carer boosting me up after I messed up.*

Pablo pouted until Colleen pulled out of the Southside car park. He looked at his ball for a while before throwing it at Tony's head. *Thwack.* I had to chomp my bottom lip to murder my chuckles. Sharyna let loose a mad laugh.

"Pablo!" Tony raised his tones. "The ball!"

"What ball?"

"Pablo!"

"I haven't got a ball." He picked it up from the footwell.

"The ball, Pablo."

"No need to raise your voice, Tony," Colleen said.

Bursting into laughter, Pablo finally handed the ball over. Tony spun it around in his hands and squinted like he was thinking of the world's hardest math equation. "It's about time we introduced Naomi to my mum and dad," he said.

"Are you sure, Tone?" Colleen replied. Some sort of mad trauma filled her eyes.

I wonder what that's all about.

"Of course I'm sure," Tony said. "Besides, they haven't seen Pablo and Sharyna for a while. It's been weeks, if not a couple of months. Mum will be cussing."

"Does your dad even know about Naomi?" asked Colleen.

This convo is getting interesting. I leaned forward.

"Er . . . not yet," Tony answered.

"Don't you think you'd better tell him?" Colleen pressed. "Tell him *everything*?"

Tony turned around and looked at me. He grinned like an ice-cream man on a hot day. "Fancy seeing my parents?" he asked me. "They'd love to see you. My mum makes a serious cheesecake and she'll spoil you crazy."

"They got Sky?" I wanted to know. "All the movie channels? A DVD player?"

"Er . . . yeah."

"Can I bring a couple of my DVDs in case I get bored?"

"Er . . . not the X-rated ones," Tony replied. "Especially that driller-killer one—I don't know why we let you keep them."

"I do," I laughed. "Cos if you took 'em away I'll take away some of your stuff. And I always try to do good by Sharyna and Pabs."

Sharyna busted out a giggle before she slapped a palm over her gob.

"Hmmm," Tony replied.

"Tone . . . Tone," Colleen mumbled. The stress cells took over her forehead. *What's this all about?* "Are you going to call your dad?" she asked. "Let them know we're coming. I don't want to turn up out of the blue and your mum has five more mouths to feed."

"I'll call Mum when we get home," Tony said. "It's Saturday, so Dad will probably be at his allotment."

"Make sure you call him later," Colleen said.

"Granddad's got a forty-eight-inch TV screen on the wall," Sharyna said to me. "We can take our Wii and do our dancing."

"Sounds good," I nodded. "Your grandparents are Jamaican, aren't they?"

"Yes, they are," Sharyna replied.

"Do they talk in a funny accent?" I asked. "There was this ancient Jamaican that my real dad used to go drinking with. He was on point and everything, always lending us funds for the gas meter and giving us milk, but I couldn't make out a diddly what he was saying. It was sort of Irish, yeah, kind of dancehall, reggae-rapper Irish."

Colleen couldn't resist that one and laughed out loud.

"They have a bit of an accent, Naomi," Tony said. "But you'll be able to understand them."

"As long as your dad doesn't start swearing in patois," said Colleen.

What's pat raw? Maybe it's some kinda Jamaican cussing that only Jamaicans understand. Cool.

"I've had a word with him about that and so has Mum," said Tony. "No bad words will come out of his mouth."

"I hope so," said Colleen. She didn't look too convinced. "Don't forget to call your dad. If he's not home then call him later on."

"Okay, Colleen," Tony said. "I'm not going senile yet. I don't have to be told twice or three times."

"Hmmm."

On Sunday, we hot-wheeled southbound on the Crongton circular on our way to Tony's parents' place. I had convinced Colleen to tune in to a grime station for the ride. Sitting in the backseat, I stared through the window as I bopped my head to Lynch Turkey and Brat-Tail. *I can't wait to tell Kim that I rode through Shank Town not once but three times now.*

Red-faced runners wearing headphones and thick watches foot-slapped the pavements. Young mums pushed mega buggies with their shopping bags hanging off the handles. Graffiti covered every bridge and tall slab. The streetlights weren't so long like where we lived. There were loads of off-licenses and discount stores. *Dad would've loved living around these ends.*

Sandwiched between Sharyna and me, Pablo played with his bald tennis ball. Sharyna looked very happy at her reflection in a small mirror. I twirled the braids that Colleen had twisted for me the previous evening. *Monkey getting stage fright.*

"How old are your parents?" I asked Tony.

"Mum is sixty-eight and Dad is seventy-three."

"Seventy-three," I said. "He's almost as ancient as my

nan. Does he forget stuff? Go to the bathroom all the time? What do I call him?"

"There are a few names I can think of," chuckled Colleen. "*Difficult* is one."

"His name's Milton but you can call him Granddad," replied Tony.

"And what's your mum's name?" I asked.

"Bernice. She'd love you to call her Gran."

"And what's Bernice cooking?" I wanted to know.

"Rice and peas, mutton, sweet potato, greens from Granddad's allotment, and lots and lots of salad," answered Sharyna. "And cheesecake for dessert."

"What's mutton?" I didn't like the sound of that word.

"It's, er . . . sheep," said Colleen. "Very tasty, especially the way Bernice seasons it."

I pulled a face, imagining getting wool caught between my fangs. I turned to Sharyna. "On the level, does it taste up to spec?" I asked in a whisper. "Hasn't got bits of stale wool on it, has it? I mean, I eat lamb cos the wool on lamb is not fully grown. It's cleaner."

"I love Gran's mutton," replied Sharyna. "She spices it up."

"Really?"

"I *really* love it.

"And what's sweet potato? It's not potato with sugar on it, is it? That's just all wrong. Aren't you supposed to put mint or a liccle slob of butter on boiled potatoes?"

"No, no, no," Sharyna laughed. "It's . . . potato that tastes . . . sweet. It's got a sort of orange color to it."

"Orange? It's not a pumpkin, is it? I don't love pumpkin. Pumpkins are not for eating—they're meant for Halloween."

"It's better than boiled or roasted potato," Sharyna said.

"You're not just saying that?"

Sharyna flashed her number one smile. "No, trust me, sweet potato is all good."

"If I get a wobbly gut then I'm blaming you, Sharyna," I warned. "And you can kiss good night about watching my DVDs . . ." I checked myself, realizing I'd leaked too much info. Tony and Colleen didn't seem to notice. I was still confused about the orange-potato thing when Colleen pulled up outside a neat house somewhere near Crongton Park. I scoped the street. Kim was wrong. Everybody in Crongton didn't step with a bandanna wrapped around their face and a samurai sword in their hands.

Colleen, Tony, and Sharyna climbed out of the car. Pablo jet-toed to the black-painted door and smacked the knocker eight times. He slapped the doorbell twice. Seconds later, the door opened to reveal a black woman with a heavy piece of waistline. I guessed that she loved to sink her own cheesecake. She had kind eyes. Happy vibes shone from her cheeks. Only saying a quick, "Hi, Gran," Pablo brushed past her and flew into the hallway.

Meanwhile, the living furies had cranked up my nerves. I couldn't move. Colleen turned around and smiled at me. *I should've brought my meerkat with me.* "Come on, Naomi," Colleen said. "Everything will be all right."

Still waiting under the doorframe, Bernice flashed her molars at me as I stepped out of the ride. I snail-toed to the front door. "Good afternoon, Naomi," she greeted me. "Me been looking forward to see you. Of course you mus' be ah liccle nervous coming here for de first time, but no worry yourself, me only get cranky if somebody don't like me cheesecake. It's nice to have children come to visit every once in ah while. Otherwise, me and Misser Golding will nag each other until we cyan't nag no more."

Despite the furies performing a zombie stomp inside my belly, I managed a half smile. Her accent wasn't as thick as Dad's Jamaican liquor buddy.

"Hi, Bernice," I said. "Thanks for having me over for dinner today. I'm sure the food's gonna be the living deliciousness. And I can't wait to sample your cheesecake. What flavor is it?"

"Strawberry."

That'll go down well before I sink a long glass of Coke. I licked the corners of my mouth.

Walking along the hallway, I noticed a painting on one side of the wall of Jesus serving bread and wine to his bruvs at the Last Supper. *Nan would've liked that.* "Their hair looks better than mine," I said. "They must've had good shampoo back then."

There was another frame hanging from the wall. This one had words in fancy writing in it. I read it to myself.

God is the unseen guest at the dinner table
God is the unseen listener to every conversation
God is the unseen witness to every sin

The Man Upstairs is very nosy, I thought.

Leading us into the lounge, Bernice said, "Make yourself comfortable. Me soon come, me jus' gone to de garden to let Misser Golding know you reach. Only the Lord knows what he's been doing out there from early morning."

I hope the Lord doesn't tell Bernice what DVD I was watching last night.

"Six ah clock him get out of his bed!" Bernice continued. "You want ah cup of tea, Colleen? Or someting wid ah bit more devil in it? I tink we had some red wine but me not sure if Milton drink it off last night. When him come to bed last night his mout' did smell ah liccle frowsy."

I don't know what frowsy *means but Bernice has jokes.*

I looked around for Pablo. *Where did he go?*

"A cup of tea is fine," replied Colleen. "Remember I'm driving on the way home—Tony drove here."

"I'll help you, Mum," Tony offered.

The first thing to catch my eye was the forty-eight-inch flat-screen TV. It showed some ancient feds show called *Heartbeat*. It lamed my brain. If the politico peeps and the feds are serious about stopping young bruvs from getting into a life of crime, they should threaten them with box sets of *Heartbeat* they'll have to watch on lockdown.

I wondered how long I'd have to wait until I could plug in Sharyna's Wii dancing game. I wanted to practice the routine Ms. Almi taught me during the week. *Un, deux, trois, quatre, cinq.* My French ratings were on the rise.

I dropped into a neat, three-seater leather sofa and scoped the black-and-white photographs of Tony's fam staring out from wall cabinets, shelves, and a fancy glass coffee table. The older peeps in the pics looked like they'd just seen a ghost. Souvenir plates from Jamaica, Trinidad, Tunisia, Sardinia, Istanbul, Paris, Rome, the Pope's Palace, and Turin were fixed to the walls. Looking out from the opposite wall, beside a crucifix, was Martin Luther King. I remembered Richard going on about him during one of our Black History Month lessons at the PRU—everyone paid proper attention in that class. Four lines of his "I Have a Dream" speech appeared below his portrait.

I remembered watching *Twelve Years a Slave* with Kim and Nats. I had to turn away from the whipping scene. It was living agony. Nats bawled like social wankers had taken her baby away. When she stopped crying she was raising tones about how bad-mind the bruvs in the film were. Kim just sat there unable to move. She went through a gobful of cancer sticks during that movie. That lashing part of the film paused in my head as I heard Pablo's excited voice coming from out the back.

Bernice returned and asked if Sharyna and I wanted a drink.

"A Coke, please," I replied.

"Apple juice," said Sharyna.

"Can me and Sharyna plug in our Wii to the TV and do our dancing?" I asked.

"Yes, of course you can," Bernice said. "Just don't ask me where you plug in the wires, cah me nah know."

Sharyna jumped up. "I know!"

Sharyna plugged in the Wii as I did my stretches—Ms. Almi would've given me a *fantastique!*

Five minutes later, Sharyna and I high-kicked, belly-juggled, moon-glided, and foot-blitzed around Bernice's front room. She and Colleen rocked their shoulders and clapped along. I spotted Tony entering from the hallway.

"Girls, girls," Tony called. "Granddad's here."

Turning around, Sharyna stopped dancing and skipped to her granddad. She bounced into his arms and Milton gave her an all-gums-out smile. "Granddad! You need a shave!"

"So your grandmother keeps telling me, but it keeps me chin warm inna de winter."

"But it's spring now," said Sharyna.

"I might consider shaving it come de summer," Milton said. "If we ever have another decent summer in this country. But your grandmother don't even want to talk about going *home*. The winters here will start snapping me very bones, but does she tink about that? No sah!"

"I'm tinking about wanting to see me grandchildren grow," Bernice said. "Going to their graduations and seeing dem get married. So if you're cold, put on a woolly sweater! You have plenty of dem."

"Hmmm," Milton grumped. He carefully placed Sharyna down and rubbed his back. He scoped me hard and looked a bit confused.

What's that all about?

"And who do we have here?" he asked.

I stared at his hands. He had thick fingers that could've choked a lazy hippo. "Good afternoon, Mr. Golding."

"Good afternoon, Miss Naomi," Milton replied. There was a dose of fakery in his smile. His gold tooth glinted. "So pleased to meet you, me dear."

Sharyna and I busted a chuckle at Milton's attempt at chatting first-class English.

An hour later, Bernice served Sunday dinner. I tried the sweet potato and loved it, as well as the spicy mutton. I didn't sink any of Milton's rabbit food though. Whenever he sipped from his glass of red wine, he gawped at me. The furies in my stomach had woken up and started to fling petrol bombs at each other. My cheeks roasted.

"More Coke, Naomi?" Bernice offered.

"Yes please, Gran," I accepted.

Milton scoped me again. My eyebrows itched.

"So how is school, Sharyna?" asked Bernice.

"Going well, Gran. I got a good mark for my Spanish Armada work the other day."

"Dat is good to hear," said Bernice. "Remember, education is de key. Never forget dat. It will lead you to ah good job and ah good life."

Bernice looked at me and smiled her kind smile. "How is school for you, Naomi? How old are you? Fourteen? You will be taking your exams soon so you better get de revision in."

I don't wanna burst her expectation bubble but I'd better drop some reality on top of her.

"I go to a PRU," I said. "For kids who get expelled."

Bernice's smile jumped ship and hot-swam to the nearest island. It went all quiet for a couple of seconds.

"We don't do any tests there," I went on. "No, tell a lie, sometimes we have a general knowledge quiz, if you can call that a test."

"Dat's nice," Bernice said. She showboated her teeth but her smile still hadn't returned.

"I've got two sistrens there, Kim and Nats," I resumed. "They show us stuff—films and that—and then we argue about it."

"Oh, I see," nodded Bernice.

"We do basic stuff there. Some of the other kids can't read or do their times tables but they don't wanna admit it. That's about it really."

"As long as you're getting a decent education," said Bernice. "Me eldest son, Franklyn, is now ah lawyer. Him study and him study till him eyes could not stay open. And dat all started from paying attention at school. North Crongton High he went to. So it's *not* the school you go to, it's the application you put in."

"And he's another one who forget where him family home is," Milton complained. "When's de last time we see Franklyn's family?"

"Milton," Bernice raised her tones, "you know dat Franklyn's a very busy man and him live far away in Benson Fields . . . And his wife was sick de other day."

"Hmmm," Milton grumped again. "His wife always ketch sick when Franklyn plans to visit we. You remember Christmas, Bernice? De last-minute *my belly don't feel too good* affair. She control him too much. Me don't know why he let her walk all over him. Sometimes Franklyn act like a damn footstool."

This is getting interesting. Tony's fam has issues just like everybody else's. Good! I feel a bit more on the level now.

"Dat is enough, Milton!" Bernice shouted. "Colleen and her family don't come here to hear about who wears de pants in Franklyn's marriage."

Twenty minutes later, everyone apart from Milton sank Bernice's strawberry cheesecake—he said he had to watch his sugar doses or something. I asked for a second helping.

Bernice gave me a top-ranking grin as she cut a mega slice. "Make sure you tell Tony to bring you back soon and me will teach you to make de best cheesecake inna de world!"

"I'm on that," I said.

Following dinner, Sharyna and I were put on washing-up duty. I didn't mind but Sharyna bitched about it for a little while—she wanted to flex her toes dancing. Pablo played one of his games on the big TV and Bernice persuaded Colleen to sample a bottle of prosecco or something. "Tony can drive home," she said.

Milton stropped about something and returned to his flowers in the garden. Tony followed him out there to continue whatever argument they were having. Sharyna and I watched them through the back window.

"Are they always like this?" I asked Sharyna.

"Yep. Every time. It gets on Mum's nerves."

"Do they ever start mauling each other? You know, proper fighting?"

"No, but I've heard them cussing bad words at each other."

"Jamaican swear words? Pat raw?"

Sharyna nodded.

"Cool," I said.

We watched them again. Milton's big hands almost slapped Tony's face. They both raised their voices. I put down my tea towel, quietly opened the back door, and stood outside to tune in. I was half-covered by the wall. Sharyna continued washing up. "I'm not getting involved in this," she said. She fixed her eyes on the bubbles below her.

The garden was one of the neatest I'd ever seen. The grass was trimmed razor-fine and the flowers sexed up the sides. The garden shed was big enough to house a single mum and her baby. Milton and Tony's tiff got louder. I crooked my ear.

"You're depriving ah black chile of ah decent home," Milton argued. "And it's already hard for dem. Wasn't it you who tell me dat black children who grow up in care are eight times more likely to end up inna prison or de madhouse? Wasn't it you who tell me dat black children in care struggle at school? They don't even know their left hand from de right!"

Monkey in the dock. They're raging about me.

"But Dad, if you just listen—"

"Wasn't it *you* who tell me dat black children inna care are ten times more likely to be homeless than any other chile? Sleeping under bridge, in shop doorways, and begging for change at de train station."

"I never said that!"

"Yes you did."

"This is always the problem with you, Dad. You never give me a chance to give my side. Can't you just listen for a sec—"

"After all you tell me," Milton ranted, "you come to me door wid ah white girl you're fostering? And you expect me to play happy families, put on me smiley face, and dance like ah damn clown?"

The furies tied knots in my stomach. I couldn't breathe. I should've brought my meerkat.

"She needs foster care just like anyone else!" said Tony. "She's just a kid. None of this is her—"

"Keep your voice down."

They glanced at the kitchen window. Sharyna kept her head down, staring at the soap suds. Crouching low, I stepped back a couple of paces and sat on the garden wall. I didn't think they saw me. I took a few quick gulps of air and glanced at one of the garden gnomes. Sharyna wasn't wrong—they creeped the shrieks outta me too.

"Do you know what your mother and I had to go through when we first come here?" said Milton.

"Yes, I know all that, Dad. You don't have to remind—"

"Dem call us nigger, sambo, and all dem kinda name," Milton cut him off. "You know what it's like for dem to look at you and you know they want to spit in your face? Do you know what dat is like, Tony?"

"It has changed—"

"*No!* It hasn't!" fired back Milton. "We're still at de bottom of society. Even de Asians have passed us and we were here long before dem! And you know why? Me will tell you why. *Because white people don't like us!*"

"They're not all the same," Tony argued. "Most—"

"Yes they are. They pretend they like us. Sometimes they might even buy you ah drink and shake your hand to make you believe dat they do. But deep down, they always see us as inferior, beneath dem."

"Dad, that was your time—"

"*No!* It's *dis* time. *Right now!* Our children are always disadvantaged. No matter what situation dis girl you're fostering finds herself in. What's her name again?"

"Her name is Naomi," said Tony. "She *needs* a home just like any black child in care needs a home. In fact, in

Ashburton, there are more white children on the at-risk register than black children."

Milton shook his head.

I felt the urge to stand up and defend myself but didn't know how. I'd never had to deal with an issue like this before. *Maybe monkey needs to get back to the forest. Be on its own. Maybe Louise wasn't wrong when she said it wouldn't be a good fit to stay with the Goldings for a long run.*

"She will always have better chances than ah black chile in de same situation," Milton continued. "When's the last time you read Dr. King's speech?"

"You drummed it into me when I was growing up," Tony replied. "I don't need to read it again."

"*I have a dream,*" Milton said.

"Oh God, Dad," Tony said. "Not again. You don't need to keep dragging—"

Milton ignored Tony and continued his speech. "He said, *I have a dream that my four children will one day live in a nation where they will not be judged by the color of their skin but by the content of their character.*"

"I know the words, Dad," said Tony. "You drilled that into us just like Mum taught us the Lord's Prayer. I'm surprised you didn't brand it on my forehead."

I half chuckled and slapped a palm over my gob.

Milton stared hard at Tony like he was in a boxing ring before the first bell. "His dream is still ah dream," he said. "Can't you see dat? They still can't stand us. We're still on de bottom rung. Most black people are still in de underclass society—"

"Some of us are doing well," Tony cut in.

"Hmmm! Ah whole heapa black children and refugee need looking after. But no, you decide to foster ah white pickney when white pickney have all de help inna de world. Don't you see? Their lives are always more precious than ours. Bloodclaat white privilege!"

Bloodclaat? I wonder if that's a pat raw Jamaican swear word.

Picking up scissors from the ground, Milton snipped a flower stem. Tony marched to the back of the garden and folded his arms. I watched their every move. They still hadn't noticed me.

Sharyna stood on tiptoes and gestured at me. "Come inside," she whispered. "They're gonna see you."

"No. I wanna see what goes down. There might be a fight!"

Shaking his head, Tony returned to front up to his Dad. He pointed a finger at him. "You taught me the speech well," he said. "I know it off by heart. *Now is the time to open the doors of opportunity to all of God's children.* That's what he said, Dad. Are you listening to me? To *all* of God's children. Black, white, whatever. Maybe *you* should read it again."

Milton focused on his flowers like they had put a mad spell on him. He snip-snipped away.

"You're not listening!" Tony raised his voice. "It's always that way with you, isn't it? You only like the sound of your own voice. Even when we were young, you came home from work, sat down in your chair, picked up your newspaper, and ignored us . . . until you told us off about something at the dinner table."

Milton carried on clipping as if Tony wasn't there.

"I don't remember you taking us to the park *once*. Not even one seaside trip. Not one museum. It was Mum who taught me to ride a bike. She took us to the Crongton Park funfair and she was the one who came to parents' days at school. You were always in your chair that we were all scared to sit in even when you weren't at home. You wanted top marks but not once did you ever check our homework. You never came to the school yet you wanted to kick me out of the house because I didn't want to go to uni."

"We had more hope for you than we did for Franklyn." Milton finally turned around. He took a step closer to Tony. Their noses nearly crashed. *Monkey in a wrestling ring. Is he gonna headbutt his own son?* "You could have achieved ah lot more. Had ah better career. You tink me took all de white man shit just for you to slave in their long gardens? No sah!"

I wonder what Kim would make of all this. Nan's not wrong. There's good and bad in everyone.

"It was my choice," Tony said. "I've always enjoyed working out in the open, with things that grow. I get it from you. Don't you understand that?"

"You were very bright. You could've been ah doctor or anyting you wanted to be."

"But I'm doing what I want and we will foster who we want," said Tony.

He's fighting for me. I can't lie. My respect for Tony grew like a mad beanstalk.

"As I said," Tony went on, "you taught me Martin Luther King's speech too good. *I have a dream,* he said, *that one day little black boys and black girls will be able to join hands with little white boys and white girls as sisters and brothers."*

Tony paused for a response but it never came. "That's what he said," he resumed. "Your precious Dr. Martin Luther King. Aren't Sharyna, Pablo, and Naomi doing that? Aren't they? Are you listening to me? They've accepted Naomi. It wasn't even an issue with them. Why can't you accept her? She's not calling you the n-word. She doesn't want to spit in your face."

I wanted to holler and repeat the question: *Why can't you accept her?*

"You remember de speech well," Milton said before going back to his snipping.

"You're not answering the question."

Milton remained silent. His scissors click-clacked away.

"And that's another bad trait you have," said Tony.

"And what is dat?" asked Milton.

"That you can never admit when you're wrong."

Standing up, Milton jabbed a thick finger in front of Tony's face. "You come here to my house and you're talking down to me? You forget dat me is de one who get up at five inna de morning to keep de roof over we head? Me had to put up wid white man calling me Sir Gollywog, Jam Jar Boy, and all kind of other name to put bread upon we table. You know how much me wanted to tump dem down?"

"Dad, I know all this. I do respect—"

Milton's flow couldn't be stopped. "You know how many times me sit down at break time eating me sandwiches and tinking of licking dem with someting? You know how *small* they made me feel?"

"Dad, you're doing it again," said Tony. "Every argument we have, you give me this guilt trip."

"Guilt trip? You call it ah guilt trip? Maybe you tink it was easy?"

"No, I know you had it hard. When Naomi first came to us, I admit, I had second thoughts about taking her in."

Is that why he made a big issue about a TV in my room? Maybe he and Colleen raged at each other before I stepped in.

"But I kept on going back to Martin Luther King's speech," Tony went on. "That's the future."

Milton screwed up his face. "She'll be better off wid her own kind."

I'll be better off with my own kind? Milton could sit down and nibble a custard cream with Louise—she said the same sorta thing.

Tony snapped his head to glance at the kitchen window. I crouched lower. "I want my kids or whoever I foster to be a part of Dr. King's future," he said.

Milton turned his back and resumed cutting.

"You have to let it go, Dad." Tony placed a hand on Milton's forearm. I hardly heard him. "Let it go."

Tony turned around and stepped toward me. I jumped off the wall, hot-toed inside, and slammed the door behind me. Then I picked up a tea towel and went back to drying the pots and dishes. I hummed something to make it look like no big drama had taken place. Sharyna's gaze never left the sink.

Did he see me? Can't be too sure. I hope not.

Tony entered shaking his head. I kept my tongue on lockdown but the furies chomped the nerves in my fingers.

I almost dropped a plate. Sharyna didn't say anything either. He looked up and half smiled. "I don't know if you heard any of that, Naomi," he said, "but I have to say sorry for my dad. He lives in the past a bit and when he first came here he had to put up with, er . . . a lot of racism. I don't know how long you're going to be with us but hopefully, in time, he'll get used to having you around . . . Sorry again."

I could see the hurt in his eyes. I placed a pot in the drying rack and tapped his shoulder—my real dad used to do that to me when I was feeling down. "That's all right, Tony," I said. "I don't have to live with your paps, do I? My real dad had a few white friends and I remember one of 'em didn't like black peeps. Or even brown, mixed-race, and desert peeps."

Tony smiled and placed a hand on my cheek. "You're a good girl, Naomi. You've got a clean heart. I see it in the way you treat Sharyna and Pablo."

"Ha ha!" I laughed. "I've got ya fooled too."

That didn't bring a smile to his face.

He slow-toed into the hallway. Sharyna and I watched him. *He stood up for me. Wasn't expecting that. I'm gonna goo-gle Dr. King and find out more about him.*

Tony reached the lounge and opened the door. We heard the sound effects of Pablo's game. "Tone, you're going to have to drive home," Colleen said. "I've had a drop of prosecco."

"A drop?" laughed Bernice.

"Whenever you're ready to leave," Tony replied, "just let me know." He sat down on the staircase and held his head in his hands.

"We got used to their arguing," Sharyna whispered. "Sometimes Gran tells them to stop behaving like kids. I ignore it. Pablo thinks it's funny. Don't get Granddad wrong though."

"He got *me* wrong," I said.

Sharyna shook her head. "He's a nice man. He just has old-school ways."

"Is that what they say about racist peeps these days," I said, "that they have *old-school ways?*"

"He's good to me," Sharyna added.

"Yeah," I said. "He would be."

"If . . . if he got to know you," Sharyna said, "he'd be sweet to you too."

She meant well but the furies didn't settle until I was in the back of Colleen's car. No one said too much on the drive home, not even Pablo.

"Did you try Gran's cheesecake?" Sharyna asked Tony just before we pulled up outside home.

Tony didn't turn around. I checked his expression in the rearview mirror. He was still brewing.

"Yes, I did," he finally replied. "It was Mum's best cheesecake ever. And what makes it so good is the variety of ingredients she uses and the way the spices work together."

I didn't agree with everything that Louise said or did, but I knew she cared about me. The same went for Colleen and Tony. A warm vibe kissed my heart.

CHAPTER FIFTEEN

Racially Correct

"**M**y treat!" Kim insisted. "Choose anything you like."
Leaning on the counter of a chicken hut takeaway,
I scoped the display screens to see what was on offer. The
smell of fried chicken and freshly cooked fries licked the
air. The counter assistant, a black-haired man in his for-
ties wearing a white baseball cap that was too small for his
head, tapped his fingers on the cash register. His sleeves
were rolled up above his elbows. Stuck on the wall behind
him was the red, white, and green flag of a country I didn't
recognize.

"You're not gonna get me lunch?" said Nats to Kim.
"Why are you only buying for Naoms?"

"Didn't I buy you two tops on Sunday, Nats?" Kim answered. "And three pairs of socks and a pair of peacock
earrings? I didn't get Naoms any new garms so that's why
I'm buying her lunch. Deal with it."

"But I need another pound to get what I want," complained Nats. "And *I'm* your girlfriend! Not Naoms."

"What's being my girlfriend gotta do with it?" spat
Kim. "Naoms is our sistren. Cool down your toes."

*Monkey in a cage with lions. I hate it when their relation-
ship issues bust open in public.*

"But—" Nats started again.

"But what?" Kim chopped her flow. "Quit getting all green-eye on me. What d'you want?"

"A chicken sandwich meal with fries," replied Nats.

"Er, I'll have the same," I said. "And a large Coke. You sure you can afford it, Kim? Don't wanna take liberties."

"Would I be offering if I couldn't afford it? Didn't I tell ya that my mum dropped me down some funds Saturday morning?"

"Sorry," I said. "There are a lot of issues ping-ponging around in my brain."

"I remember," put in Nats.

"Obviously you remember, Nats," said Kim. "You were with me when my mum slapped our front door."

"I wish I had a mum who came down and dropped me off some funds," I said.

Awkward silence.

"She's still on her guilt trip, and while she's riding that bus I'm gonna rinse and drain her for all I can," said Kim. "She wanted to see me but I pretended I was crashing. At least she had the decency to leave me money in an envelope."

"That's all good," I said.

"Me and Nats wheeled up to Ashburton to buy new garms first thing Sunday morning," Kim said. "We took a cab and stopped by your place. Colleen told us you were asleep. The taxi meter wasn't joking so we had to take to our wheels."

"Yep," said Nats. "We had to roll on."

"I stayed up late watching films," I explained. "And I

was going somewhere with my foster fam anyway."

"Can I have a drink too?" asked Nats. "Lemonade."

Kim sighed. "I suppose so. I'm gonna be on a serious austerity by tomorrow the way you're going on. When your social worker touches down you can ask her for some funds and you can treat me."

"Deal!" replied Nats. "I *always* treat you."

Three minutes later, we bounced out of the chicken hut, sinking our meals as we walked.

"So what did you do over the weekend, Naoms?" asked Kim.

"Went to the grandparents' house. They've got a monster-inch TV. It was like being in a cinema. Sharyna took her Wii dancing game and she and I flexed toes and juggled bellies for most of the time."

"They're Jamaican, right?" said Nats.

"Yeah, but not as hard-core Jamaican as the guy who used to swig around with my paps."

"What did you eat?" asked Nats.

"What's it called again? Sheep, rice, and sweet potato. Oh, and untold salad."

Nats shook her head. "You mean mutton, rice, and sweet potato. I used to love that. They tried cooking mutton in the unit once. It went all wrong."

"Yeah," Kim agreed. "I don't think it was mutton. Could've been crocodile ribs or something."

Nats and I busted out a chuckle.

"So what were these grandpops like?" Kim wanted to know. "Weren't too jurassic, were they? I don't love the smell of old people. Didn't have to poke them with the remote control to check if they were still alive, did ya?"

Nats burst out laughing again. A couple of chewed fries flew to the pavement.

"They were cool," I said. "The gran . . . what was her name . . . Ber . . . Bernice. Yeah, Bernice. Apart from her Team Jesus issues, she was on point. She makes her own cheesecake and she's gonna teach me how to bake it the next time I'm around."

"*Boring!*" said Kim. "Dunno what I would've done if I was there."

"I don't think the granddad had too much love for me," I said.

"Why not?" Kim asked. "What's his issue? You didn't squeeze your jamrag juice into his cocoa, did ya?"

"Eeeeeww! No!" I swallowed a dose of saliva. *Monkey in pantomime. One day Kim's gonna kill me with her one-liners.* I cleared my throat before I let the rhino do its business on the marble floor. "His issue . . . his issue is that I'm white."

"White?" Nats repeated. Her eyebrows kissed her fringe.

"Liberties!" shouted Kim. Her eyebrows almost went over the back of her head. "Did he call you anything? Didn't hit ya, did he? What did the gran do? Did Tony and Colleen take you away ASAP? They should've done."

"No, it didn't go down like that," I said. "Tony was arguing with his paps and his paps said something . . . he said a few things."

"What did he say?" Kim asked. "Come on, Naoms! Let the hippo yawn."

"He doesn't like my foster fam fostering white kids," I said. "They were raging about Martin Luther King."

"Martin Luther King," said Nats. "Didn't Richard talk about him in Black History Month?"

Kim stood in front of me and wouldn't let me pass. "Is that really what he said, Naoms? That he didn't love white foster kids coming through his gates?"

I felt the heat of Kim's hard-curb gaze. I nodded.

"If he did, you have to spill the full mug on that one," Kim said. "Don't fruck about. See your social worker and let your tongue loose. She'd have to do something. What did he say exactly?"

I tried to remember Tony and Milton's argument. "The granddad . . . he said . . . he said he didn't want no white girl in his house or something and that Tony should only foster black kids."

"*No!*" Nats called out. "Outta freaking order!"

"Listen to me, Naoms," said Kim. "Perk up your ears. Tell your social worker—wassername?"

"Louise."

"Give the full movie to Louise, even the deleted scenes, and don't let them know you're telling her. And *don't* say anything to Sharyna and Pablo."

"But I like staying there," I said. "I'm like Sharyna and Pablo's big sis. They let me cook, even after I messed up, and do my own thing . . . well, sort of do my own thing. Tony had my spine and Colleen's had a hard-curb life too. She tells me about it when the kids have gone to bed. I was gonna say to Tony and Colleen to take a holiday and I'll babysit for 'em. And I don't have to live with the granddad, do I? And who's gonna nice up my hair?"

Nats put her hand up. "Er, me," she said. "I can braid neatly—"

"You can't allow it," Kim interrupted. "What's gonna happen when this racist granddad visits ya? Say he stays for the weekend or longer? He might be filling ya brain with all kinda racist malarkey. You haven't got anywhere to escape."

"I don't think Colleen will let him stay," I said. "Not while I'm there anyway."

Kim shook her head. "What will happen if the gran drops dead after making a cheesecake? The granddad might have to move in with ya. He'll be telling you crap 24-7, the first to the thirty-first and from January to December. Can you imagine that, Naoms? It'll do your head in."

I didn't know what to think. I didn't feel hungry anymore. I tossed my chicken sandwich and fries into a bin.

"What d'you do that for?" moaned Nats. "I would've ate that."

"Sorry," I said.

"You should've listened to me and then none of this drama would've happened," Kim went on. "You should've stayed at our unit so me and Nats could look out for ya. As Nats said, she can plait your hair."

"I hear that," I said. "Thanks."

"I can go wherever you are and bless up your hair," put in Nats. "Don't have to be at the unit."

"All this moving about with foster families," Kim said, "where the fruck has it got ya? You're at *nowhere o'clock*!"

"I . . . I dunno," I mumbled. "Colleen cares about me. So does Tony. I'm not gonna lie about that one."

Kim moved out of my way. I rolled down the street in silence as Kim huffed and puffed beside me. Five minutes later, we turned into the school grounds. Nats checked the time on her mobile phone. "We're twenty minutes late," she said.

"So?" Kim said. "We've got to deal with Naoms's grand-dad issue. Richard can wait and fiddle with himself. And you know I always have a smoke after I eat something."

"It's not a big issue," I protested. "He didn't say anything off-point to me. He was raging at Tony."

"That's not the point!" said Kim. "The granddad doesn't like white kids. That's the skidmark in your pink knickers. You can't allow that."

I found myself nodding in agreement.

"Listen to me this time, Naoms," Kim said. "If you crooked your ear to me in the first place you wouldn't have ended up in that perv's yard where that prick fiddler, Mr. Holman, was standing outside while you're having a shower. You should've stayed here, like I said."

"But . . . but," I stuttered.

"No buts," Kim said. "When you see Louise, tell her you wanna stay in our unit, with us. *No* flib-flobbing about. Tell her straight and don't fall for the *but we'll have to investigate and have meetings*. Bomb the meetings and the inquiries, Naoms."

"I'll miss Sharyna and Pablo," I said.

"They can visit you," Kim replied. "It won't be an issue. Colleen can bring 'em down to our unit and they know how to bounce on a bus, don't they? I'll dye Sharyna's hair or something if she wants and tell her what garms will suit her. Might bring her up to Ashburton on one of my shopping missions and jack her a pair of sneakers. What size does she take?"

"Er . . . three, I think."

"Not a problem," said Kim. "Nats or you can be my lookout and before you can say *name-brand* I'll be sitting pretty on a bus with a sweet pair of sneakers and a glam pair of socks. By the time I finish my project with Sharyna, she's gonna look well sexy—"

"She's *not* a teenager yet," cut in Nats.

I can't believe the way this convo's going.

"And what will Pablo do while we're shopping?" I asked.

"I'll find him a game or something," said Kim. "Or we can give him a DVD. We'll just drop his ass on a couch with something to watch and he'll be cool."

"I . . . I don't know."

"You're not scared of Louise, are ya?" Kim shook her head. "How can you be scared of a first-class, high-nose bitch like her? Every now and again you should always give 'em a cuss attack. It keeps 'em on their toes. It makes 'em scared of ya, and when they're scared of ya, they do what you tell 'em to do. Trust me on that one. I've got a degree in it."

"Louise tries her best for me," I said. "I don't agree with everything she does but—"

"You sound like one of them now," said Kim. "You've fallen for all their fake compassion."

"No I haven't," I argued.

"Yes you have, Naoms!" yelled Kim. "They work for *us*.

Remember that. They're s'posed to do what we tell 'em to do. Let her work for her Gs. They're on about fifty grand a year."

"Fifty grand a year?" said Nats.

"What's a matter with you two?" said Kim. "Don't you know that? Has someone been renting out your brain space? A lot of 'em dress down and drive cheapo rides to try and hide the big Gs they earn. They've got those double-door fridges in their mega kitchens and pay one of them refugee slaves to wash their clothes and do their ironing."

"One of my social wankers went on holiday to Australia once," said Nats. "She brought me back a boomerang."

"That's standard for them," nodded Kim. "They've got movie screens in their front rooms and they eat at first-class restaurants. Have you ever seen a social wanker munching fries and chicken nuggets in a chicken hut?"

Nats and I thought about it and shook our heads.

"No!" Kim answered her own question. "Don't think they're doing you a favor when they take you out for something to eat—they get paid extra funds for all that game."

"I've seen Louise take out her own money when she's treated me," I said.

"That looks all good, Naoms," said Kim. "But it's all fake. The next day, she's giving her receipts to her boss and she's getting paid back double. Trust me on that one, Naoms. As I said, your best option is to bounce back to us. Nats and I have your heel, your spine, and the back of your head. You know that."

"Louise is coming to pick me up later," I said. "Breaking news: she's taking me out to get something to eat."

Kim grinned. "Good! Don't let her go cheapo on you and *make sure* you tell her the whole movie. Don't delete anything out."

CHAPTER SIXTEEN

Biggin Spires

When school finished, Kim, Nats, and I parked on our usual bench—Kim wanted to give me the get-down of my situation so I wouldn't mouse out about the granddad issue. A car horn blasted and I spotted Louise's ride reversing into a parking space. She waved to me and climbed out. I was about to stand up but Kim pulled me back down again. "Burn her," Kim snapped. "Finish your fagarette first. Let her highty-tighty bones wait."

"Naomi!" Louise called. "Naomi!"

Ignoring her, I sucked hard on my cancer stick. Kim and Nats laughed.

"I haven't got all afternoon, Naomi," moaned Louise. She crossed her arms.

I took one more pull before killing my smoke with my heel.

"Remember what I told you," said Kim. "*She* works for *your* best interest, and your best interest is to bounce back to the unit. Don't let her get away with any crappety-crap."

"May . . . maybe," Nats started, "they could slap an injunction or what they might call it so the granddad can't wobble within a mile of Naoms. Then she could stay with the Goldings."

"Not gonna work," Kim raised her voice. "Don't listen to Nats, Naoms. Stick to my program on this one."

Nats gave Kim a Terminator-like look and I thought I'd better take strides before them two raged at each other again.

Opening the passenger-side door, Louise greeted me with an *I'm having a good week* smile. "So how was your day, Naomi? How have you been?"

I shrugged as I dropped into the passenger seat.

"So where would you like to eat?" she asked. She seemed desperate for me to feel her joy.

I secured my seat belt and shrugged again. "You never wanna go where I wanna go, so what's the point of you asking me? You're too much of a cheapo."

"Try me," smiled Louise.

"Okay." I creased my forehead thinking about it. "Biggin Spires," I said after a while. "Never stepped there before. Kim went there once. They've got a Wag-a-waga or something in the shopping mall there—some Chinese or Thai place."

"It's a bit of a drive," Louise said. "I hope the traffic's not too bad on the Crongton circular."

"You better juice up your ride."

Louise checked her gas needle. "Okay," she said. "Why not? Biggin Spires it is. And if we get stuck in a jam it'll give us a chance to speak."

She pulled away. I found my fave grime radio station and spanked up the volume. *Bomb giving us a chance to speak. I'm not feeling that idea.* I nodded in time to the drumbeat.

"How's the dancing coming along?" Louise asked after a short while.

"I'm getting to do the same moves as the other girls," I replied. "It's complicated, not easy. Some of them other chicks are just *toooo* good—their legs are well flexible. But I've only had two lessons."

"And you'll get better," Louise put in.

"I like Ms. Almi," I said. "She's a proper pro. There's no jokes in her sessions and not much talking. Everyone pays attention cos they wanna be in the next show. When we finish, I can hardly walk up the stairs. My bones turn into thick smoothies."

"Perhaps you should think about giving up smoking?"

I gave Louise one of her *really* looks. "Seriously? You're telling me to quit my smokes? What about *you*? There must be a cancer-berg in your chest. I'm surprised you don't get an asthma attack when you step to your car every morning."

"I see your point," she chuckled. "But I'm a lost cause. If you want to carry on dancing you have to think of your health."

"If I give up then *you* have to give up too," I said.

Louise thought about it. "Okay. Mind you, I've tried meditation, patches, vaping, and all sorts."

"I'll tell you what," I said. "Every time you think about buying another box of smokes, just give the money in your purse to me. That'll work. If you get yourself good ratings, I might put the funds in a post office account for ya."

Louise couldn't block her giggles. "That *won't* work."

"Cheapo!"

* * *

Biggin Spires was a small town on top of a hill. I imagined Susan, the bike freak, riding up one of the steep inclines and doing a *Rocky* shadow-boxing thing when she got there. *I wonder how Emily's flexing. Must remember to ding her. Need funds for my phone.* It had the same shops as Ashburton but not as many. It had a mega church with a long tower—peeps used their mobiles to take pics of the ancient graveyard. *Maybe a celeb was buried there recently.* All the streets seemed to have three words in them: Bishop Park Avenue, Friar Gorge Chase, and Abbot Lawn Way. The buses were blue and the sidewalks were wide with little skinny trees sticking out of 'em. High Street was five brooms cleaner than Ashburton's. *If I was a dog I'd look over my shoulder and think twice about shitting here.*

I stared at a dress in a charity shop window.

"Everything okay?" Louise asked.

I shrugged. "S'pose so . . . just a bit peckish. I didn't finish the takeaway chicken I had for lunch. I flung half of it away."

"Why are you spending money on takeaway when the school provides a decent meal for you?"

"Didn't pay anything for it," I replied. "Kim bought it for me. She's been treating me better than you have lately. And she hasn't got as much funds as you."

Louise raised her eyebrows. I could see the tiny veins above her eyelids. *She's getting old.* "Oh, she treated you, did she? That's very kind of her but you need to stick to school meals, Naomi."

I gave Louise a hard-core glare. "Can you just quit lecturing me today, please?" I said. "I just wanna have a good dinner. I'm well peckish."

Five minutes later, we found the Wagamama restaurant in the Spires shopping center. Louise made her way to a corner and we parked on a bench. Louise ordered a large Coke for me and a black coffee for herself before reading the menu. "What takes your fancy, Naomi?"

"Chicken curry and Singapore rice."

Louise went for a chow mein dish.

The waiter returned with my drink but Kim's words rattled in my brain. *Should I make an issue outta what Tony's dad spilled? I could do with less drama in my life, but Kim will cuss me out if I don't leak anything.*

"Are you okay?" Louise asked.

"I'm good," I lied.

"Something happened at school today?"

"No."

"You sure?"

"For fruck's sake, Louise! Take a day off."

The meals were served ten minutes later and hardly a word dropped between us as we sampled our food.

"How did it go with Tony's parents?" Louise asked after a while. "By all accounts, Tony's mum's a great cook. I know Pablo and Sharyna love seeing them."

I dodged Louise's gaze and sank a big glug of Coke.

"Naomi?"

I carried on eating and didn't answer till I finished a mouthful of rice. "There was a mega argument," I said.

"Between who?"

"Tony and the granddad."

"About what?"

"I heard it from the back door. They didn't know I was tuning in. Sharyna was washing up . . . I wanna go back to the unit."

"Hold on for a minute, Naomi." She placed her cutlery on her plate. "What was this argument about?"

"Me." I stared into my chicken curry.

"You?" Louise looked proper confused. "Can you be more specific?"

"I wanna go back to the unit," I repeated. "Isn't that specific enough for ya?"

"But I thought you were enjoying your stay with the Goldings?"

"You're not wrong on that one," I said. "I was all good with that till the argument."

"Can you please tell me what this row was about?"

"I told ya . . . it was about me."

"Naomi! *Stop it!*"

I fed myself another gobful of curry and ran that down with a long slurp of Coke. Louise gave me an intense glare. *If I don't spill, something steamy's gonna gas out of her ears. She'll probably suck out half a box of smokes before she drops me home. I better give her a liccle relief.*

"The granddad," I said.

"Tony's dad?"

"Of course it's Tony's dad," I said. "What other granddad is there? Colleen doesn't know her paps."

Louise leaned back in her chair and thought about it. "Met him only once," she said. "He seemed all right. Loved his garden—"

"He doesn't like white kids," I corked her flow.

"Excuse me?"

"Are you going deaf on me, Louise? Do I have to perform sign language on this one? Let me replay this in HD. *He doesn't like white kids.* Comprendy? I'm not chatting grime so you should be able to understand me."

Louise's left cheek twitched as she sipped her cold coffee. "How . . . how do you know this, Naomi? Did he speak directly to you?"

"No! Aren't you listening? He was raging at Tony. That's when he came out with it. He said he didn't want Tony fostering white kids and didn't want white kids polluting his house. At the dinner table, he was looking at me like I had squeezed my jamrag juice into his cocoa or something."

I had to use Kim's line. It was too good not to.

Louise shook her head. "I'll have to carry out an investigation."

"I don't want an investigation," I raised my tones. "Just wanna go back to the unit. How many times do I have to say it?"

"You've just made a serious allegation, Naomi."

What's an allegation? *It sounds like a boy alligator that has had his bits chopped off.*

"I can't ignore it," Louise went on. "I'll have to talk with Tony, his father, and anyone else who heard the conversation. If what you say is true then I can't allow Tony and Colleen to bring you along to see him. You'll have to stay somewhere when they take Sharyna and Pablo to visit. Maybe I'll take you out somewhere."

Monkey in a cage. I don't love it when Louise drops into her social wanker zone. The furies had woken up and pricked their needles into my ribs. "You're not listening, Louise! Do I have to spell it out for ya? I WANNA GO BACK TO THE UNIT!"

A world of eyes switched my way but I didn't care.

Louise dropped her tones. It was almost a whisper. "There'll have to be an investigation, I'll grant you that, but there really is no need for you to move—"

"You're not freaking listening!" I yelled. "I don't want any investigation. You can eat it and fart it out on the top of the Smeckenham Hills for all I care."

Louise took out her phone and made a note in it. I tried to read it but she covered the screen with her hand. She looked up at me. The stress lines in her forehead had doubled. Delete that—they had tripled. "Naomi, can you at least give it a few days and think about—"

"*No!* I don't have to think about it. I WANNA GO BACK TO THE UNIT!"

"Has Kim put you up to this?" Louise wanted to know. "I have to say, I don't like the influence she has on you."

"It's nothing to do with Kim," I lied.

Louise gave me a hard-core *really* look.

I lowered my voice. "I wanna go back to the unit."

Louise closed her eyes and puffed out a few breaths. *She really needs to quit smoking.* She eventually opened her eyes. "Okay," she said. "I'll see what I can do."

"Good." I picked up the menu and flipped it over to scope the dessert choices. "When I finish my curry and rice, can I have a chocolate sundae?"

Louise's eyes weren't at home. The joy she had when

she picked me up had been murked with the granddad issue. *When I grow up I might be a dancer or a foster carer but I'll never be a social worker. I'm gonna flush that idea down the shit ride.*

"Er, you what?" Louise stuttered. "Yes, of course you can have a chocolate sundae. If you promise not to shout again—"

"Then listen to me," I cut in.

"But . . . but getting back to the point," Louise said, "I'll still need to speak to Tony to hear . . . to hear what he has to say."

"Whatever," I shrugged. "But I'm rolling back to the unit. Don't put a world of red cones in my way."

"Can't you wait until I speak with Colleen and Tony? I'll make sure that you never have to be in the presence of Tony's father again."

"I can make sure myself," I said. "I'll miss baking cheesecake with Bernice though. Anyway, at the unit, at least none of the staff there hate white kids. They have to like everybody, black, white, brown, mixed race, and even desert kids."

Louise slurped her coffee again but screwed up her face at the chill of it. She raised her hand to attract the waitress's attention. "Can I have a chocolate sundae, please, for the young lady—"

"And another Coke," I added.

"Anything for you?" the waitress asked.

"Another black coffee, thank you."

CHAPTER SEVENTEEN

A Heavy Piece of Guilt

I didn't mind the corked traffic on the ride home. I even allowed Louise to listen to her old-school pop radio station.

"I'll speak with Colleen and Tony when I drop you off," she said. "I don't want to do it over a phone call."

"I get that," I said. "Best to be one-on-one with these kinda issues."

"Do you want to be there when I tell them?"

"No, no. Wait till I'm in my room before you start spilling everything."

Louise turned to look at me. "Are you sure, Naomi? You've accused me of doing things behind your back in the past."

"You're good to go on this one," I said. "I'll sign a form for you if ya want." My brain was sweating so I wound down the window.

"I don't even know if a room is available at the unit," Louise said. "I'll call them tonight but don't expect them to have it ready by tomorrow."

"I can wait," I said. "Just put the kid on the top of the slide on this one."

I peered through the windshield. Cars were bumper to bumper as far as I could see. I wanted to ask Louise if I could stay over at her place but I thought better of it. No way would she go for it. Her boyfriend wouldn't love it.

"Naomi, are you sure you want to move from the Goldings' home before I find you a permanent foster family? We're still looking at potential families."

I wasn't sure. Kim's voice was in my head. *If I lose her as a sistren, who else have I got?*

"Yeah, I'm good to go," I replied. "I'll have to check out from the Goldings' sooner or later anyway. That's the reality of my situation."

Louise nodded. "Yes, it is."

"I'll be sorry to leave. They're good peeps."

"Yes, they are."

Not too many words were swapped till Louise pulled up outside the Goldings' house. It took me a long second to climb outta my seat. Nerves rat-a-tatted inside my belly.

"Don't worry," Louise said, "Colleen and Tony will understand."

"They might think I'm ungrateful. But I'm thankful—to the max. They actually care more than a dose about me and they found that dance club for me."

Louise angled her face and half-smiled. We rolled slowly to the front door. It only seemed like yesterday when Louise first brought me here. I didn't wanna get outta her car on that night either.

I pushed my key into the lock. *I'll never tie Pablo's laces again before he skips to school. I'll never fix the ribbons in Sharyna's hair before she steps out in the morning. I won't get to try out new dance moves with her with the Wii game. I'll have to say a long goodbye to everybody. I'll have to give the key back. They are all normal. What have I done? Monkey took a swing on the wrong branch. I can't bounce back on it now. They'll never take me seriously again.*

As we walked in, Colleen stepped down the stairs. Her smile rippled her cheeks. I felt horrible and stared at the floor. "Hi, Louise, Naomi," she greeted. "You ladies have a good time?"

"Yes, we did," Louise replied. "We drove out to Biggin Spires."

"Lovely," Colleen said. "What did you eat?"

"Naomi had a chicken curry and rice and I had chow mein."

"The last time I had Chinese food it ran my belly," said Colleen. "I hope your stomachs are made of sterner stuff than mine."

"I want to try and get rid of the softer stuff on my waistline," joked Louise.

"So, you ladies had time to catch up about things?" asked Colleen.

Louise took in a breath. "I need to have a word with you about that. Something needs to be discussed."

Colleen started for the kitchen. "I'll put the kettle on," she said. "We'll chat in the kitchen—Sharyna's in the front room."

I can't take any more. Don't leak tears in front of 'em, Naoms. Don't!

"I . . . I need to use the toilet," I said.

I hotfooted upstairs, bolted the toilet door, and parked on the bog. Tears filled my eyes and covered my face. Untold snot came outta my nose too. *What have I done?*

There I stayed for the next fifteen minutes. My breathing Darth Vadered for a little while but I managed to eventually control it. I must've used half a roll of toilet paper.

When I came out, I quick-toed to my room, closed the door behind me, and found my meerkat. I held it close to my throat as I curled up on my bed. *I hope Colleen and Tony don't think I'm some kinda snitch.* For some reason, I put my thumb in my gob—hadn't done that for the longest time.

Five minutes later, someone tickled my door. I ignored it. It tapped again. "It's me, Pablo. Open the door, Nomi."

I jumped up and opened the door. Pablo stood there with a game console in his hands. Judging by his face, whatever game he was playing I didn't think he was winning. "Sharyna doesn't wanna play," he said. "She's got her stupid homework to do. You're not as good as Sharyna but can I play you?"

"I dunno, Pabs," I replied. "Maybe not today."

Pablo dropped his head. "Why?"

"It's been a mad day," I said. "My head's chocko-blocked with so many things, so I dunno if I can focus."

"Why?" Pablo repeated.

"Cos when you get to my age there's a lot of issues that can clog up your head and you need time to review situations."

Pablo thought about this for a long second. "Why?" he asked one more time.

"Cos . . . cos . . . oh all right."

How can I give the big NO to eyes like that?

As I followed Pablo to his room, I wished that a simple

game could make me happy. I'm not sure how life slapped Pablo and Sharyna before they bounced into the Goldings' house. One time I overheard Tony and Colleen talk in the lounge about refugees and boats or something. They put a fat full stop to that convo when they realized I was in the kitchen pouring myself a long glass of Coke.

I wanted to be Pablo's age again. A time when I stood on a box to help Mum bake a cake. A time when Dad took me out to pubs on weekends and bought me cheese-and-onion crisps and Coke. All I worried about back then was if my fave act would make it to the final of *The X-Factor* and would their dancers be on point. That was my world.

Later that night my phone bleeped. It was a text from Nats. I didn't want to open it but curiosity slapped my want-to-know buds.

If u r hppy at the Gldngs you shud stay there. Kim and I r going thru a bumpy patch. We need time n space to sort shit out but if u r here we won't get that. You'll be in and around our business. Do u get what I'm saying?

I thought about my reply for twenty minutes.

I won't get in your way, I texted back. *I won't breeze into your business. When you two are together I won't bounce into her room or yours. I'll keep to myself.*

Nats texted back immediately: *Promise me you'll keep out of our radar. We need our time.*

I thought it was a bit strong that she wanted me to promise, but I texted my reply: *It's gonna look wrong if Kim invites me to her room and she wants me to watch TV or something with you guys but I won't blip on your radar if I'm not asked.*

Thanks, Nats responded. *Good night.*

I didn't know how much time passed before I finally crashed out that night, but I spent most of it crying.

CHAPTER EIGHTEEN

Casino Ashburton

It had been two weeks since I moved from the Gold-ings' to the unit. The Goldings had visited me once and they brought with them two slices of Bernice's strawberry cheesecake. I appreciated that to the max. Pablo wondered why I couldn't go home with 'em. I can't lie, when they left, I hot-stepped to the toilet and the tears hosepiped out—I didn't wanna do that in front of Kim and Nats.

Louise visited me twice and I had to give her rat-ings cos she had quit smoking for real. One of them tree air-freshener things blessed the air in her car and she had developed a mad craving for extra-strong mints and gummy bears. Whenever I was in her ride I swiped a few of them and shared 'em out with Nats and Kim. Old habits were hard to quit. I sensed there was something off-key about her though. I couldn't quite put my thumbnail on it or maybe my jokes weren't up to spec.

The social-worker-mother in charge of the unit was Samantha. She and I had got off on the wrong toe cos she wouldn't let me help out in the kitchen. She kept on blah-blah-blahing about risk assessments and health and safety issues. I launched a cuss attack at her, blitzed a plate in the dining room, and she put my TV on lockdown for a couple of days. I bruised her ears with my hollering on that one but she just sat there behind her desk with her arms folded. It gets kinda tiring screaming till your throat turns dry. I guess Samantha was used to that kinda tonsil-bashing, yelly drama—Kim lived in this unit.

So, my new life was standard living for me. I kept my promise to Nats and spent as little time as possible in Kim's room, but Kim was forever asking me to come down for this and that. It was there where the drama of my life booted off into the Premier League.

Keri Hilson's "Pretty Girl Rock" smoked out of Kim's pink boombox. The breeze rushed into her bedroom from an open window. The grimy net curtains blew in and out. Sitting cross-legged on Kim's unmade bed, Kim, Nats, and I scoped each other hard. We each held a hand of cards—Kim had tickled my door and invited me down to play. She said it was proper boring with just two players.

Kim bopped her head to the beat. Nats juggled her shoulders and I tried to focus on my cards—I didn't wanna lose another round.

"You show first, Nats," Kim said.

"Nah, let Naoms show first."

"I showed first last game," I protested. "Why don't you show your hand?"

"I'm the banker," said Kim. "Bankers always show last. Didn't I say that in the rules before we started?"

"How come you're always the banker?" I asked.

"Cos I'm always the banker. You two's mathematics skills are not on the level."

"But we're not playing for funds," complained Nats.

"But I'm shuffling and dealing," Kim said. "And we're playing for beats and dares."

Monkey waiting for his bananas. "All right, all right!" I said. "For fruck's sake! I'll show ya what I've got." I laid down my cards. I had the queen of diamonds, a six of spades, and the three of clubs.

"Nineteen," Kim counted. "What you got, Nats? You bust?"

Dropping her cards, Nats had a jack of spades, a two of diamonds, and a six of hearts.

"Eighteen," added up Kim as she put down her own hand. She had two kings. "Twenty! I win again."

"Shit!" shouted Nats. "You're always getting kings and queens."

My relief dropped into a deep, snug pillow.

"What's it gonna be, Nats?" chuckled Kim. "Beats or dare? And you got five losses now. It's a mega dare or a mega beat."

"My arm's proper swollen from the last time." Nats rubbed her left bicep. "Don't wanna go through them agonies again."

"So it's gonna be a dare then?" I asked.

"I dunno," said Nats. "You two punch *solid*. And you might get me to do something cadazy for a dare."

"Make up your mind!" demanded Kim.

Nats thought about it. "Dare," she whispered after a while.

"Okay, okay," I said. "I've got one! I've got one!"

Nats closed her eyes.

"What have you got?" asked Kim. "It better be a top-of-the-chart mission for a mega dare."

I took in a deep breath. *Will Kim go for this?* "For Nats to go downstairs into Samantha's office and spit in her fish tank."

I couldn't lie. I was still raging at Samantha for not letting me help cook the lamb shanks we had for dinner the day before. I would've sexed it up with spices and herbs the way Colleen did. Kim, Nats, and the others would've given me top ratings.

"No, no, no!" said Nats. "That's farting on liberties, sistren. You can't expect me to do that. That's messed up. And I like them fish. They're pretty and they color up the place. Nah, I can't do that."

"That's dare-o-licious!" Kim's eyes sparkled with a mad pleasure. "Can you imagine the look on her fat face? It's a queen of a dare! Yeah, you gotta do it, Nats. That's the pain of the game."

"It's too far," said Nats. She scoped me hard, expecting me to have her spine.

I kept silent. I was just super glad it wasn't me who lost the last game of cards.

"I haven't had any beef with Samantha for a while," Nats said. "She'll get me to scrub it out with a second-hand toothbrush. Nah, I'm not doing it. She'll take my TV away forever and put me on lockdown till my eyelashes turn gray."

Kim and I drew back our fists.

"This is nuts," said Nats. "Spit in her fish tank? It'll probably murk all the fish. They don't deserve to die."

"Then take the licks," said Kim. She tightened her fist. A knuckle cracked.

Colleen would put a block of full stops to this. No way would she let me play this with Sharyna. But I had nodded a fat yes to the rules. So had Nats.

"I'm not taking another beating," Nats decided.

"Then you have to play the dare," insisted Kim. "So bounce downstairs, slap on Samantha's door, look at her fat face, close your eyes, think of the grimy ends of Ashburton, and gob in her fish tank."

"Eeeeeeww," I reacted.

"Make it a real proper coughy-chesty one," Kim said. Her eyes got bigger like an old-school cartoon character. "Heave it up from your belly till your throat hurts. Pollute her friggin' fish. She cares more about them than us. If it was me, I'd flick some bogey, drop some toenail dirt, and fling a liccle bulldog shit in that mother too."

"That'll definitely murk the fish," moaned Nats.

I wasn't sure if Kim was serious but she dropped her head onto my lap with a big grin splitting her cheeks.

"You don't really expect me to play this, do you, Kim?" Nats said. "Please tell me this is just jokes, right?"

Kim sat up. "I don't joke when I'm playing games," she said. "You know me, Nats."

We swapped glances. Any second I expected Kim to bust out a laugh. But she didn't.

"So . . . so you really want me to go into Samantha's office and spit in the fish tank?" Nats said.

"Yep!" Kim nodded. "If I didn't mean it, I wouldn't have flashed a green light to it. Why don't you have a practice spit out the window? As I said, heave it up from your belly, suck it up from every corner of your throat. Drag up all the phlegm from any toxic cold you've ever had."

The bedroom door knocked twice. Nats opened it. Samantha stood in the doorway. She adjusted her glasses. Her oversized cardigan couldn't hide her heavy ring of waistline. Her jeans screamed for mercy and we couldn't kill our giggles.

"What's so funny?" asked Samantha. She sniffed the air. "Have you been smoking in here again? *Kim?* How many times do I have to warn you?"

The ashtray sat on the edge of the bed. It was full. Samantha did her proper best to pretend she didn't see it. Her warning was ignored. She had to wait till our chuckles quit before she spoke again. "Natasha, your new key worker, Ms. Alvarita Moreno, is here. She's waiting in my office."

"Tell her to bust open her purse," said Kim to Nats. "Don't accept any *let's go for a cheapo coffee.*"

"She's taking me to Nando's," said Nats. "I'm gonna sink some barbecue wings and chips."

"Remember the Nando's rule!" shouted Kim. "Come back with cheesecakes for us or more licks!"

"I'll . . . I'll remember," Nats responded.

"I'm waiting, Natasha," said Samantha, standing there with her hands on her hips.

"See you later," said Nats.

"*Don't* think you're getting off your mega dare," said Kim. "You have to complete that mission later on tonight or tomorrow morning."

Samantha angled her eyebrows. She always did that

when she didn't know what was going down. I chuckled and Nats half grinned.

"Close the door behind you," said Kim.

Before Nats shut the door, she gave me a funny look. *After the next game I'll bounce up to my room and watch a horror movie on my own.* Kim got up and secured the lock.

Louise had tried to set up a key worker to see me. Some mixed-race woman called Patrice. I had to yell out a fat no cos I didn't really want one. I didn't even tell Louise everything and I had known her for the longest time. So I couldn't work out how she expected me to spill personal biz to this Patrice. *She'll be like a friend to you*, Louise said. *She can offer you more time than I can. You can discuss your problems with her. She's a very good listener.* I told Louise she could lick the envelope, slap a first-class stamp on it, and send that idea to a pumpkin farmer in North Korea.

I watched Kim shuffle the cards. She looked up every now and again to catch my eye. Laura Mvula's "Green Garden" grooved from the boombox. Kim dealt the cards then lit a smoke. She offered me one but I declined—I wanted to stick to my deal with Louise. I picked up my two cards. I had a six of diamonds and a five of clubs. Kim pulled hard on her fagarette. She puffed smoke rings into my face.

"You sure you don't want one?" she asked.

"Nope."

She then stubbed her cancer stick out although it was only half-smoked. She looked at the cards in my hands. "What's it gonna be, Naoms?"

"Twist," I replied.

My next card was the four of spades. I counted my total. Fifteen.

Kim leaned forward. Her eyes locked on mine. Today, she bragged silver eyeliner and mustard-colored lipstick. Our noses nearly touched. Her tobacco breath polluted my nostrils. "You sticking?" she asked.

I thought about it.

"Well? What's the play?"

"Twist," I said.

I picked up the eight of clubs and shook my head. Kim laid her two cards down faceup. She had the ten of diamonds and the queen of spades. I screwed up my face.

"What you got?" she asked. Her mouth curled ready for victory.

I closed my eyes and cussed bad words under my breath.

"Come on!" said Kim. "Show your hand."

I dropped my cards on to the bed. "I'm bust."

"Five losses," said Kim. "You're at mega-dare o'clock or super-beats o'clock. Choose which way to die."

"You punch like a crusty man," I said.

"Then go for a dare."

"I'm not spitting at anything. And I'm not doing anything to jump on Samantha's tits. Don't want my TV on lockdown anymore. I won't be able to watch my DVDs."

"Who says I'm gonna ask you to spit at anything?"

"Then what?" I asked.

Kim thought about it and smiled a devious smile.

Monkey in the witches' pot.

"Don't know why, Naoms, but you're always saying that

you wanna find a guy when you're fifteen. That's not too far off."

"Yeah," I said, "that's the program."

Kim side-eyed me. "So you wanna link up with him and later on be a mum to his screaming babies, right? And then live happily ever after. It's all very Walt Disney but that's what you're always on about, right?"

"Er, yeah," I replied. "What's that got to do with a dare?"

Kim moved up close to me. "If you wanna get one of the good bruvs," she said, "one of the decent ones who stays with ya and doesn't hot-leg it to another bitch, you're gonna have to learn to do certain things."

"Like what?"

Kim side-eyed me again.

Where's this going?

"First of all, you're gonna have to learn how to kiss him right," she said. "You have to get that down. Have you ever smacked tongues with a bruv before?"

I haven't kissed anyone before. I didn't even peck my mum or dad on the cheek. My fam weren't like that.

I dunno why I took the longest time in answering. "Er . . . no. Haven't met a bruv that could stir my love cells yet."

Kim grinned a dangerous grin. "Then your mega dare is to let me teach you how to kiss on point."

What did she say? I scoped her for a very long second, but she wasn't playing.

"It's easy once you know how," she said. "Trust me, by the time I finish with ya, you'll be curling tongues like how they do at the end of lame rom-coms. Bruvs won't be able to sample enough of ya."

"You're gonna *teach* me? Nats won't love that. She . . . she definitely won't love that. And I don't swing that—"

Kim shook her head and busted a little chuckle. "I'm only teaching you," she explained, "so don't hype it up. There will be no tongues. Nats won't mind. We're sistrens, aren't we?"

"Yeah, yeah, we're sistrens."

"So stop getting your G-strings in a tangle," Kim said. "This older chick who was here taught me. Trust me, Naoms, there's nothing more tragic than when you first kiss a bruv and you mess it up slobbering all over him like some retarded hound. And you don't wanna fill his gob with your spit."

"Of course I don't," I said.

"But nuff girls make that mistake. They open their gobs, all this spit gushes out, and they end up monsooning the bruv's tonsils."

I couldn't kill my giggles but I was still worried about Nats. "But . . . but . . ."

"And you don't want your tongue drilling into his throat," Kim cut me off. "Some girls kiss like they're digging for oil. That'll choke him and you might have to do some lifesaving shit on his ass. You think he's gonna want to know you after that? Fruck no! He's gonna hotfoot it outta there and leave you standing like a statue with a mad pout. Trust me, Naoms, you don't want that on your personal résumé."

"No," I agreed.

"Happened to me once, Naoms. It was mega embarrassing. I didn't go out of my gates for ages. I wish I had known what to do. Trust me, luck blessed my skin when this older chick taught me. Nancy Skellington was her name—pretty chick. She had a top half to claw eyes out for but her legs were kinda broad. You could've put babies to sleep on her calf muscles."

"All right then," I nodded. "What . . . what d'you want me to do?"

"Wait a sec," said Kim. "Let me clear the bed."

Picking up the ashtray, she emptied the butts out the window. She didn't check if anyone stepped by on the sidewalk below.

"Why didn't you empty it into your bin?" I asked.

"Cos Samantha would have the evidence that I'm smoking."

"But she knows you're blazing fagarettes anyway."

Kim collected the cards and pushed them into their cardboard box before rejoining me on the bed. "Put your head at an angle," she instructed.

I did as I was told. It felt strange. *Am I really gonna do this? Never thought I'd bump lips with a chick. But it's best I know what to do. Don't want decent bruvs hot-toeing it away from me. And she said Nats wouldn't mind.*

"Not *that* much of an angle," said Kim. "You'll give yourself a crooked neck. Won't look good when you slurp him and you end up in a neck brace. That'll be well sad . . . A little straighter."

I readjusted. I looked at Kim hoping I had it right.

"That's perfecto," she said. "Now, relax and close your eyes. When you feel my lips, don't chew 'em off and don't suck 'em like it's a fat cough drop. Just go with whatever motion I do, okay? Take it slowly. Don't rush it."

"Okay," I said.

I shut my eyes. My heart woke up and left-hooked my ribs. *It still feels weird. Doesn't seem right. But it's a dare. That's all. Just a dare. It's not a biggie. Don't set fire to your stress cells, Naoms. It's one of the things teenage chicks have to learn to get the ticks and ratings into womanhood.*

Kim placed her hand behind my head. "Your mouth follows mine, right. Go with the flow. Keep your eyes closed."

I nodded.

Her lips brushed mine and then she pulled away. I stayed still and kept my eyes closed. "Just go with the flow," she said. Her voice was softer. My lips felt dry. *Is it too late to slap on some lip balm or something? Nah, go with the flow.*

She kissed me a dose harder, forcing my mouth open. Her lipstick tingled my senses. I sniffed perfume behind her ears. I half opened my eyes for a short second but didn't move my lips. Kim pushed my head firmer into hers. She was sort of opening and half closing her mouth. Then I felt her tongue gate-crash into my mouth. It curled around my own tongue. We swapped saliva. I gulped and swallowed. It creeped the fillings outta me.

My body stiffened. My heartbeat vibrated inside my throat. It felt off-key so I opened my eyes. Kim still held the back of my head, pushing her face into mine. Her eyes were still closed. I felt a hand on my breast and then a squeeze. For a long second I froze. Only my toes moved.

Naoms, Colleen would shake a big no on this one. You gotta quit. She's taking liberties. But she's my sistren? No, she's not! If she was my sistren she'd keep her paws to herself.

I pulled away. "What the fruck you doing?"

Leaping off the bed, I made for the door. Kim chased me. She tried to pull me back. I snapped my arm away.

"Naoms, don't . . . don't go," she stuttered. "*Please.*"

For the first time since I had known her, I sensed some kinda weakness in Kim's eyes. Couldn't explain it.

"Please don't go, Naoms," she said. "I've . . . I've liked you forever. I . . . I thought you knew. I've been dropping nuff hints."

What's she saying? What does she mean? She knows I like guys. She needs to drink some reality juice.

I spun around, fiddled with the key, opened the door, and high-toed to my room on the next floor. I locked the door behind me and grabbed my meerkat from my pillow. I crashed on my bed and held the meerkat tight against my chest. I closed my eyes when I heard a mad banging on my door.

"*Naoms! Naoms!* I'm sorry. I got carried away. It won't happen again. Trust me."

"Leave me alone!"

"Let me in!" shouted Kim. "Let's talk. I'm super sorry. I thought you were into me."

Why would she think that? It's not like I've been scoping her butt for the longest time. She's got Nats. Why she wanna slurp tongues with an extra? Nats loves her to the core . . . I pulled on my shoes.

"Naoms! Come on! It's me! Your best sistren. We're soul bloods. You know that. Nats and me are on our end credits. I'm waiting for the right time to tell her. You know I'll always have your spine. Open the freaking door."

"Leave me the fruck alone!"

I tied my laces.

"I was just doing what a bruv would do," said Kim. "Didn't mean to upset ya. Sorry it went a bit extreme but I just wanted you to know what it's like and what a hungry bruv might try. They're all like that."

"D'you expect me to believe that fruckery? What dragon pills d'you think I'm taking?"

"Let me explain, Naoms. *Please.*"

I pulled open a drawer in my bedside cabinet. I grabbed some cash and pushed it into my jeans pocket. I took out my phone from another pocket and scrolled down to Emily. My hands shook and I couldn't punch the right buttons on my first attempt. I tried again. "*Pick it up! Pick it up!*" I whispered.

"*Naoms!*" Kim cried out.

My call went into Emily's voice mail. *No branches for monkey to swing on.* "For fruck's sake!" I waited for the bleep so I could begin my message. It seemed to take forever.

"*Naoms!*" Kim shouted again.

I pressed *End Call.* I took a mega breath and closed my eyes. When I opened them I went to the door. My heart-beat vibrated inside my toes. I swear it echoed along the floor. *She's been a good sistren but I have to drop it to her. Don't mouse out, Naoms. Tell her straight.*

I opened the door. Kim's eyes spilled with tears. Her cheeks had collapsed and her lips were doing this shakey-shake thing. I'd never seen her cry before. "Just frucking leave me alone!" I yelled.

I bumped Kim aside and flash-heeled down the stairs.

I reached the ground-floor hallway. Some Spanish-looking woman stood there adjusting the strap on her handbag. I paid her no mind and brushed by her.

"What's the matter?" she asked.

"What's the matter?" I repeated. "*She* stuck her tongue down my throat and touched me up! That's what's the frucking matter!"

"What's going on outside there?" Samantha called from her office. "What's with all the shouting?"

Someone came out of the kitchen. *Nats. Oh God. Oh no!* She gave me a long hard-curb, drain-corner glare. *She's gonna murk me.* I couldn't move. I closed my eyes but she slowly walked past me. Then she flew up the stairs. *What have I done? I have to hot-step it outta here.*

I opened the front door and slammed it as hard as I could behind me. Samantha came out and was just about to launch a cuss attack on me but a mad shriek cut the air from above. I thought it was Kim. It was a horrible sound. I looked up to her bedroom window. The light shade swung. Shadows clashed. Something banged. Samantha quick-stepped back inside.

I can't stop for this drama. Gotta fly. Nats might wanna do me something grievous next.

I hurried down the street till my lungs quit. It was a long road. *I should've stopped smoking a long time ago.* I covered two hundred meters or so till I pulled up and puffed hard. When my breathing got back on the level, I counted the funds I had. Twelve pounds sixty. *Where am I gonna rest my bones? I can't roll to Nan's. That'll be the first place where they'll hunt for me. Let me try Emily again. Maybe she can come and get me and take me away with her. She might even let me go to Australia with her. It'll all be nice sinking Coke, kicking back, and watching crocs chase kangaroos in Woola-Boola-Bong or somewhere. Her mum doesn't have to know.*

I dinged Emily once more but her phone was still on answer mode. *Damn. You haven't got any friends, Naoms. No real sistrens. You're all alone in this frucking cruel world. That's how it is. That's how it'll always be.*

I speed-walked to the end of the road. When I got there this ambulance whooshed by me. It almost launched into orbit over the road ramp. Its sirens screamed. *Oh God! I hope it's not for Kim or Nats.* I thought about going back but I couldn't. Truth be told, my want-to-live cells didn't want me to. I turned left and then took a right that led to Ashburton High Street. I stepped into an off-license and bought a liter bottle of Coke. The miserable man behind the counter took my funds. I parked on a red bench at a bus stop and thought about high-footing it back to the Goldings'.

Nah, Louise and Samantha would sniff me out there and I don't want them on my radar for now. They'll probably slap a Parcelforce label on my butt and fax me back to the unit. What if Kim denies she tried to kiss me and feel me up? Can't deal with that. Have to think. I'm not going back tonight. Not going back anywhere. I'm gonna go ghost on 'em. Fruck 'em all.

A 133 bus pulled up. Its final destination was North Crongton. My brain quick-flicked through my options. Before the doors closed, I jumped on. The female Asian driver smiled at me. I didn't return it. I paid my fare, bounced up to the top deck, and parked on the backseat.

There were only seven other passengers around me. One was a mixed-race guy with a super-duper Afro who sat two seats ahead of me. He glanced over his shoulder and grinned at me. I ignored him and stared out the window. I opened my bottle of Coke and let it fizz before sinking a quarter of it.

There weren't any friendly peeps out there. There wasn't anyone who I could trust. When the fat lady has had her cocoa and is ready to crash, I haven't got anybody who I can depend on in this frucked-up world. *I might as well find some grimy spot, curl up, and let the earwigs have their way. What have I got to live for?*

The bus slow-wheeled through the traffic. It picked up a bit of speed as we left South Ashburton and joined North Crongton Road. There were fields, bushes, and trees on either side. *Maybe I should get off here and find a tree to crash under. Nah, I don't want worms crawling all over my business in the morning. I hate freaking worms and I don't wanna be an ugly corpse. I'm sure I can find an empty slab in North Crongton to crash for the night. They won't find me there.*

It had just gone past eight thirty p.m.

For some reason, Mum gate-crashed into my head. I tried to boot her out and delete her from my memory cells but it was no use. The front doorbell kept ringing on that one.

I was back inside our flat. Back to that *dreadful* day.

Dad tried to keep me out of the bathroom but I saw medical peeps in day-glo uniforms lift Mum out of the bath. Their surgical gloves were stained with her blood. Their eyes were empty. They might as well have been carrying out a mannequin. My screams bruised my tonsils. Dad couldn't hold onto me. I scrambled up to her and told her to wake up. No response. I tried again, this time splitting my vocal chords. She looked very peaceful—the most calm I had ever seen her. Even when she slept she had stress lines crisscrossing her face. *Wake up!* Nothing.

Apart from me, everyone else was composed. There was no rush. It all happened in slow motion. They put her in a black body bag.

Maybe she couldn't take any more. Maybe that's the way I'll go. The girls in my fam don't last too long—except Nan. I'll find a beer bottle or something, smash it, and then red-sketch my wrists with it. I hope it's not too painful. When Mum did it, I didn't hear her squeal.

I looked out of the bus window as we neared North Crongton. I imagined that the Man Upstairs created these ends on a wet Sunday. I got off the bus at the final stop. Some bruv with a scraggly beard was giving out newspapers. There was a row of shops beside the bus terminal. I stepped into a food mart and bought a bottle of beer and a packet of bourbons. The man behind the counter didn't even look at me, let alone ask me my age. The liquor was the brand my dad used to buy.

I wonder where that waster is tonight? He might sober up when he hears the get-down about me. Mind you, he might use it as a reason to sink even more liquor. I remembered his lame excuse: *It helps me get through the day.*

Walking along North Crongton High Street, I swigged my beer on the way. Rough sleepers had already taken up their bookings in shop doorways. Graffiti squiggled up every bus stop and wall that I passed. A small *n* within a bigger *C*. I wondered what that meant.

I spotted tall buildings in the distance so I headed toward them. There was a spit of rain in the air. *I should've brought my hoodie.*

Kim told me once that in Crongton, dangerous peeps swaggered with swords and machine guns. The murk rate was one young bruv every two weeks. Every six months or so, some gangster chick would get deleted too. They'd usually get murked or raped for snitching or blasted in a gone-wrong drive-by. That didn't scare me anymore. I nibbled my bourbons, slurped my beer, and stepped on.

I came to a stop at a row of black-painted garages behind a couple of long tower slabs. One of 'em was open so I made for it. The pull-down door was dented and the handle was broken. Paint tins were piled in a corner. There were bits of wood, broken chairs, and ripped cushions on the floor. Flies buzzed around a grimy stain near the back. The place stank of piss and mold but I didn't care. I sat down against a wall, put my bottle of beer in front of me, and stared at it.

Two minutes later, I smashed the bottle, drained away the beer, and held the glass in my hand. I stared at my reflection. *I'm fourteen years old. My future was frucked up before I was even born. What a frigged-up, sad grime of a life I've had. If there is a man or a woman upstairs, they need to come down to earth quick-time and start listening to prayers from young peeps like me on the streets—not those who roll to church, synagogues, and mosques in their best clothes, name-*

brand handbags, and their nice clippety-clop shoes. They don't need any friggin' help. And most young peeps only care about the ratings they get on their social media selfies and what brand of shoes Kim Kardashian's smoking on her red carpets. This world and its mum can go and fruck themselves.

I rolled up my sleeve, flexed my fingers, and watched the veins dance in my wrist. I studied my wedding finger and thought no bruv in this world would ever put a ring on it. That didn't happen to chicks like me. That didn't happen to women like my mum either.

My bum felt numb. I wriggled about to try to get more comfy. A faint buzzing of flies filled my ears.

They told me Mum had used a bread knife. *This broken bottle will have to do. I hope it doesn't hurt. I hope it happens quick-time. It'll be proper embarrassing if it doesn't quite work and the meds save my sad self. I don't wanna step around with bandages covering my arms and peeps pointing at me. "That's the off-key girl who tried to murk herself."*

If they can find him, Dad will have to sober up to bury my ass. Maybe Ms. Almi can get the girls to do a dance at my funeral. Colleen and Tony can put on their Afro wigs. Pablo and Sharyna can get their groove on. That'll be a neat way to go.

I tensed my arms and closed my eyes. Soft rain pitter-patted on the roof.

"You're not using drugs, are ya?" a voice called out.

I looked around. There was a man standing outside. He wasn't too tall. He was wearing a flat cap. A blacky-gray beard scratched his chin.

"Er, no," I replied.

"This is *my* garage," said the man. "Been waiting for

over a week for the council to give me a new door. They
said they were coming yesterday."

"Sorry," I said.

"I've had young druggies in here taking their dragon
pills. It's like I have to be out here 24-7 to keep an eye on it."

"Sor . . . sorry," I repeated.

"Go on, get out of it," the man demanded. "Find somewhere else to take your drugs."

I stared hard at the broken bottle before standing up. I
dropped it before hot-toeing away.

"Take your friggin' mess with ya!" the man yelled after me.

I gave myself a cuss attack for leaving behind my biscuits. I wandered around for a while. The area was full of
sidewalks, dead ends, alleyways, little greens, and skinny
trees. I couldn't really tell where roads started or quit. I
heard whoops and hollering coming from behind a wide
row of apartments. I headed toward the noise.

When I turned a corner, young bruvs wearing black
baseball caps, black head rags, black T-shirts, and name-
brand sneakers played a serious game of basketball on an
open-air court. It was surrounded by a high-meshed fence
and watched by chicks wearing platform sandals, tattooed
eyebrows, black berets, and white lipstick. I thought I was
well down with cuss words but listening to these bruvs
playing b-ball taught me a new dictionary.

For a few minutes, I quit worrying about where I was
going to crash tonight and watched the game.

"Naomi!" someone called.

They can't be calling me. No one knows me in these ends.

"*Naomi!*" the female voice hailed again.

I turned my head and tried to locate where the tone came from. This pretty chick rolled toward me. She had long black hair and a red dot between her neatly shaped eyebrows. *Who's she?*

"Naomi," she said again. "It's me. Sunny from the dance club. Ms. Almi's class."

"Oh, yes," I pretended to remember. *Gosh, Naoms! You really need to start paying proper attention to the chicks in your dance class.*

Relief tasted good.

"I thought you lived in Ashburton ends," she said. "What are you doing in North Crong sides?"

"Er . . ." I couldn't think of a reply that worked.

"You look a liccle lost," said Sunny.

"I am," I admitted. "A friend dropped me down here. I wanted to go to the club and fill out some forms and stuff." I couldn't tell if Sunny was falling for my spin. "And I think I took a wrong turning and got lost," I explained.

"It's easy to get lost in the North Crong projects," Sunny said. "It's all mazes and alleyways. When I moved here it messed me up too. I think it made my mum cross-eyed."

I tried a half smile. "My inner sat nav is way off dial," I said.

"Anyway," Sunny said, "don't sweat your brains. I'll walk you there."

"Thanks." My heart quit banging my ribs.

While Sunny led me out of the projects, she told me about how she loved Bollywood movies, reggae, and street dancing of all kinds. Her dad drove a taxi and her mum worked in a cupcake shop on Crongton Broadway. She bust a laugh when I said I loved ancient Hollywood musicals, baking, and horror movies.

I felt bad about wanting to chop my veins. *There are nice peeps in this world, Naoms. Don't let the bad-mind ones force you to murk yourself.*

"Okay," Sunny said. "We're very close. Just take the next left and you're there."

"Thanks," I said. "You're a legend. I owe you big-time."

"The center usually closes at ten. It's ten to now so you'd better flex your toes and get a rush on. I've gotta step home. I'm not meant to be out at moon o'clock."

"Thanks again," I said.

I hot-stepped to the end of the road and broke into a jog when I turned left. I recognized where I was. The community center was on the other side of the street. There were no lights on. *Monkey standing in the rain. Gonna need a plan C.*

Crossing over to the center, I slapped a bell at the side of the front door. No response. I waited for five minutes. I don't know why but I pressed again. Tears ran down my cheeks and dribbled over my lips. I could still taste Kim kissing me. *This is not going well. But I'm not heading back. Why don't I have Ms. Almi's number in my phone? Maybe she could foster me. Learning to speak French would top off my ratings neatly.*

I looked around. No one was about. High above me the moon was fat. I stepped to the side of the building where there was a short driveway. A black Range Rover was parked there and behind that was a dumpster filled with cardboard boxes, office papers, and trash bags. There was a window that overlooked the dumpster. It wasn't that high. *That's* my answer.

Climbing into the dumpster, I picked up a piece of wood. I could just about balance on the dumpster's edge and blitz the window. Making sure my footing was secure, I covered my face with my left hand and koofed the window. I glanced over my shoulder to check if anyone had heard the smash. The hole was just big enough to allow my hand go through and turn the handle. I pulled it open. I didn't hear any burglar alarm. Relief once again soaked my arteries.

Flicking away the glass on the ledge, I then pulled myself up and through the window. I landed on the dance floor. I saw a dark reflection of myself in the long mirror. *I s'pose this is a better option than lying murked on some cold garage floor that's polluted with piss.*

In my head, I could hear Ms. Almi tapping her cane on the floor. *Un, deux, trois, quatre, cinq! Fantastique, Mademoiselle Brisset! Très bien!*

Yes, I can crash here tonight.

There were mats that they used for yoga piled up against the far wall. I pulled two off and placed them in a corner. *It's better than a park bench. Do you remember that night, Naoms? You hot-toed into the night and it freaked the jumping jilly-beanies outta Dad. Maybe I should've done that more often. It might've sobered him up.*

I didn't want to think about Kim, Nats, Louise, Colleen, Tony, or Samantha. Not on this night. I just wanted to be on my own. *And I hope Mum doesn't gate-crash my dreams.*

* * *

Some hours later, I heard a noise.

Someone came through the window. Something dropped to the floor.

I sat up. My heart dropped and punched my stomach. *It might be the feds. Even worse, it could be Kim and Nats coming to delete me.*

"Naomi!" someone called. It was a man's voice. It was Tony.

I lay back down.

"Naomi!"

"Is she there?" asked another voice from outside the window.

"It's too dark to see," replied Tony. "I'm gonna drop down."

He landed with a crunch of broken glass on the floor. I felt the vibrations beneath me. His footsteps approached me. I kept perfectly still.

"She's here!" he called.

Tony crouched over me. I didn't wanna admit it but I was glad it was him. "Naomi," he said again, this time softer.

I opened my eyes. "What took ya?" I said. "Think you're getting too ancient to climb through windows—you almost landed chin first."

"I've come to take you home," said Tony.

I sat up. "*Home?* I haven't got a home. I haven't had a home for the longest time. And I'm *not* going back to the unit. You can rip up the page on that one and burn it. Not with *her* there."

"You don't have to go back there."

I brushed off the dust that covered me. "I just had to fly away from there," I said. "All the prick fiddlers she warned me about, but she didn't warn me about herself. How messed up is that?"

"Are you okay?" Tony asked. "You're not hurt, are you? I was just about to leave but I spotted the smashed window."

I wasn't okay but I nodded anyway.

"How did you know I was here?" I wanted to know.

"Colleen said I should check the dance studio out. In our relationship, she not only has all the beauty, she has all the brains too."

"You've got a dose of sense too," I said.

Tony smiled. "Can I help you up?"

"Tone," I said, "I just high-flied it away for the night. I haven't lost my legs."

He busted half a chuckle.

"Can . . . can I stay here for a couple more minutes?" I asked.

"Why?"

"Just to chat."

"Oh . . . okay. Chat about what?"

I hesitated. "Er . . . my mum."

Tony sat down beside me and gave me an awkward smile. Another two minutes went by until I spoke.

"I could've saved her," I said finally. "Been thinking about it while I've been lying here. To tell you the ugly truth, I've been thinking about it every day since it happened. I can't help but think about it. It's a living film inside my head."

Tony's voice was soft and calm: "None of us expect you

to forget about what happened to your mum, Naomi. It'll probably stay with you for the rest of your life. That's natural. Your mum was the closest person to you in this world and you'll always miss her. To still grieve her is okay."

He wasn't wrong.

"But it doesn't mean you can't be happy," Tony went on. "You were very young. She wasn't your responsibility. *She* was responsible for *you*."

"What's going on in there?" yelled Louise from outside. "Are you coming out?"

"Just a minute!" shouted Tony.

"But I could've saved her," I insisted. "If only I checked in on her. She was taking the longest time having that bath."

Tears rolled down my cheeks. Tony placed an arm around my shoulders. I'm not sure how long I sat there leaking tears. Five minutes, ten minutes. It could've been half an hour.

Eventually I found my voice again. "We better get in motion, Tone," I said. "If Louise tries to get through that window it could all end up tragic."

"She's very worried about you," Tony said. "We all are. Sharyna was in tears earlier."

Bless Sharyna. I shoulda really taught her some more dance routines.

My stomach remembered it was peckish. "If I go back to your place tonight, can I make myself a ham omelet?"

"Of course you can."

"And you got some Coke, right?"

"If we don't, we can stop off somewhere and buy some."

"All right, let's make strides before Louise goes into one," I said. "She's all right, really."

We left through the front doors of the building. Louise was waiting outside. "Sorry for getting ya out of your bed," I said to her, "but Kim really freaked the tonsils outta me."

Louise and Tony swapped a long, knowing look. I could tell something was very wrong. My insides chogged and churned. They didn't say anything as they climbed into the car, Tony in the back and Louise in the driver's seat. I dropped into the front passenger seat. Louise turned the ignition and I tuned the car radio to a dance station.

"It'll be good to see Sharyna and Pabs again," I said. "I've missed 'em."

"They've missed you too," said Tony. "I'm going to text Colleen to tell her we're on our way."

"So you want to go back with Tony and Colleen on an emergency placement until I find something more permanent?" Louise asked.

"Yeah . . . I do."

"I'm thinking of a new start for you, Naomi," Louise said. "It's going to be new beginnings for both of us."

I glanced over my shoulder to look at Tony. He shrugged. I turned around to face Louise again. "What d'you mean, a *new start*?"

She ignored me and focused on the road ahead.

"Louise!" I raised my voice. Then I turned to Tony. "What's going on?"

He wound down a window. "It's a bit stuffy in here," he said.

"Louise!" I raised my tones even louder.

She slowed and parked on a terraced street. She turned off the engine and switched off the radio. I didn't complain. For a long second, she just stared at her feet. My stomach cramped up. *Shit! This is serious.*

"I'm moving on," Louise said.

"What d'you mean?" I said. "You're gonna work in far-off ends?"

Louise shook her head. "No."

"Then what?"

She sucked in a long breath and glanced at her glove compartment where she used to keep her smokes. Instead, there was a bag of gummy bears there. She offered me and Tony some but we both declined. She chucked one into her gob and started chomping.

"This job gets to you after a while," she said. "The stress builds up. It starts affecting your personal . . . I need a break to think about *me* and what I want out of life."

"What?" I said. "You're flaking outta your job? What about all the kids you're responsible for?"

Louise nodded. "Flaking? I guess you can call it that."

"But who's gonna be my social worker? You haven't quit cos of me, have ya? I know I can be too gobby some-times and I'm sorry if I've been stomping on your stress cells lately but—"

"Naomi," Louise cut in, "it's not you. It's me. I want to try new things in my life. Think about starting a family and so on. I'm thirty-eight. I have a good man with me who wants—"

"But . . . but . . ."

I can't believe I'm hearing this. Louise gets on my tits at times but . . . but she's my social worker. She can't leave me. I didn't know what to say. I stared through the windshield. I fought the tears building up behind my eyes with everything I had.

Louise placed her hand on mine. "You'll be all right," she said. "You're a survivor. That's what I love about you. You're so resilient."

"What does *resilient* mean?" I asked.

"That, er, that you're a survivor."

"So it's nothing to do with what went down tonight?"

"No, not at all," Louise replied. "Me and my boyfriend have been talking about it for a while. He . . . he deserves more of my time . . . my attention."

"So you've quit raging at each other?"

Louise gave me a standard *really* look. "I wouldn't call it raging, Naomi . . . Sometimes . . . sometimes he felt I brought my work home a bit. Well, not a bit."

A grin split my cheeks and I couldn't help busting out a mad chuckle. If I didn't laugh I'd be bawling lakes. "So things are back on the level with Mr. Man," I said. "And you're ready to make babies. If I was you, I'd stop at two cos any more than that and your stress cells will be ringing. Trust me on that."

"One would be nice," Louise said.

"And you gotta have me as one of the godmothers," I said. "I'll be the top-ranking godmother out there. Trust me on that. I'll take your baby out for walks in the park and make sure you breastfeed it for the longest time."

Tony and Louise grinned.

"What's so funny?" I asked. "If I'm godmother I won't forget birthdays, Christmases, school prom, and school play nights."

Louise restarted the car and I switched the radio back on. I couldn't really bop my head to the music though. It smacked me hard that this might be the last time I rode in Louise's car. I couldn't blame her for wanting a normal life. I wanted that too.

No one said anything till Louise turned onto the Goldings' street.

"You spoke about a new start for me as well," I said. "How's that gonna go down?"

Louise didn't reply till she parked and switched off the engine. "I take it you don't want to go to another unit in Ashburton?"

"That's not happening," I said. "You'll have to pollute my insides with nerve gas and conk me on the head with a slab before I say a wide yes to that."

"There's a new unit in South Crongton," she said. "It's run by a man I know—Mr. Cummings. I used to work with him. He's very compassionate and experienced. The rooms have en-suite bathrooms and—"

"South Crongton," I broke her flow. I remembered how nice Sunny was to me. "There're some nice peeps in Crong Town. It's not all about bruvs with shanks and guns."

"And if you do agree to go there," Louise said, "I think it's about time you went back to a normal school. I was going to bring this up at our next meeting."

I looked at Tony. He nodded. "You think I'm ready?" I asked.

"Yes," Tony and Louise replied together.

We climbed out of the car. My belly twisted again. *I've just got to stay on the level for a few secs and then I can let it out. God, Naoms. Leaking tears over a social wanker. What next?*

Colleen waited for us outside the front door. For a second I thought about Colleen and Tony being my new mum and dad. That would be a neat new start but I knew it could never happen. Then Kim and Nats flashed into my mind. The cramping in my stomach got worse but I had to ask.

"What happened to Kim and Nats?"

No response.

"What happened?" I pressed. "You can't block me out on this one."

"There . . . there was . . ." Louise faded out. She glanced at the sky and shook her head. I think I saw a tear in her eye.

Tony's voice was as low and slow as I'd ever heard it: "I'm really sorry to tell you, Naomi, but Kim suffered a serious head injury. She's in a—"

"TONY!" Louise cut him off. I'd never heard her yell so loud.

There was a long pause. We had all stopped walking. I'm not gonna lie, I didn't wanna hear any more. My stomach quit crunching. I just felt numb all over. *Kim! Poor Kim.*

"Maybe it's not that bad," I said. "She'll be up in the morning wanting to try on garms in charity shops and all that."

Tony shook and dropped his head once more. "I'm really sorry, Naomi," he said in a whisper. "Kim won't be shopping for . . . well, not tomorrow morning."

"It's not the time to talk about this, Tony," Louise said.

She started again for the Goldings' front door. Tony and I followed her.

"I . . . I had no idea this would happen," I said. "She . . . she always tried to be good to me."

"Nobody else expected this to happen," said Louise. "I don't want you to think that you're responsible in any way."

"I . . . I hope Nats will be okay," I said. "Can you keep me up to spec . . . on where she is?"

Tony and Louise swapped another long look.

"Of course," Louise replied. "But it might not . . . it might not be for a while."

Colleen hugged me extra tight as I entered the house. When I scoped her eyes I knew for real that Kim was in a bad place.

"I'll put the kettle on and make the coffees," I said.

"No coffee for me," Louise said. "I have to head home."

I embraced her, though she wasn't expecting it. She gripped me hard. "You'll have to put up with me for a few weeks yet," she said.

"Will you take me down to this new place in South Crongton?" I asked.

Louise nodded. "Yeah, I won't leave before that. It'll take around two weeks or so to get all the paperwork done. You'll be under the care of the Crongton council. But I'll make sure you're settled in okay."

"Remember, I wanna be a godmother," I said. "So hurry up and get pregnant."

"I'll try," Louise said.

Then she was gone. It was better that way. We didn't wanna spank up the trauma.

I spilled more tears as I made Tony and Colleen their late-night coffees. I tried to stop but all this mad emotion gushed outta me. Colleen made me my ham omelet and I chased that down with chocolate biscuits. She led me to my bedroom later on and kissed me on my forehead.

"Never forget this, Naomi," she said. "No matter what happens, your life is as valuable as anyone else's."

She closed my door but left the light on. I didn't have my meerkat to cuddle up to but I wanted what Colleen, Tony, and Louise had. A proper home with nuff love in it.

I wanna find some good sistrens, sistrens who'll be there for me. Is that too much to ask? The Man Upstairs owes me on that one. Maybe in South Crong I might find a decent bruv too. I'll be fifteen in a couple of months. I'll be old enough. Yeah, I'll meet a bruv and we'll hot-toe it away to somewhere like Biggin Spires where, if we do foster kids, they can go to a decent school. No grimy ends or PRUs for them.

Acknowledgments

I'd like to thank my tireless agent, Laura Susijn. I've benefited from twenty years of your careful steering and wise counsel. Thanks for putting up with my strops and rants in all that time, and here's to at least another two decades.

A big Crongton knuckle bump to the numerous librarians, schools, colleges, prisons, and literary organizations who promote and share my work.

Special mention to those who have supported me and stood by me when I felt down: Courttia Newland, Lemn Sissay, Vanessa Walters, Andrea Rhoden, Denise Rhoden, Amaka, Carol Brown, Tony Parkes, Pauline Gocan, Pauline Caitlyn-Reid, Irenosen Okojie, Grace Wilson, Yvvette Edwards, Joy Francis, Words of Colour, and so many more.

Thanks to my cowriters in the anthology *SAFE: On Black British Men Reclaiming Space* and its editor, Derek Owusu. It was a pleasure being part of the project and it fills me with great confidence that there is a new generation of black writers emerging who will tell their stories and make their mark.

As the Wailers sang, we must pass it on.

And thanks to the most important group of them all, those who have read an Alex Wheatle book. It's been twenty years since the publication of my debut novel, *Brixton Rock*, and I still can't believe I'm doing this writing thing for a living.

If I was blessed with the talent to pick out a decent melody, I'd write a song about the moment I picked up a Biro in a youth hostel in Brixton and wrote my first poem, "Dear Nobody." More of that later—watch this space.

One love,
Alex Wheatle